## Praise for *Letters from My Sister*

"A nuanced and heartwarming tale of sisterly love and community, based partly on the author's family history, from a master of Southern fiction similar to Lisa Wingate or Lauren K. Denton."

*Library Journal*

"Rich with historical details, Luesse's fascinating glimpse into the Old South combines an engaging mystery with sweet romance and social justice."

***Booklist*, starred review**

"*Letters from My Sister* drew me in on the first page with the delightful Callie Bullock, and Luesse's lyrical style and wonderful characters kept me glued to the story. Meals, shopping . . . everything waited until the last page."

**Patricia Bradley**, *USA Today* bestselling author of the Natchez Trace Park Rangers series and the Pearl River series

"Winsome and sweetly haunting, *Letters from My Sister* brims with family love, humor, romance, and mysterious insights into the meaning of memories. A thoroughly engaging novel that probes deep."

**Sarah Sundin**, bestselling and Christy Award–winning author of *The Sound of Light* and *Until Leaves Fall in Paris*

# the light on horn island

# the light on horn island

*A Novel*

## VALERIE FRASER LUESSE

**R** Revell
a division of Baker Publishing Group
Grand Rapids, Michigan

© 2025 by Valerie Fraser Luesse

Published by Revell
a division of Baker Publishing Group
Grand Rapids, Michigan
RevellBooks.com

Printed in the United States of America

Library of Congress Cataloging-in-Publication Data
Names: Luesse, Valerie Fraser, author.
Title: The light on Horn Island / Valerie Fraser Luesse.
Description: Grand Rapids, Michigan : Revell, a division of Baker Publishing
    Group, 2025.
Identifiers: LCCN 2024044854 | ISBN 9780800741617 (paper) | ISBN 9780800746780
    (casebound) | ISBN 9781493448685 (ebook)
Subjects: LCGFT: Christian fiction. | Novels.
Classification: LCC PS3612.U375 L54 2025 | DDC 813/.6—dc23/eng/20240930
LC record available at https://lccn.loc.gov/2024044854

Most Scripture quotations, whether quoted or paraphrased by the characters, are from the King James Version of the Bible.

Some Scripture quotations, whether quoted or paraphrased by the characters, are from the Holy Bible, New International Version®, NIV®. Copyright © 1973, 1978, 1984, 2011 by Biblica, Inc.® Used by permission of Zondervan. All rights reserved worldwide. www.zondervan.com. The "NIV" and "New International Version" are trademarks registered in the United States Patent and Trademark Office by Biblica, Inc.®

Cover image © Silas Manhood / Trevillion Images

The author is represented by the literary agency of Stoker Literary.

Baker Publishing Group publications use paper produced from sustainable forestry practices and postconsumer waste whenever possible.

25  26  27  28  29  30  31      7  6  5  4  3  2  1

*For the sister-friends and girl cousins*
*I'm blessed to have in my life*

*one*

**GOOD PIMENTO CHEESE IS A REASON TO LIVE.** It tastes like everything just might turn out fine after all. Somewhere between New Orleans and the Mississippi line, I had stumbled onto some.

I pulled into one of those great old stores with clapboard siding and a tin roof, where the entrance is a cantankerous wooden door pinned shut with a wobbly metal knob, the parking lot is more dust than gravel, and the two Texaco pumps out front have been there since sock hops were all the rage. What made me hit the brakes was a wooden sandwich sign right at the edge of the road: "Cold Drinks. Good Tomatoes. Aunt Letha's P.C." In this part of the South, "p.c." stands for pimento cheese, a down-home delicacy I have loved since childhood. Not just anybody can make it. Too much of this or too little of that, and it'll taste as sorry as a mushy Better Boy. But I had high hopes for Aunt Letha.

Standing in the old store, with frosty air blasting from a couple of duct-taped Sears window units that looked older than I am, I placed my order and watched a woman behind the counter lightly smear mayonnaise on two thick slices of white bread, then add a generous slathering of unadorned pimento cheese.

The woman looked about seventy, her gray hair bobby-pinned into a French twist and a pencil stub tucked behind her ear. "That gonna be all for you, cher?" she asked as she put my sandwich in a paper sack and filled a Styrofoam cup with a fountain Coke.

Have mercy, I had missed that accent. "Could I get a basket of tomatoes too, please?"

"Sure can." She began ringing me up.

"Are you Aunt Letha?"

"Naw, dahlin'. That was Mama's sistah. I'm Rema—Rema Guillory. But I try to do Aunt Letha proud when I make her pimento cheese."

"Nice to meet you, Rema. I'm Edie."

"It's good to meet you too, Edie. That'll be fifteen dollahs even. Five for your sandwich and Co-Cola, then another ten for the tomatoes. Just pick you out a basket over there by the door."

I slid a twenty onto the counter. "You keep the change."

"Thank you, honey. Travel safe—and don't forget your tomatoes. Folks are forever doing that, and then I have to chase 'em down in the parking lot."

"I won't forget," I said as I headed for the door and grabbed a basket.

Rema's tomatoes smelled like rich black dirt and hot Louisiana sun and green leaves just rained on. A brass bell on the door jingled as I went outside, back into the kind of heat that makes you wonder how the cicadas have the energy to chirp. It was only May—usually a mild month—but summer had come early this year, and I had the sweat to prove it.

Getting situated in the dullest car I'd ever rented, I took a bite of my sandwich. Bless Aunt Letha, she knew what she was doing. She and Rema just might cure my faltering appetite, with a little help from Punk—that's my grandmother.

About a month ago, Punk called and said, "Sweet girl, why are you up there hurting all by yourself in New York City? Come on down here and let these gulf waters heal you." Punk believed there was no wound the Gulf of Mexico couldn't salve.

Once I made up my mind to leave the city, I sold what little furniture I owned, packed my biggest suitcase with summer clothes, and shipped the rest of my belongings to my parents' house in Birmingham. Then I caught a flight to New Orleans, in part because I wanted a few days in a city I had always felt way down in my bones, but also because I wanted to savor the coastal road I was on—every salty, windy, hot, humid mile of it.

Eventually, the marshes, bayous, and fish camps of Louisiana gave way to a string of coastal towns fronting the gulf in Mississippi, where the humble byway I had been traveling transformed into touristy Beach Boulevard. From Pass Christian to Ocean Springs, live oaks stood like sentinels guarding grand old Southern homes, their massive branches protectively spread, daring the water to come one step closer to the azalea bushes and the family silver.

Stealing occasional bites of Rema's p.c., I at last made it to the final leg of my journey, a narrow, southerly strip of pavement snaking toward Punk's tiny waterfront hamlet of Bayou du Chêne, home to so many Louisiana transplants that locals call it Little Lafayette.

I pulled into my grandmother's shady driveway and drove up to her Creole cottage on the southern tip of a channel connecting the bayou to the gulf. Before I could even shut off the engine, the front door opened and Punk raced down the porch steps, her arms outstretched. I breathed in her perfume as she wrapped her arms around me and held me tight.

At last, she stepped back, her hands on my shoulders. "How's my girl?"

"I've been better, Punk."

She nodded and took me by the hand. "Come inside, Edie. We'll worry about your things later." At the top of the steps, she squeezed my hand and winked at me. "You're in luck. I just happened to make gumbo."

I kissed her on the cheek and followed her into her kitchen on a back corner of the house. Adjoining it and filling the opposite corner was not so much a dining room as Punk's answer to a French salon, a place for lively conversation fueled by her cooking. The exterior wall facing the gulf was lined with floor-to-ceiling windows, always open to cool breezes even when the air conditioner was running, while the interior wall held a bank of overflowing bookcases. A mix of unmatched upholstered chairs—all of them comfortably worn from countless gatherings, large and small— surrounded Punk's long cypress farm table, brought here from Louisiana many years ago. Behind the far end of the table, opposite the kitchen, was a wall hanging that Punk had needlepointed before I was even born. It was the second half of one of her favorite Bible verses, from Hebrews: "For thereby some have entertained angels unawares."

"Want me to fix the tea?" I asked.

She nodded as she spooned a layer of white rice into two soup bowls, topped it with chicken-and-sausage gumbo—my favorite—and put a small scoop of potato salad in the center.

Punk still had those old-school metal ice trays with the

lever you pull to loosen the cubes. She put our bowls and a French loaf on a tray as I grabbed the tea, and we headed out to a small table and chairs tucked into a corner of her back porch, wisely screened against the buggy seasons. It ran all the way across the back of her house, offering spectacular views of gulf sunsets.

I dipped my spoon into the gumbo, being careful to capture a little chicken, a bit of andouille sausage, and a touch of potato salad. Tasting those familiar and long-missed flavors, I leaned back in my chair and sighed. "Now I'm home."

Punk reached over and patted my arm. "Yes, you are, sweet girl! Yes, you are."

"Don't tell Mama, Punk, but I've always felt misplaced. This is where I'm the most at home. It's where I'm the most myself."

She took a sip of her tea. "You get that from me."

When I first told my big-city friends about my grandmother, they asked if she was like all those old Southern women in the movies—feisty and eccentric, with big jewelry and an even bigger mouth. I guess it was the nickname, bestowed on her by her older brother. Truthfully, my grandmother—real name Adele—could give Grace Kelly a run for her money. Tall and slim, she had the bone structure of a *Vogue* model and a sense of style to match. Her eyes were sky blue, her shoulder-length silver hair worn in a neat chignon. Her uniform of choice was a pair of cigarette pants or clam diggers ("nobody wants to see an old lady's knees") and blouses of crisp cotton or soft linen. Minimal jewelry. Revlon Persian Melon lipstick. Chanel No. 5. She often said she was "kicking down the door to ninety" but was barely eighty and didn't look a day over sixty.

"So did you decide?" she asked before blowing on a spoonful of gumbo to cool it. "Are you taking a leave of absence or leaving New York for good?"

"Leaving for good."

She plopped the spoon down in her bowl. "Well, hallelujah! Not that you can't live anywhere or do anything you set your mind to. You're perfectly capable. It's just that you've always had such a connection to this place. Even your Pop wasn't as smitten as I was, and he's the one who wanted to move here. You're the only one who loves it as much as I do, Edie."

I propped my elbows on the table and rested my chin in my hands—a faux pas not to be committed in your finer French Quarter restaurants, but perfectly acceptable on this forgiving old porch. "What am I gonna do, Punk?"

She reached out and squeezed my arm. "Whatever is meant to happen will happen, Edie. I pray about it every night. You should too. God expects a little conversation from us."

We watched as a V formation of pelicans flew low over the water. I loved the look on my grandmother's face, at once serene and awestruck, as her eyes followed those birds in flight. "Can we go, Punk? Can we go right now?"

She tapped the tip of my nose with her forefinger. "Boat's already packed."

*two*

"YOU'RE THINKING ABOUT A BOY with wild blond hair, aren't you?"

I turned to see Punk smiling at me, the island breeze stirring a few loose tendrils around her face. That lady could always read my mind. "You have to admit, Punk, he was something special. Still makes me a little wistful to think about him."

"Yes," she agreed, "he was special. But that hair, Edie . . ."

"Oh, come on! He was a California surfer boy. That was the look."

We laughed together at the memory of my first and only summer boyfriend, whom I'd met right here on Horn Island. An older man, seventeen to my sixteen—well, almost sixteen— Cole Donovan came here from Santa Barbara when his dad got a temporary assignment at Keesler Air Force Base. After he went back to the West Coast, we wrote to each other for a while, but teenage boys being teenage boys, the letters eventually trickled out. I was heartbroken. But I still had a soft spot in my heart for him and fond memories of moonlit kisses on the beach.

"They say men get better with age, but I'll tell you what, Punk, I have yet to see a guy in his twenties or thirties who could hold a candle to Cole at seventeen."

She smiled and dusted some sand off the top of her foot. "Imagine what he would've looked like with a little snip-snip of that hair."

"Stubborn," I said, nudging her with my elbow. "How about a fire?"

"Plenty of time for that," Punk said. "Go and give Horn a proper greeting. We'll build a fire when you get back."

I grabbed my camera and set off down the beach. The island's north shore faces the Mississippi Sound, where gulf waters, corralled between the mainland and a string of barrier islands, are flat and river colored. But Punk and I had anchored on the southern shore, near Horn's eastern tip, washed by the open gulf, its salty waves curling against white sands.

Slash and swamp pines blanketed the island's interior, giving it a scruffy beauty. Their tall, bare trunks hoisted tufts of green into a sky now mellowing into the pastel watercolors of sunset, less than an hour away. This time of day, the surf grew calm and flat as a mirror. Terns and sandpipers scurried across the sand, right at the water's edge, with seagulls spiraling like a live mobile hanging high above a cradle of sand and sea. Listening to gulf waters lap against the shore as a stiff island breeze blew my hair away from my face, I took pictures of one soul-soothing scene after another, trying to capture the tranquility of this place.

Lately, that had been mighty hard to come by—tranquility, I mean. I'd go to church and cry because all those hymns about everlasting love cut too close to the bone. Go to the grocery store and cry because something stupid like the boxed macaroni and cheese we lived on in college triggered too many memories. I could turn on the radio and cry because a local station played the Go-Go's, and it took me back to a sunny spring day when laughter poured out of an AMC Gremlin bound for a pretty state park, where we would lie on a quilt Punk gave me, crank up a boom box, and work on our tans as we dreamed about a place of endless promise called the future.

I closed my eyes, turned my face to the sky, and took a deep, long breath, turning down the noise in my brain so I could hear soothing island sounds—the splash of a jumping fish, the flap of pelicans' wings, the wind in the pines. Peace. That's what Horn sounded like to me. Everlasting peace.

Walking barefoot in the hard-packed sand washed by the surf, I let myself reminisce about my long-ago summer with Cole, which I hadn't done in a long time, certainly not since Leni got sick. Truthfully, it was Pop's boat and not my ravishing teenage self that first got Cole's attention. I had forgotten my suntan lotion when I dropped anchor and waded onto Horn. As I went back for it, I saw the most gorgeous boy I had ever laid eyes on, checking out the boat. If I was honest with myself, I had never felt anything like that arrow-to-the-heart first glimpse of him, a tall, tan dream with golden-blond hair, blue eyes, and a right-dimpled smile to die for.

I heard a splash and looked out over the water to see where it came from—a couple of dolphins playing together in the gulf. That's what Cole and I were like back then—just a couple of carefree dolphins living it up under a summer sun.

I was about to turn around and retrace my own footprints when I spotted some writing in the sand. Even before I got close enough to read it, I could predict what it said. Likely some variation of "Brian Loves Ginger" or "Dave Wuz Here." As it turns out, I was wrong.

Kneeling beside the writing, I lightly ran my finger across

it, not words at all but symbols, or maybe they were letters, but not from any alphabet I could read. Touching it made my skin tingle. I stood up, took a few steps back, and felt the tide lap at my feet. Raising my camera, I took several shots of the sand message, which had an ancient look about it. Odd for something destined to be erased by the wind and water any second now.

The sky was slowly dimming. Punk would begin to worry if I didn't get back soon. Over the years, I'd observed one logical flaw in my otherwise rational grandmother: When someone she loves doesn't arrive at her expected hour, Punk's mind goes straight to death and/or dismemberment without stopping for "probably stuck in traffic." I checked the screen on my camera to make sure the pictures were in focus and then hurried back to our spot.

Punk waved as she watched me approach. "And how did you find our friend Horn?"

"Intriguing and mysterious." I sat down beside her on our quilt.

"In what way this time?"

"I found a peculiar message in the sand. Look." I showed her the images on my camera screen. "Are they symbols or letters, do you think?"

Punk took a closer look. "That's Hebrew."

"Really?"

Punk grinned as she studied the picture. "Do I have to break out my slides and make you watch them all again?"

"No! No! Anything but that!"

We both laughed about the infamous slide show—four trays loaded to the gills—that Punk had put together after she and Pop toured the Holy Land. The whole family had to sit for hours watching as she clicked through them, meticulously narrating each one. She'd spent twenty minutes on the Western Wall alone.

"How about that fire?" she said.

We dug a pit in the sand and laid a fire with split logs I had carried from the boat. Punk handed me some matches from a straw tote bag with orange leather straps and a bright yellow pineapple embroidered on the front. When it came to her clothes, Punk preferred ocean-washed colors—seafoam green, pale aqua, soft cream—but, she always said, "We can be bolder with our accessories."

Punk and I sat together, listening to the surf lap against the sand as our fire crackled under a sky growing softer and darker by the minute. Staring into the flames, I pulled my knees to my chest and wrapped my arms around them, just as Punk was doing.

After a long, quiet while, I finally asked, "Why'd it have to be her, Punk? How could such a light just go out?"

Punk reached over and stroked my hair. "Leni's light didn't go out, Edie. It just moved to a place where you can't see it, for now anyway. Same as Pop. And even though every preacher from here to yonder will say we should rejoice in their reunion with the Almighty, that's a tall order when your heart is breaking. *They're* in a better place, but you're in a mighty painful one."

I used a long stick to punch up our fire. "My grief counselor says time heals all wounds."

"Your grief counselor's an idiot."

I couldn't help laughing, despite the somber weight of our conversation. As always, Punk took no prisoners.

"Some wounds never heal, Edie, and that's a fact. We never get over them. But we do learn to carry them with us, to move along, broken wings and all. Remember that tote bag I brought back from Italy when Pop took me for our anniversary?"

I smiled and nodded. "Hand-tooled leather in a color you called cognac."

"That's right. It was stunning—still is. And it could hold all the shopping I could do in a day. Trouble was, once I carried it all over the place, I'd need a BC Powder for my back at night."

"But you kept carrying it."

"Of course I did. So what if it weighed a little heavy and caused me pain? It was beautiful and filled with wonderful memories from our trip. They bring me even more joy now than they did back then. Grief is the same. It may take you a while to get strong enough to carry it, but one day you'll wake up and realize it's not so heavy anymore. The happy memories lighten up the hurt. It's the proverbial mixed bag, sweet girl. To completely get over Leni, you'd have to leave her behind, forget what it meant to have her for your best and truest sister-friend since childhood. That would be a far greater loss than what you're experiencing now."

"I just feel so stupid."

"Why?"

I punched at the burning logs again and sent a spray of orange glitter into the darkening sky. "Because we couldn't see it, Punk. Leni used to say, 'Miracles can happen, even on a Tuesday.' That was her version of 'Anything's possible.' We believed it too. We just didn't understand what it meant. We saw only the *wonderful* things that might come our way, not the awful ones. We never saw the awful coming."

I felt a familiar sickening swell rise up from some deep pit in my stomach, stinging my eyes and making me queasy. I hated that swell. I hated my fear of it even more.

"Edie," Punk said, taking my face in her hands. She put her arms around me and let me cry till I didn't need to anymore.

Together, we watched the glow of our campfire, listening to it pop and crackle as the gulf swished and sighed against the shore. Tomorrow would bring a new day. But right now, on our favorite slip of sand in the whole wide world, Punk and I were in no hurry to let this one go.

# three

MY BEDROOM AT PUNK'S was pure heaven. Cypress floor, shiplap walls, a poufy sleigh bed, and the dreamiest linens I'd ever slept on. They smelled like distilled springtime. Then there was my favorite part—tall windows overlooking the gulf, with a window seat big enough for two. I couldn't believe I was actually here, in this bedroom, this house, this place.

A burst of laughter floated up the stairs. The Ten Spots had landed. That's what I called Punk and her three closest friends, sisters Sugar Vansant, Cookie Harris, and Coco Menard. They were far too frugal, not to mention Presbyterian, for the gaming floor, but they did enjoy the restaurants and shopping promenades at your better casino resorts. The Ten Spots had an ongoing contest to see who could score the best loot for ten dollars (hence the nickname). Punk was the current champ, having landed an elegant print scarf marked seventy-five percent off at "the Beau," one of the ladies' favorite hangouts.

I grabbed a quick shower, put on a blue and white kaftan dress Punk bought me on my last visit, and bounded downstairs with wet hair and bare feet.

"Edie!" Sugar jumped up from the table and ran to me,

squeezing me in a tight hug. I kissed her on the cheek. "How *evah* are you, honey?" A few summers back, Sugar spent a month with friends in Selma and insisted that she could not shake the South Alabama accent she picked up there (*evah*, *buttah*, *sugah*). The accent, however, tended to appear sporadically, leaving the rest of us to suspect that Sugar intentionally conjured it whenever the notion struck her.

"I expect Edie was a whole lot better before you squeezed the life out of her." That was Cookie, who got up from the table and joined her sister in checking me out. I hugged her before she took a strand of my wet hair in her hand. "You've let your hair grow long, darlin'. I think it's beautiful."

"Oh, me too," Sugar said. "And it's the most *gaw-uh-geous* colah! That deep chestnut with those green eyes . . ." Sugar was Miss Louisiana of 1941, and it showed. She was always "done," her chin-length bob professionally blonded and styled just so to frame her face, which never saw the light of day without full-on Estée Lauder.

"Nonnie Tucker's granddaughter dyed her hair purple," Cookie was saying. "And I understand she's dating a young man in the illegal substance industry."

Sugar closed her eyes and shook her head. "He wears leather in the summertime. That has to smell."

It was hard to tell which of the boyfriend's flaws left Sugar more horrified—his line of work or his wardrobe.

"If my granddaughter started going with somebody like that," Cookie said, "I'd tie a rock around my good leg and jump in the bay."

Cookie's short crop and straight bangs looked all the whiter against her year-round tan. She favored pedal pushers, sandals, and men's shirts, insisting that "the boys shouldn't be the only ones who get to be comfortable."

Punk herded us all back to the table and set a bowl of shrimp and grits in front of me, along with a steaming mug of coffee.

"Did y'all eat already?" I asked Punk before taking a long sip.

"We did," she said, "but I wanted you to catch up on your sleep, so I wouldn't let these hooligans wake you up for early breakfast."

Punk's shrimp and grits was transformative. Some cooks left the shrimp bland and smothered the grits with what Punk called "tomatoey nonsense." But my grandmother flavored her crustaceans with bacon, lemon, garlic, and Tabasco, while keeping the grits creamy and cheesy. Nothing on top but a light sprinkling of crumbled bacon and scallions.

"Have mercy, Punk," I said as I tasted a big spoonful. "Nobody can beat you at shrimp and grits."

"Not so fast," Sugar said. "You've never had mine."

"That's true, Miss Sugar. I'm always available for a tasting. I'll even bring my own fork. Or spoon. I never can make up my mind which one shovels more shrimp and grits into my mouth."

Sugar's real name was Collette. Cookie's was Corinne. Their daddy nicknamed them both, as well as their older sister, Marguerite, whom he called Coco. She graduated high school with Punk. My grandmother says Coco and her sisters have been her closest friends "since Methuselah was a toddler."

"Where's Miss Coco?" I asked.

"Torturing her only child," Cookie said as Punk freshened everybody's coffee. "She's got a sickly sago palm she's tired of, and she's been nagging Francis to get rid of it. He finally went over there early this morning with his backhoe."

No sooner were the words out of Cookie's mouth than we heard the front door slam and an unmistakable loud, raspy voice. "Punk Cheramie, where are you? And where's the kid?"

Into the kitchen came Coco Menard. Coco was like a hurricane. She didn't just arrive. She made landfall. Taller than her younger sisters and rail thin, Coco dyed her hair strawberry-blond and wore it short, swept away from her face in smooth waves. She was fond of animal prints, dangly earrings, and bright coral lipstick. Her go-to accessories were a pair of black cat-eye sunglasses and an enormous shoulder bag, which she had been known to weaponize. Though she hadn't smoked in years, she would often press an unlit cigarette between her lips, "just for the feel of it," which she was doing right now.

"Hey, Miss Coco." I got up from the table and kissed her on the cheek as she came into the room.

She stepped back and looked me over. "Good to see you, kiddo," she said, the cigarette flopping up and down as she spoke. She took it out of her mouth and stuck it behind her ear. "I hear you hit a snag."

"Yes, ma'am."

"Well. Don't you worry." She reached out and lightly touched her fist to my chin. "Snags stink, but they'll put hair on your chest." It was the kind of sympathy you might expect from a football coach consoling his team after a big loss. But I knew she was doing her best.

"Coco, would you like some breakfast?" Punk asked, pouring a cup of coffee and setting it on the table for her newly arrived guest.

Coco shook her head and sat down next to me, across from Sugar and Cookie. "I was up before the roosters hit the snooze button. Had breakfast hours ago. But I'll take a little coffee cake if you've got some."

Punk always had coffee cake and brought some to the table. "Did Francis take care of the sago?"

Coco selected a slice from the plate. "Bless my soul, if I didn't know better, I'd swear I've raised a snob. It took him two weeks to 'get to me,' as he put it. Get to *me*! His *mother*! The way he carried on, you'da thought I'd asked that boy to move the Biloxi lighthouse instead of a li'l ole palm."

"Coco, 'that boy' is fifty-six years old," Cookie said. "I expect he's got the beginnings of arthritis by now, just like the rest of us."

"Pfft!" Coco shook her head and took a bite of cake. "When I was his age, I could ride a mule from here to New Orleans and whistle all the way."

"You were always musical, even as a child," Cookie said with a sly smile. "I'm surprised you didn't give Shirley Temple a run for her money. Lucky for that little show-off, your hair won't curl."

All the women laughed except Coco, who pulled the cigarette from behind her ear and pitched it at Cookie. "What's the game plan?"

"I thought we might take Edie shopping," Punk suggested. "Maybe drive up to the pass and work our way down the beach—have a nice lunch somewhere along the way?"

"I'm for that," Sugar said.

"When we make it back to Biloxi," Punk said, "we'll introduce Edie to The Trove."

"Is that new?" I asked.

Punk took a sip of her coffee. "Well, that's the thing. Up until a few weeks ago, nobody had ever heard of it. The place just sort of appeared out of nowhere. But once you're inside, it looks well established, like it's been in that spot for years and years."

"Yes, and it's just overflowing with *delightful* curiosities," Sugar said. "Antiques, old books, *fabulous* jewelry . . ."

"Don't tell me y'all are abandoning Paige and Miss Katherine?" I asked. The mother-daughter proprietors ran a family-owned shop that Punk and company loved.

Coco shook her head. "Our loyalties remain steadfast. The Trove is just a dalliance."

"It's tucked away in a narrow two-story on Howard Avenue," Cookie added.

"The owner is named Jason Toussaint," Sugar said. "Nonnie told me there's a rumor going around that he's a distant relative of Jean Lafitte." Nonnie owned the general store. She fancied herself the Barbara Walters of Bayou Du Chêne.

"Nonnie?" Coco huffed. "You know good and well her biscuit's not done in the middle."

"Oh, it is too!" Sugar countered. "Well, almost. Might be a little gummy here and there. But her story fits—the descendant of a pirate with a *trove* of treasures for sale."

Coco shook her head. "For all we know, Jason Toussaint started that rumor himself, just to move more candelabras."

"I think he's quite handsome in a . . . oh, what's the word . . . *disturbing* sort of way," Sugar said.

I had to ask. Of course I did. "Disturbing?"

Sugar tossed her head and pushed her hair away from her face. "Well, you know what I mean, dear. He's one of those men with an alluring face—*very* alluring—but there's something in those piercing eyes that makes you wonder whether he might ride up on a black steed under cloak of darkness, throw you over his shoulder, and carry you off to a schooner bound for New Orleans, where you'd live in a French Quarter mansion with a secret tunnel to the Mississippi River."

"Why, Miss Sugar!" I said. "I think you've led a more interesting life than I have."

She winked at me and giggled.

"Somebody's been dipping into the romance novels again." Coco fished another cigarette out of her purse.

"I have *not*," Sugar protested.

"Now, ladies," Punk interrupted. "Let's remember we're here to show Edie a good time."

"Punk's right," Cookie said. "Y'all can catfight anytime, but while we've got Edie with us, you two put on your happy pants."

"Fair enough." Coco's cigarette bobbed up and down as she spoke.

"How could we be anything but agreeable on such a *gaw-uh-geous* day?" Sugar said.

I glanced at Coco, whose eyes narrowed as she pressed the cigarette so tightly between her lips that it shimmied.

Punk stood up and tapped the table with her hands. "Then it's settled. Y'all grab your purses. We'll follow Edie to Gulf-port so she can drop off her rental at the airport."

# four

STANDING WITH THE TEN SPOTS, I watched in awe as Punk opened the door of her garage, removed the cover from Pop's prized convertible, and backed it out. She asked me to put the top down while she distributed headscarves to the others.

"You sure about this, Punk?" I asked her.

She smiled and handed me a scarf. "Rosetta needs some air."

Rosetta was Pop's 1959 Chevy Impala, painted "Roman red," an official Chevy color back then, with the famous cat-eye taillights, chrome to die for, and a big bad V-8. He'd bought her brand-new, and Punk had Rosetta completely restored as a retirement present for him. That car was big as a football field and could flat-out fly.

Punk and her friends wore their scarves tied under the chin, while I found a ponytail holder in my pocket, corralled my hair into a bun of sorts, then tied the scarf into a headband. Punk nodded with approval. "Suits you," she said. "Tastefully bohemian. You go on ahead. We'll meet you out front at the airport."

I knew why she gave me a head start. Punk was not a timid driver. She enjoyed horsepower. It was all I could do to stay ahead of her till we got to Gulfport and dropped off the Ford I had rented in New Orleans.

Approaching the Impala, I could've fainted when my grandmother slid over to the passenger's seat and motioned for me to take the wheel. Although I had ridden in Rosetta many times, I had never been allowed to drive her—not unless you count all the times Pop let me sit on his lap and help him steer to Abel Mouton's marina when I was a little kid. He probably would've gotten pulled over for that on the main highway, but Bayou du Chêne is not exactly high on the county sheriff's patrol list, so we got away with it.

For a minute, I just sat there, taking it in—the red steering wheel and dash, the chrome, the low, throaty rumble of a muscled-up engine straight out of Detroit.

"Well? Are you gonna drive or do I need to go find somebody to smooch with in the back seat?" Coco asked from her spot in back.

"Don't be shy," Punk assured me. "Rosetta embraces a heavy foot."

I eased the majestic beast onto Beach Boulevard and hit the gas.

"That's more like it!" Coco shouted over the wind noise.

I tried my best to focus on the road, but it was hard to resist stolen glimpses of the water, with a brilliant blue sky overhead and a warm summer sun lighting up the gulf. Through the rearview mirror, I could see Cookie and Sugar giggling like teenagers. Coco held a cigarette between two fingers as she draped her arm across the doorframe, ever the cool girl.

I ferried us to all our favorite Gulfport shops before we

stopped for lunch and ate enough shrimp to kill us. At last, we were bound for Biloxi and the mysterious new antique store that had so fascinated Punk and her friends.

The five of us walked together down Howard Avenue until we came to the skinniest building on the block, two stories of white brick with black shutters flanking the upstairs windows. The only window on the ground floor, a great big one right in front, held a sampling of the shop's eclectic merchandise. Behind the display was a black curtain ensuring that passersby could see nothing of the store from outside, but the unusual window display was enough to make anybody stop: a set of three delicate crystal perfume bottles resting on a baroque purple velvet footstool, a small wooden chest tipped over with an array of striking gold jewelry arranged to spill out of it, an ornate Mardi Gras crown and cape, and a tall silver art deco candle stand with mother-of-pearl wings molded down either side.

"I swear I don't remember this building at all," I said. "How did I overlook the only white-brick storefront on the whole street?"

"Well, it does look freshly painted," Punk pointed out, "but even so, I can't place it in any other color. For the life of me, I just can't remember what was here before."

Cookie stepped onto the front stoop and into an alcove that sheltered the entry door. "Dare we enter, ladies?"

"We dare," Punk said.

As Cookie pushed the door open, a chime sounded. The rest of us followed her inside.

"Please come in," called a male voice from somewhere above us. "Make yourselves at home."

"How'd he know there's more than one of us?" Sugar whispered.

"Maybe the cat told him," Coco said, pushing past Sugar for a closer look at the most regal animal I'd ever seen this side of the Bronx Zoo. "It's a Maine coon," she said over her shoulder. "They get huge. Isn't he a stunner?"

"How do you know it's a he?" Sugar asked.

"I checked," Coco answered, keeping her eyes on the cat.

Coco's affinity for felines was well-documented. She found dogs far too needy. It was the aloofness of a cat that appealed to her. This one was silver-gray with streaks of white. He had sapphire-blue eyes and must've weighed at least twenty pounds. Coco laid her hand on the oak counter, where the cat was lounging next to an antique brass cash register. He rubbed his head against her hand, bringing a rare smile from Coco as she stroked his cheeks and lightly scratched under his chin.

The front of the store was so tight that the five of us could barely squeeze in between the counter where Coco stood and the display shelves lining the opposite wall, but a high tin-tiled ceiling gave it breathing room. Just beyond a spiral staircase maybe fifteen feet or so from the front door, the back of the store opened much wider. Tapestry rugs in pale blue and silver topped plank floors painted white. Lamps and chandeliers replaced the usual fluorescent lighting of retail shops. The whole place smelled of rich leather, old books, chamomile, and lilies. I heard the faint splash of a fountain and the soft music of wind chimes but couldn't see where they were coming from. A grandfather clock chimed three.

"I see Pierre has greeted you more properly than I have."

We followed the voice, and I saw, just as Sugar said, a man who was handsome but a little unnerving standing on the bottom step of the stairs, his hand resting lightly on the polished wood rail. As he came toward us, I immediately flashed back to sophomore lit class and the otherworldly Dorian Gray, wondering whether our host might've struck a deal with the dark side to look the way he did. His high cheekbones left dramatic hollows on the planes of his face, which was as chiseled as a statue, the jawline strong and square. He had full lips, flawless skin, and ice-blue eyes with long lashes. His hair was dark brown. His clothes—a white linen shirt, pale gray slacks, and fine leather shoes—had a Charleston look about them, simple but expensive. I would guess he was in his forties.

"Pierre's a real looker." Coco kept petting the cat.

"And very popular with the ladies," the man said with a smile as he stepped behind the counter. That smile transformed his face completely, melting the ice with warmth and kindness, which changed his whole demeanor. It was the strangest thing I'd ever seen. "Welcome back to you all. And I see you've brought a friend."

"This is my granddaughter, Edie," Punk said. "Edie, this is Mr. Toussaint."

"No need for 'Mr.' Please call me Jason. Welcome to The Trove, Edie."

"Thank you." I was trying very hard not to gape. I had never seen anybody anywhere who looked like him.

"Ladies, you'll find refreshments near the French doors in back. Please have some while you browse and let me know if I can be of help. Otherwise, I'll not hover and spoil your fun."

We thanked him and soon split up, each of us drawn to a different nook or cranny of the store, which, I now realized, felt much more like the private library of a grand old home than a retail shop. I followed the sound of splashing water past the staircase and into the large room in back, where tables and display cases were arranged in a maze of sorts that kept you from seeing everything all at once. You needed to wander—slowly at that—to take it all in. From somewhere in the maze, I heard Sugar shopping with Coco.

"Oh, sister, isn't this just a *fascinating* menagerie?"

"For heaven's sake, Shug, why can't you just be like everybody else and say he's got a lotta stuff?"

"Why would I want to be like everybody else?"

The sound of water grew louder as I approached the French doors, slightly ajar, and I smelled chamomile tea wafting from a silver service beside a platter of macarons. Next to them was a tall crystal pitcher filled with water, ice, and thin slices of lemon and blood orange.

Stepping beyond the doors, I found something every bit as impressive as the store itself—a lush courtyard garden framed by high brick walls draped with ivy and moss. Stepping stones laced with creeping Jenny made a serpentine path through the garden. A pergola laden with passionflower vines sheltered about three-quarters of the courtyard, diffusing the sun's heat and light even on a hot afternoon. Wind chimes stirred by gulf breezes dangled above. The back fourth of the garden was open to the sky. Two fig trees, one in each rear corner, lifted their fan-like green leaves into the blue. All along the garden walls were palms and elephant ears underplanted with colorful tropical flowers. At the center of the garden, a shallow round pool probably six feet across formed the base of a three-tiered fountain topped with a copper replica of a celestial globe, the kind old-time mariners once used to navigate. Four rectangular raised beds, all made of stone, overflowed with roses and fragrant lilies. They lay at the top, foot, and either side of the fountain, like the spokes of a wheel.

Leni would've loved all this. She would've called it "a storybook place." She and Punk were the only reason I knew a daffodil from a tulip. Mama wasn't much of a gardener.

I sat down on the ledge of the fountain pool, held out my hand, and let the cascade trickle through my fingers. Looking into the water, I watched my own reflection as ripples set it in motion, reshaping my image second by second. Just then, I had not so much a vision of Leni as a sense of her. I felt my friend in my heart and soul, and I could see her—not literally, but in my mind. Or maybe my heart. I'm not sure. Nothing like this had ever happened to me before. And it wasn't a memory. The Leni I sensed was different from the one I remembered, the one I had adored since childhood. That Leni was in constant motion, so eager to experience and embrace life that she couldn't take it in fast enough. This one was still, peaceful, wise, and distant. Leni wasn't just gone. She was transformed. I knew it, felt it, whatever you want to call it. Maybe I didn't understand it, but I didn't imagine it either.

"I see you've found my favorite spot in all of Biloxi."

I turned to see Jason standing at the entrance to the garden and tried to collect myself. He joined me beside the water.

"I can understand why you like it," I said. "It's so serene."

He nodded and held his hand under the cascade just as I was doing. "I wanted to give my guests a reminder that there's peace at the center."

"Of what?"

"Of everything." He took a white handkerchief from his pocket and dried his hand, then gave it to me so I could do the same. "May I show you something upstairs? I think it might be what you're looking for."

I frowned as I dried my hands and returned the handkerchief. "I'm not really looking for anything in particular."

He turned his face toward the sun and closed his eyes for a few seconds. "Perhaps I had it wrong," he said, smiling down at me. "Maybe something is looking for you. May I show you?"

I followed him inside, through the maze in the back of the store. We passed Punk, who was studying a wooden bread bowl, and Sugar, admiring an Old Country Roses tea service. No sign of Cookie, but Coco was sitting in a brocade armchair with her feet propped on a wooden stool, a cup of tea on a small table beside her. She calmly stroked Pierre. Stretched out as he was, the cat covered Coco's torso, his front paws resting on her shoulders, his face nuzzled against her neck. Coco looked like she'd died and gone to heaven. It was the first time I realized how unhappy she usually appeared.

The spiral staircase was so steep that I clutched the handrail as I followed Jason, who confidently glided up the steps. Upstairs, I found a completely different environment from what lay below. Wood-paneled walls and a coffered ceiling were lit by two brass chandeliers and evenly placed wall sconces. Jewel-toned, velvet wingback chairs dotted the walls, and a cart in the center of the room held another tea service. The heart pine floor was stained a rich walnut and dressed in maroon tapestry rugs that looked very old. The whole space felt like a cross between a ship and a church.

Tall bookcases wrapped all the way around a long reading table at one end of the room. They displayed antique books with rich leather bindings, gold embossing, and script typefaces. Scanning them, I saw sections on Mississippi, maritime history, Southern folklore, art, religion . . . At the other end of the room were all kinds of vintage photographs and maps, neatly arranged and well organized. I walked over and peered into a glass case displaying antique navigational tools—a telescope, quadrant, astrolabe, and celestial globe. I thought of my brother, a mechanical engineer obsessed with maritime history just as Pop had been. This display would make him hyperventilate.

Looking up, I saw my guide smiling at me. "Was I right to bring you here?" he asked.

"Definitely."

Jason poured us each a cup of chamomile, then took two red leather-bound books from one of the shelves and pulled out a chair for me.

"Start with this one," he said, sitting next to me and sliding one of the books in my direction. I lightly ran my fingers over the title: *Confessions*. Opening the book, I read its title page and saw that it was published in London in 1880. On each page inside, I found a column of questions to the left, with space for answers to the right. The questions had been repeated over and over, answered by different writers who initialed and dated their responses. *What is your favorite color? What do you most appreciate in your friends? If not yourself, who would you be?*

"What *is* this?" I couldn't take my eyes off the swirls and slants of inked answers to questions large and small, committed to this very paper over a hundred years ago.

"It's a parlor game, very popular in the Victorian era," Jason explained. "A form of entertainment in a time with no televisions or movie theaters. Marcel Proust is its most famous practitioner. Do you know his work?"

I shuddered. "One of my college professors went on and on about Proust and those 'petit madeleines' of his. Turned me off petit fours there for a while."

That brought a laugh from my host. "Understandable.

This isn't the exact confessional that Proust answered, but it's very similar. What I find fascinating about these books is that they can turn from light to dark and back again very quickly and unexpectedly, based on either the questions or the answers. A simple 'What is your favorite flower?' breaks your heart if the answer is 'The gardenias my wife kept at her bedside as she lay dying.' On the other hand, 'What is your deepest regret?' becomes a light question if the answer is 'That dreadful yellow hat I wore to my sister's wedding.'"

I scanned an unsigned page and read a regret aloud: "'I did not marry for love. I fulfilled expectations.' How sad is that?"

Jason's face grew somber as he looked down at the script handwriting. "I imagine that happened a lot in those days, Victorians being how they were."

I read a few more answers out loud. "Someone with the initials S.S. loves blue hydrangeas because they remind her of her grandmother. E.N.F. loves yellow roses best of all." I looked up at Jason. "It's strange, isn't it—how knowing that a woman prefers yellow roses to red tells you something important about her?"

"I had a feeling about you, Edie," Jason said. "Somehow I knew you would appreciate *Confessions*. And I have a gift for you." He slid the other red volume to me. It was the same book, but without any answers to the questions.

Running my hand over the empty space, I asked, "I get to answer them?"

"Yes," he said. "When you're ready."

"Should I answer them myself first and then ask other people?"

"I would recommend a more communal experience. Perhaps share it with the ladies." He took a small white paper bag from a shelf behind us and tucked the red book inside, then helped me with my chair.

"Thank you for this," I said as he handed me the bag.

"My pleasure." He led me back downstairs, where Punk and the other Ten Spots were waiting by the counter.

"I knew you were taking that home the minute I saw you with it," I said to Punk, who was cradling the bread bowl.

"It's misplaced," she said. "It wants to be on my table."

Jason rang up the bread bowl for Punk, an iron dinner bell for Cookie, who said she meant to hang it on her dock, and the tea service for Sugar.

"Coco, are you ready to go?" Punk asked her.

Coco didn't answer, riveted as she was on Pierre, who was licking her hand.

"Sister!" Cookie said loudly.

"What?" Coco barked, clearly aggravated to have her attention torn away from the silver cat.

"Well, are you *buying* anything?" Cookie asked.

"Of course." Coco took a twenty-dollar bill out of her purse and laid it on the counter, pushing it toward Jason. "You take that and buy my friend here anything he wants. Does he like fresh crab off the docks?"

"He does." Jason was watching Coco stroke the giant cat. She looked stricken at the thought of leaving him. "I believe your twenty dollars will cover your selection," Jason said as he reached behind the counter and pulled out a silver harness and leash, then fastened them to Pierre. He handed the leash to Coco, now uncharacteristically dumbstruck.

"What are you doing?" she asked.

"I'm sending Pierre to his new home," Jason said.

Pierre stood up on the counter and rubbed his head against

Coco's hand, now holding the leash, as if he wanted her to get on with it.

She shook her head. "But—but this cat's worth a lot of money."

"All the more reason to give him the home he deserves." Jason scratched the cat's neck. "He's grown weary of the shop and all the traffic in and out. He has done a fine job of charming my customers, but he's ready to retire. And he deserves his rest. You can offer him suitable accommodations, yes?"

Coco could only nod.

"Excellent." Jason took a small bag of cat food and two bowls from behind the counter and put them in a bag. "These will do until you and Pierre can visit the docks."

"But are you sure you want to—"

"I'm very sure," Jason insisted.

It was the first time I had ever seen Coco speechless. It was probably the first time *anybody* had ever seen Coco speechless.

"Cookie, can you—can you take—take the bag for me?" she stammered. "I'll carry Pierre. We can't let him burn his paws on that hot sidewalk."

Cookie grinned and took the bag. "No, we can't."

Jason picked up the tea service. "Allow me to carry this for you, Mrs. Vansant."

Sugar smiled and clasped her hands together. "You're too kind, Jason."

He held the tea service in one arm while he opened the door for us with the other. "After you, ladies. And I hope you enjoy the rest of your afternoon."

# *five*

**"COME ON, EVERYBODY,"** Punk said. "Let's go out on the porch so we don't miss the sunset. Edie, why don't you bring your book? I've mixed us up a batch of Liz Taylors."

Years ago, Punk heard Elizabeth Taylor interviewed on TV after a substantial weight loss. The movie legend reported that she had traded unhealthy drinks for sparkling water with a splash of cranberry juice on top. Punk said if it was good enough for Cleopatra, it was good enough for her. She had been serving Liz Taylors ever since.

Following our adventure at The Trove, the Ten Spots had stayed for a supper of leftover gumbo and French bread. I cleared the table while Punk got her crew situated on the porch. Then I grabbed my book and a pen, designating a page for each of us, and poured Pierre a saucer of cream before going out to join them.

"Pierre thanks you," Coco said as I knelt down and set the cream on the floor beside her rocking chair. The cat purred and rubbed his head against my knee while I scratched his neck.

"Now, don't get distracted by that scruffy ole tomcat, Edie," Cookie said. "Let's tear into your book."

I took a seat next to Punk in her porch swing and had a

sip of Liz. "Okay, here we go. First one's easy: What's your favorite color? Punk?"

"Aqua."

"Miss Cookie?"

"Yellow."

"Miss Sugar?"

"Pink. But not a deep, rosy pink. What I love best is the palest, most delicate of pinks, like the pink of a dogwood blossom. Not the darker tips and edges, of course—"

Coco slapped her palm against her forehead. "Dear people! By the time she's done describing that pink, I'll be laid out at the funeral home with you old birds leaning over the casket, crowing about how natural I look."

Even Sugar had to laugh. That's one of the things I've always loved about her—Sugar will be Sugar, but she knows it.

Pierre leaped onto Coco's lap and licked her cheek.

"What about you, Miss Coco?" I asked her. "What's your favorite color?"

"Silver."

"I thought it was orange," Sugar said.

"I've changed." Coco smiled down at Pierre and scratched his neck.

I turned to Coco's page and recorded her answer. "Next question: What's your favorite flower? Punk?"

"Hold on, now," she said. "What's *your* favorite color, Edie?"

I grinned at my grandmother. "Horn Island. That's my favorite color."

"I might've guessed," she said.

"I think I can answer the flower question for you," I told her. "*Camellia japonica*, white empress. But that's just a wild guess."

All of us laughed. Punk loved those white blooms so much that she planted them all the way up both sides of her driveway.

"Miss Cookie, what about you?"

"Daffodils. They're always in a good mood, and they don't ask for much."

"Miss Sugar?"

"I just love Rosa 'the Fairy.' It's such a striking pink rose."

"Miss Coco?"

"Bougainvillea. It shows off when it's good and ready, and it's thorny as all get-out so nobody messes with it."

"Edie?" Punk prompted. "What's your favorite flower?"

I thumped my pen against the page with my name on it. "I never really thought about it. But I love morning glories. I like the way they bloom wherever their vines take them. And you can count on them to open again when the sun comes up."

"Oh, honey, those vines will eat your house," Sugar said.

"That's true, Miss Sugar. Maybe I'll just ask Punk to paint me some. Y'all ready for a few more?"

"Shoot," Cookie said.

"This one's kind of interesting," I said. "What quality do you most value in your friends? Punk?"

"Kindness," she said.

"*Kindness*?" Coco asked her. "Then what am I doing here?"

Punk laughed at her. "I said you have to be kind, Coco, I never said you have to be sweet. You're very kind, much as you hate to admit it."

Some of us had short answers—honesty for Coco, a sense of humor for Cookie, "love you, warts and all" acceptance for me. Then it was Sugar's turn.

"I need an appreciation for beauty in my friends," she said.

"Anybody who can look at a Walter Anderson painting or a beautiful old church or even a lovely rose and not be moved by it—well, I just don't understand them, and I don't want to be their friend. I think they've got a loose screw, if you want to know the truth."

We kept the game going, confessing our favorite writers, names, and prized possessions until all of us were starting to yawn.

"Y'all want to do one more and call it a night?" I asked.

"Sounds good," Coco said. "I'm about ready for the sandman to break out his shovel and whack me over the head with it."

"What is your greatest fear?" I asked the group. "Anybody want to go first?"

"I will," Sugar said. "I'm afraid that one day I'll stop caring about myself—how I present myself, I mean. That I'll stop going to the beauty shop and getting my nails done, and I'll turn into one of those dreadful women who go about in flip-flops, with dirty feet and cracked heels. They wear sloppy clothes and let their hair get wild. Women like that don't care at all about making the world a pleasant place for those around them. They just don't think enough about other people to offer their best. If I ever do that, y'all will know I'm ready for the home."

"There could be earlier signs," Coco mumbled, which made Cookie snicker, as much as she tried to remain neutral between her sisters.

"How about you, Miss Coco? What's your greatest fear?"

"Fire ants. They'll ruin your garden and sting you to death on the way to it."

"Miss Cookie?"

She looked out at the water, darkening now that the sun

44

had dipped below the horizon. "Losing my independence," she said, turning back to the group. "I'm afraid I'll break a hip or dislocate a knee or something and that'll be that. Everybody'll say, 'Bless her heart, she went down so fast.' And I won't be able to take my boat out to fish or work in my garden or play golf—all the things I did with Grady when he was alive, things that keep a little part of him with me still. I'm very afraid of that."

"I imagine we all are," Punk said.

"Even you, Punk?" I asked her. "Is that your biggest fear too?"

She frowned as she thought about it. "Not exactly. I'm most afraid of having to leave this place. I think I could handle needing help or even being bedridden as long as I'm here. But if I couldn't wake up every morning and look out at the water or raise the window and feel the salt air—if I couldn't do that, I believe I'd ask God to take me." She looked at me and smiled, putting her arm around me. "I guess it's your turn, sweet girl. What's your biggest fear?"

I saw the first star twinkling in the early evening sky. "That I'll never make peace with what happened."

## Six

ABOUT A WEEK AFTER our first round of *Confessions*, I woke up to find a small gift box on my nightstand. It was beautifully wrapped, Punk style, in pale blue paper with a narrow white satin ribbon tied into a perfect little bow. The minute I opened it, I jumped out of bed and ran downstairs.

"Punk! Punk, where are you?" I found her in the kitchen, a mischievous smile on her face. "Punk, you can't do this!"

She gave me a big hug. "I'm pushing ninety—shoving it even. I can do what I want."

"But Rosetta?" She had wrapped up Pop's keys.

Punk kissed me on the forehead. "Something as special as that car wasn't meant to be hidden away. Your brother prefers boats, and Pop's will be his when I'm too old to take her to Horn. But nobody was ever more excited to ride in Rosetta than you. Pop got such a kick out of that. When we completely run out of fun things to do, we'll go down to the courthouse and get the title transferred into your name. In the meantime, you take her and enjoy her as much as your Pop did. I've got Bluebell to keep me warm."

Bluebell was a 1958 Eldorado Biarritz that Pop bought

Punk for her birthday decades ago. She loved it so much that she refused to even entertain the possibility of a replacement.

"I don't know how to thank you, Punk." I kissed her on the cheek.

"Remember your Pop with a smile every time you drive her. That'll be thanks enough. Let's go out on the porch and have our breakfast with the cranes and the pelicans."

————

I tried to talk Punk into coming with me for a top-down beach cruise, but she said I needed a day to myself after spending all my time with a bunch of old women. Honestly, Punk and her friends were more fun than most women my age. I think at a certain point—and the Ten Spots had reached it—women throw decorum to the four winds and do exactly as they please. They aren't the least bit self-conscious about anything. Maybe you don't notice it as much in other places, but in the Deep South, where "pretty is as pretty does," you notice.

I drove Rosetta around the bay to Abel's marina on the eastern side of the bayou and heard a familiar *ding-ding* when I ran over the long black rubber hose reaching out from two gas pumps. It had been alerting him to the arrival of his customers since 1957.

"Great land o' livin', it's Rosetta!" he exclaimed as he came outside.

"Hey, Mr. Abel. How's it going?"

He leaned against the doorframe. "Better now that I've got a pretty girl in a sweet ride to tend to. What brings you down, Edie?"

"Just long overdue to spend some time with Punk. And I think I might've had enough of New York. How's Miss Margie?"

Abel shook his head and grinned. "Meaner'n a snake with a toothache."

I laughed and pointed a finger at him. "You better take good care of Rosetta, or I'll tell your wife what you said."

As Abel gassed up the Impala and cleaned her windshield, I saw a flash of candy-apple red out of the corner of my eye and turned just in time to catch the rear end of a mint-condition '62 Thunderbird driving by. I whistled at the sight of it. "Man, did you see that?"

Abel finished cleaning my windshield and dried his hands on a towel hanging from his belt. "You mean the T-bird? Oh, yeah, she's a beaut."

"Local car?" I asked.

Abel scratched his head. "Not sure. I've prob'ly seen it two or three times now, always in Biloxi. Never seen it around the bayou till today. Maybe the driver finally heard about Nonnie's muffalettas."

"The legend lives on," I said. Everybody this side of New Orleans knew about Nonnie's to-die-for muffalettas. She claimed her secret was "making them with love." Punk thought it had more to do with the shot or two of Tabasco she detected in Nonnie's olive salad and the French bread she bought fresh from a Biloxi bakery every day.

"I might have to cruise around and see if I can get a closer look at that car," I said.

Abel winked at me and grinned. "I'd done forgot you were a born gearhead. You could spot a fine set o' wheels way before you were old enough to drive one. Can you spare me fourteen dollars?"

"Sure can." I handed him my money. "Thanks for looking after Rosetta—and tell Miss Margie I said hey."

"I'll do that." He tucked the money into his shirt pocket

and waved as I drove away, following the path of the T-bird until I hit Beach Boulevard and let it carry me all the way to Bay St. Louis.

I've always loved the way the bookend bridges on this highway give you such a sense of arrival, like they're lifting you out of one world and dropping you down in another. Drive east and a bridge takes you away from Biloxi's glitz, with its casino lights and splashy resorts, and into the quiet, tree-lined little jewel that is Ocean Springs. Drive west, where I was headed, and another bridge leaves behind serene Pass Christian, landing you in Bay St. Louis, a fun-loving mini New Orleans, where locals don't mind one bit if you dance barefoot in the street.

I trolled the galleries downtown until lunchtime and then made a beeline for my favorite beach hangout, where the rear deck had a view of the train trestle crossing the water. This place had been here forever. I found a table on the deck and looked out over the bay to see if I could spot any trawlers.

Somebody had left a newspaper on the table next to me, and a headline near the bottom of the front page caught my eye: "Horn Island Light Remains Mystery." Sliding the paper over to my table, I read that some local shrimpers had reported several sightings of a light on the eastern tip of Horn around midnight. The spot would appear to glow very brightly, they said, and then go completely dark. Must be a powerful light for shrimpers to see it from their boats out in the gulf.

"Got any theories?"

I looked up to see a waiter with a neatly trimmed beard and a short ponytail standing by my table. He smiled as he laid down some silverware wrapped in a paper napkin and set a glass of water on the table.

"Not a clue," I said. "Guess I'll go with pirates. You?"

He shrugged as he took a pad and pen out of his apron pocket. "Stuff like that usually turns out to be campers, fishermen, or teenagers up to nonsense. Need a menu?"

"That's okay. Could I get a medium-rare burger all the way, with fries and a Coke?"

"You got it." He jotted down my order and headed for the kitchen.

I took another look at the article. The light had been spotted three times so far, never when anyone was there to locate its source. The local marine guys reported no involvement on their part. The paper had even contacted NOAA to see if they were up to anything on Horn, but they said no.

I had just caught up on all the high school sports when the ponytailed waiter delivered my lunch, taking a bottle of ketchup out of his apron pocket and setting it next to my plate. "Anything else I can get you?"

"No, this looks great," I said. "Thanks a lot."

Having been spoiled by Punk's cooking, which is positively life-affirming, I wasn't easily impressed by restaurant food. But the burgers here were something special, quality beef flame-broiled nice and juicy with the bun lightly toasted on a flattop. The sandwich was dressed with melted cheddar, fresh lettuce and tomato, dill pickles and red onions, and a house-made mayo-ketchup blend. Hand-cut fries. Nothing frozen, pressed, or otherwise automated.

I took my time savoring both the food and the view, watching a couple of trawlers way off in the distance. The official state line between Mississippi and Louisiana extends into the gulf. You can see it on maps, but I have no idea how watermen keep up with which side they're on. I doubt the fish give it much thought. Sometimes I feel like I'm navigating invisible lines myself, like the one between how things were and how they are now, the line between Leni up there and me down here.

"All good?" The waiter stopped by to check on me.

"Perfect," I said, giving him a thumbs-up.

The first time I ever came to this place, I must've been twelve or so. Pop and Grady loved the burgers, and they'd let me tag along. During my summer with Cole, they'd bring the two of us in the Impala. After lunch, Cole and I would dance to Otis Redding on the jukebox if the band wasn't playing, while my grandfather and his friend swapped fish tales with the older guys who came here daily for that very purpose.

After Leni and I graduated high school, she stayed a few weeks with me at Punk's. We spent several afternoons on this deck, dancing with cute boys and watching the trains go by.

Now another train was crossing. The jukebox was playing "Sittin' on the Dock of the Bay," just like it did back then—just like it had a million times before. The empty chair across from me seemed suddenly threatening, as if it meant to take this perfectly pleasant afternoon and turn it on its head. I flagged down my waiter, got the ticket and a to-go box, then packed up the remaining half of my food and paid my bill.

Driving Beach Boulevard, the water on one side and Pass Christian on the other, I felt a gradual ebb in the swell of whatever it was—call it grief, call it panic—that had begun rising at the restaurant. Maybe this was what I could expect for a while—the mixed bag, as Punk called it. One minute, a wave crashing against me; the next, that same water peacefully retreating to its source.

I decided a trip to The Trove was in order. I could tell Jason about our experience with *Confessions* and find a million distractions in his store. I was beginning to think that's

51

what I needed most of all—some sort of distraction, and maybe a big one, like a new job. I couldn't expect Punk to fill every waking minute for me. I had leaned on her long enough. Much more of that and I would become completely disgusted with myself.

In Biloxi, I found a parking spot near The Trove. I was just about to get out of the car when I had an idea and grabbed my camera from the glove compartment.

Jason wasn't behind the counter when I stepped inside. "Please come in," I heard him call from upstairs. "I'll be right with you."

"It's just me, Edie," I answered. "Take your time."

I spotted an antique brooch Sugar would love. It was shaped like a rose and made of pink—make that *delicate* pink—rhinestones. Before I could check the price, I heard footsteps on the stairs and turned to see Jason.

"What a pleasant surprise," he said. "What brings you in today?"

"I've come to report on *Confessions*," I said.

"Ah! And how is it going?"

"We're all enjoying it—my grandmother's friends and me—and you were absolutely right about the way the answers can turn when you least expect it."

Jason nodded. "That's what drew me to it. That and the investment of time and courage it takes to record those answers, revealing as they are. Can I help you find something today?"

"Not unless you're hiring," I said.

"As a matter of fact, I am."

The phone rang, and he stepped behind the counter to answer it. When he finished, he jotted a few notes on a pad next to the phone before turning his attention to me.

"About the job," he said. "I'm surprised you're looking. I was under the impression you were vacationing with your grandmother."

"More like transitioning," I said. "I was working in New York until, well, until I needed a change. Punk came to my rescue."

"I doubt the job I can offer would compare to anything you had up there."

"That's kind of the point. I'm not really looking to start a new career right now. But I'm a hard worker and a pretty quick study. Is that what you need, though? Or are you looking for someone longer term to run your store for you?"

"Truthfully, I'm not sure. Up until now, I've had no trouble handling everything by myself, but I've just acquired a sizable cache of Hurricane Camille photography that will need to be cataloged as best we can and displayed somehow. I'm afraid it's a bit more than I can handle along with everything else. So for now, I need a part-time assistant, likely three days a week, at least through the end of the year. Are you interested?"

"Very."

"Then you're hired. I'm certain we can agree on a fair salary. Why don't we say Tuesday, Wednesday, and Thursday? That way you'll have long weekends."

"Perfect."

He glanced at the camera around my neck. "Did you need to take pictures of something in the store?"

"Actually, I wanted to show you a picture I took on Horn Island and see if you might help me figure it out."

"Happy to." He stepped from behind the counter as I took off the camera strap, looked through the screen, and scrolled to a few pictures I had taken of the writing in the sand.

I handed him the camera. "Punk thinks it's Hebrew?"

Jason stared at the writing and then slowly nodded. "Your grandmother is correct."

"Can you read it, by any chance?"

"Possibly." He looked more closely at the picture and then spoke the words in Hebrew.

"What does that mean, Jason?"

"'Help one, save one, lead one home.'"

I repeated the words. "What on earth does *that* mean?"

"I'm afraid I can't say. I wish I could."

"No, that's okay. I really appreciate your help." I thought about what I'd just said and smiled. "I guess you've helped one. Now all you have to do is save one and lead one home."

Jason stared blankly at me for a moment, then smiled and nodded. "Yes, I suppose that's all I have to do. I'll put it on my calendar."

# Seven

**THE NEXT DAY WAS GRAY AND RAINY,** so Punk and I decided to relax and spend the afternoon reading on the back porch.

"Hey, Punk, did you see that story about Horn in yesterday's paper?"

She looked up from her book. "No, honey, I never got to it."

"It said shrimpers have seen an odd light out there around midnight—three times so far. They said it looked like the eastern tip of the island was glowing for a few seconds and then it went dark. That's the same part of Horn where I found the writing in the sand."

"I'm sure there's a sensible explanation," Punk said. Then she grinned and pointed a finger at me. "But that's no fun, is it?"

"No, ma'am, it's not." When I was a kid, the two of us made up stories all the time about anything and everything—a shrimp boat on the horizon, an old earring uncovered in the sand, a feather floating on the water . . . absolutely anything.

"A flash of light on Horn could mean only one thing," Punk prompted.

"Pirates, obviously," I said.

"Obviously," she agreed. "But the truly shocking part is the identity of their ship's captain, the mild-mannered yet inscrutable . . ."

"Jason Toussaint."

"And his bloodthirsty first mate . . ."

"Nonnie Tucker, a.k.a. the marauding muffaletta maven of Jackson County, Mississippi."

Punk laughed and shook her head. "Sweet girl, I think you need more time on Horn if the most intriguing accomplice you can conjure for poor Jason is Nonnie Tucker."

"Agreed. I'm pitiful. And I think I hear a car pulling up."

Punk set down her book. "I guess we'd better go see who it is."

We walked through the center hallway to the front porch, and I couldn't stifle a girlie squeal when I saw our guest step out of a taxi, suitcase in hand.

"Charly!" I ran out into the rain and hugged her tight before grabbing the suitcase as we hurried onto the porch. "I can't believe you're here, chouchou!"

She kissed me on both cheeks. "Oh, chouchou, neither can I!"

*Chouchou* is a French version of the Southern "honey," "baby," "sugar," etc. Charly taught me to say it when I was a little girl, and we've been chouchou-ing each other ever since, always with very heavy, very bad French accents.

She held my face in her hands and stared at me just like Mama always did. "Look at you! I'll bet your mama's proud enough to pop."

"She and Daddy are on assignment across the pond."

"I hear he's advising on something hydroelectric?"

"That's the scuttlebutt."

Punk gave her a hug. "Did I forget to tell you Edie was here?"

Charly laughed and shook her head. "Just like you forgot to tell Edie I was coming."

"And how did you leave North Carolina?" Punk asked.

"Behind. For now."

"Good for you. Let's go inside."

Charly's real name was Charlotte—Charlotte Moran. My godmother, she has always been Mama's Leni, the two of them thick as thieves since third grade. When I was first learning to talk, all my "sh's" came out as "ch's," and she became Charly to me. Now it would seem weird to call her anything else.

My mother's best friend is not someone you'd overlook in a crowd. Her fair skin is flawless, her bone structure delicate, while her hair is curly, unruly, and deep copper, almost down to her waist. She has periwinkle eyes, a slightly upturned nose, and a smile which, now that I think about it, reminds me of Jason Toussaint's in that it transforms her whole demeanor. But unlike Jason, who can appear downright menacing without a smile, Charly has what you might call resting melancholy. She looks like she belongs someplace with moors and castles and poets penning odes to random birds.

"Now that you're both here," Punk was saying, "we might as well fire up the coffeepot. Charlotte, honey, are you hungry?"

"No, ma'am. But a piece of your Mudpie sure would be good."

Punk put her hands on her hips. "What makes you think I made one?"

Charly mimicked her pose. "Because you did."

"I sure did." They laughed as Punk hugged her again. "I

have missed you so much, lovebug." Punk kissed her on the forehead. She'd probably been doing that since Mama and Charly were kids. Watching the two of them made me feel an unexpected pang of loneliness for both my mother and my best friend.

After we went inside, I took Charly's suitcase upstairs while she and Punk made coffee. Together, we went out to the table on the back porch where we could look at the water and listen to the soothing sounds of rainfall, surf, and gulf breezes stirring the live oaks.

Charly took a bite and closed her eyes, as if she wanted to shut out everything except the taste of what had become Punk's signature chilled dessert, named Mudpie by my older brother. Two layers, one of chocolate pudding, the other a blend of cream cheese and Cool Whip, were spread over a nutty, buttery crust. Punk topped the whole thing with more Cool Whip, chopped pecans, and chocolate curls.

"Miss Punk, promise you'll make this for my last meal."

"Honey, I doubt I'll be around," Punk said, "but if I'm still here, you can count on me."

All three of us heard thunder and looked out at the water. "I had almost forgotten how beautiful it is down here," Charly said.

"It's my great pleasure to remind you," Punk answered.

"Your table has always been the safest, happiest place in the world to me," Charly said before taking another bite. "Can we eat this every day till I have to go?"

"Of course," Punk said. "But why would you have to go?"

Charly narrowed her eyes and pointed an accusing finger at Punk. "You never change." Then she laughed and added, "Thank goodness for that." She spotted *Confessions*, which I had left in the chair next to her, and picked it up. "What's this?"

"It's a Victorian parlor game." I explained how it worked as she opened the book and thumbed through a few pages. "I got it at an antique store here in town. I've been playing it with the Ten Spots."

She laughed at the nickname. "I had forgotten you call them that."

"Edie, why don't you read Charlotte the questions that the rest of us already covered and get her caught up so we can all play together next time the crew comes over?" Punk suggested.

Charly made a face like she had just bitten into a lemon, immediately putting the book on the table and pushing it away. "You know I'm not big on soul-bearing, Miss Punk. I wouldn't even go back to church camp with Libba after that one time she talked me into it."

"Remind me, honey. What was the trouble with camp again?"

"They paired us up with total strangers and declared us prayer partners for the week." Charly shuddered at the memory. "I had to pray with an opinionated Baptist girl from Opelousas. She felt compelled to critique my supplications."

"Ah! Now I remember," Punk said, patting Charly's hand. "Don't you worry. We'll let you skip any questions you don't care for. And in my house, you can pray with anybody you like—or nobody at all."

I grabbed the book, which still had my pen tucked inside, and jumped in before Charly could protest. "First question's painless. What's your favorite color?"

"Peacock blue."

"Favorite flower?"

"Gardenia."

She was answering so quickly that I could barely jot down

her answers before she wanted the next question. "Favorite writer?"

"Eudora Welty. Or Toni Morrison. Definitely one of those two."

"Favorite name?"

She winked at my grandmother. "Punk."

"Most prized possession?"

"This." She reached inside the neck of her blouse and pulled out the gold heart necklace my mother had given her at their high school graduation, engraved with "Sisters" on one side and "Always" on the other.

Punk reached over and lightly touched Charly's cheek.

"What trait do you value most in your friends?" I asked.

"Acceptance."

"That's what I said!" I told her. "Last one and then you're all caught up. What's your biggest fear?"

Charly silently stared at the water for the longest time. Then she said, "That I'll never get an answer."

Punk and I looked at each other. "Charly, that's so weird," I said.

"What?" She loaded the last bite of chocolate onto her fork and held it in midair.

"Your answer's almost the same as mine. That makes two."

She set the fork down on her plate and leaned back in her chair. "Well, how about that?"

# eight

COASTAL STORMS ALWAYS KEEP ME AWAKE, not because I'm afraid of them but because I don't want to miss anything—not the flashes of lightning over the gulf, the rumble of thunder, or the big gusts of wind. Packed away somewhere in my parents' house, I've got a crateful of storm pictures I've taken over the years. Tonight, I took up a post in my window seat just after eleven. It was almost midnight now, and the storm showed no signs of waning. I heard a soft knock just before Charly stuck her head in my door.

"You awake, chouchou?"

I smiled and waved her in. "Wide awake, chouchou."

She sat down opposite me. I handed her a pillow for her back and a cotton throw as we watched the storm together.

"On the lookout for the Horn Island light?" Charly asked.

"I guess Punk told you all about it?"

"She did."

"It's got some competition tonight." I nodded at the window as lightning flashed several times. "Plus I doubt whoever's causing the glow wants to be out in this."

"What if it's just a big gimmick: 'Come, gullible tourists, and behold the fabled ghost light of Horn Island, Mississippi!'"

We laughed together at Charly's paranormal pitch for tourism dollars. I told her about the message in the sand that Jason had translated.

"That's the weirdest thing I've heard in a while," she said.

"I know, right?"

We stopped talking and listened to one of those long, low thunder rolls that sounds like it will never end.

"Man, it's good to see you," I finally said.

"I'm sorry it's been so long."

"No need to apologize. I'm just glad you're here."

She traced a heart on the window with her fingertip. "Me too, sweetie. These days, I mostly just want to be alone, but I could never turn down Miss Punk. And I'm so glad I get to be with you for a while."

"How long can you stay?"

"As long as I want to, I guess. About six months ago, I let my partner buy me out, so I can pretty much pick and choose projects—design only the homes I want to when I want to. Do I sound lazy?"

"We should all be so lazy."

We watched a rapid-fire triple flash over the water. Neither of us jumped the way Mama always did when she saw lightning. Charly used to tease her about it: "Are you sure Edie's not mine, Libba? Look at how much she loves a good storm!"

"Mama beats all I've ever seen when it comes to thunder and lightning," I said. "She'll just about get under the bed—and drag the rest of us with her."

"I know. She's always been like that." Charly looked at me and sighed. "I'd be lost without Libba. How are you managing without Leni?"

She always cut through the chitchat. "Sometimes I'm not." I hugged my knees to my chest. "When Leni first died, it felt like a knife in my stomach every time I thought about her. I kept going over and over everything in my head. Should I have tried to talk her into changing doctors, pushed her this way or that? Did I do everything I could to help her get well?"

Charly reached across the window seat and squeezed my hand. "I know the answer to that, and I wasn't even there. Whatever you did for Leni was your level best, and whatever you gave her was all you had. I know that because I know how much you loved her. You loved her the way I love your mother."

"The last night that she was conscious, I was the only one there. Leni had been feeling so good that her mom flew home for the first time in a month, just to check on things and pay bills." I put one of Punk's throw pillows in my lap, fidgeting with the fringe to give my hands something to do. "But then that infection came raging back and everything happened so fast. I called Leni's mother right after I called the ambulance, but she couldn't get a flight till the next day. And I can't help wondering—would things have been different if somebody else had been with her, somebody smarter, more experienced . . . somebody more . . . something?"

"Edie, Leni was too sick to get better that night, no matter what you or anybody else did."

I took a deep breath and miraculously didn't cry. "Being with Punk helps. I think what I miss most—and it's kind of hard to explain—is that Leni didn't just get *me*, she got *all* the me's."

"What do you mean, sweetie?"

"She got the family me, the one who tries hard not to disappoint or worry anybody. She got the high school me—total drama queen. She got the college me—embarrassingly earnest. She got the New York me—half the time desperate to fit in, the other half ready to chuck the city and move down here for good. All the me's, real or imagined."

Charly slowly twirled a long strand of red hair through her fingers. "We all do that, Edie—wrestle with ourselves and adjust to suit our circumstances. Sometimes we don't even realize we're doing it."

I looked out the window as I grappled with the words to explain why Leni had been such a singular part of my life. "She was the only friend I ever had who could make sense of all my pieces. She was always in my corner, one hundred percent, but wouldn't hesitate to tell me when I'd gone off the rails." I turned back to Charly. "I don't know how to keep myself on course without that—without her."

"It's only been a couple of months, Edie. You have to give this awful thing its due. Nobody has the right to tell you how long that should take. It takes as long as it takes."

We watched another flash of lightning over the water, way out against the horizon. "Have you ever lost somebody— somebody you were really close to, I mean?" I asked.

Charly looked out at the storm and sighed. "It was a long time ago. But I still feel it when I let myself, which I try not to do."

"Charly, I'm sorry," I said. "It's bad enough I've turned into a mush bucket, and now I'm dragging you down into the quagmire."

"You're not dragging me down. Not ever. Sometimes you just have to let the bad stuff out with somebody you trust. Your mama's always been the one I count on for that."

"Always?"

"Yep." Charly grabbed a pillow and hugged it to her chest. "From day one, Libba never made me feel like I needed to change anything or hide anything. She took me as I am.

Didn't even give me grief for ditching LSU. That says a lot about her, given that your grandparents had written scholarship recs for me and I was supposed to be Libba's roommate. It would've been easy for her to guilt me into doing what she wanted, but your mama put me first. That's just how she is."

"What made you give college a pass?"

"I found something better."

"What?"

"Biloxi, Mississippi."

"Well, now you have to tell me everything."

She looked out the window, watching another brilliant flash of light. Then she turned back to me with a sigh. "That was so long ago. Seems like it happened to two different people."

"Two?"

"Libba and me."

"You mean Mama was with you in Biloxi?"

"She most certainly was."

"Spill, Charly, spill!"

She laughed at my persistence. "So you want me to dish the dirt on your mama?"

"What are friends for?"

She fluffed the pillow behind her back and got comfortable. "Back then, Libba was sure of two things: She wanted a family and she wanted to teach little kids. College was an easy choice for her. Best place to get her education degree *and* her M.R.S. But I, on the other hand, had no clue. Our junior year in high school, I started taking classes at the trade school and got my beauty operator's license a few months before the principal handed us our diplomas. I knew I could make a living in a beauty shop, at least for now. I just wasn't sure where until Libba and I road-tripped to Biloxi right after graduation."

"Pop and Punk still lived in Louisiana then?"

"That's right. They moved here right after Camille."

"And Punk let Mama road-trip to Mississippi when she was only seventeen?"

"Sort of. But you know your grandmother. She always has a plan. You've probably heard Miss Punk talk about her older cousin Louella?"

"I never knew her, but I've heard the stories. Must've been a real character."

"Oh, she was—buried in a strawberry-pink suit with a matching pillbox hat. I went to the funeral. But back in the sixties, she lived in a big, rambly Victorian right on Beach Boulevard. Cousin Louella invited us girls to stay with her since we weren't exactly rolling in cash. Conveniently, that also allowed her to keep an eye on us for you-know-who."

"And what did a couple of Louisiana girls do on the loose in Mississippi?"

Charly looked so wistful that I had to wonder what she was remembering about her carefree summer with my mother. "Summer of '68," she finally said. "You can't imagine what it was like down here. The Strip was buzzing. Beach Boulevard was loaded with shops and restaurants and dance floors and bowling alleys and skating rinks—anything you wanted. We'd stay on the beach all day long. Hotels weren't as strict back then, and we loved the pool at the Buena Vista. We'd just stroll in off the beach and take a cold dip."

I reached over and nudged her. "How was your social life, Charly?"

She gave her hair a dramatic hand flip. "Honey *child*. If you wanted a date, all you had to do was step outside. Keesler was overflowing with young airmen training for their first tours. The boys were shipping out to Vietnam in droves, so there was this incredible sense of urgency. All the young people down here could feel it. And there were so many of us. You couldn't stir us with a stick."

"What were they like—all those airmen about to leave for war?"

"Some of them were just on the hunt for a wild night with girls who were, as Louella put it, 'loose as a goose.' We avoided them like the plague. Libba and I met some really sweet guys who just needed somebody to keep them company and take their minds off what they had to do when their training ended. Louella would let us invite our dates to supper so they could have a home-cooked meal while she checked them out. She'd always find a way to casually mention that Biloxi's chief of police was a dear personal friend. Then the boys would take us dancing or bowling. Sometimes we'd finagle a boat and take a sunset cruise on the bay. We'd always end up walking on the beach in the moonlight." Charly rested her head against the window. "There's nothing like romance when you're young. The right boy can make your heart jump into your throat just by holding your hand."

"You're not exactly ancient, chouchou," I said.

She sat up and looked at me. "I know. But it's different now. When you're young, every touch is a first. Every date is a will-he—will he hold my hand, will he kiss me good night, will he *really* kiss me good night . . . It's thrilling. You just don't realize how much until you're older and have all that scar tissue on your heart."

"Did you and Mama have lots of thrills with your airmen?" I teased her.

"You know it!" Charly said. "But we didn't get away with

much. The one time we were ten minutes late for our curfew, Louella met us and our dates on her front porch in her robe and nightgown—had a silk scarf tied around her pin curls and a Winchester in her hands. That lady meant business. But we still managed to have the time of our lives. I just fell head over heels in love."

"With one of the airmen?"

"No, with Biloxi. Everything about it fit me like a glove. We were supposed to leave on Sunday, but on Saturday morning, I spotted a Help Wanted sign in the window of a beauty shop near the Tivoli Hotel. Libba let me give her a bouffant while the owner watched. Her name was Maxine Gilbert—over six feet tall and wore her hair bleached blond, teased into a beehive. Maxine was so shorthanded that she said she'd hire me on the spot and advance me a week's pay if I could start work on Monday. I didn't have to think twice. She was my ticket out."

"Of Louisiana?"

"Of everything. My parents divorced when I was twelve, which was kind of a relief because they fought all the time and neither one of them paid us kids much attention. The apartment we lived in felt like one of those empty crab shells you find on the beach. No life in it. Just a hollow shelter and a hard one at that. By the time I graduated, my brothers were big enough to take care of themselves. Maxine and her beauty shop cracked open the door, and I barreled through it."

"Can't say I blame you. I'd have done the same thing. At least, I like to think I'd be that brave." How many times had I heard Punk say that you could know somebody all your life and not really know them at all? Charly had never told me much about her family before. Neither had Mama.

"Early Sunday morning, your mama drove me home,

helped me pack all my worldly belongings into her Mustang, and then took me back to Biloxi."

"Where did you live?" I asked.

"You know that thing Miss Punk does where you think you're running the show, but she's actually worked everything out to suit her and you never saw it happen?"

"Hello? How do you think I got here?"

"Exactly. Libba begged her to let us have this one last summer together before she went off to LSU and I pursued a lucrative career in hairdos. When we got back to Biloxi late Sunday afternoon, Louella offered each of us a ridiculously low rate for our room and board—no doubt subsidized by Miss Punk—and arranged a summer job for Libba in the nursery at her church, where working mothers left their kids during the week. Libba loved looking after those preschoolers. She was in heaven. We both were."

"And you got to spend a whole summer in Biloxi together, on your own?"

"On our own but under the eagle eyes of Louella. We didn't mind, though. It was still more freedom than either of us had ever had. Of course, your mama's situation was completely different from mine. She didn't need to escape her family. She just wanted to spread her wings a little bit. But I flew out of a cage and never looked back." Charly leaned her head against the window again and watched the rain drizzle down the panes. "You're working your way out of a cage too, aren't you, chouchou?"

"Trying to."

"Don't give up, Edie. It's a mighty empty feeling when you give up."

## nine

**THE NEXT MORNING,** Charly asked Punk and me if we'd mind lending her Pop's boat for a solitary trip to Horn. She hadn't been back to the island since she'd left Biloxi all those years ago. She said she wanted to reintroduce herself. We reminded her that this was Memorial Day and solitude would be hard to come by, but she wanted to try anyway. I helped her load supplies and then decided to take Rosetta for a cruise while the Ten Spots went to an art show in Ocean Springs.

I made my way to Beach Boulevard and cruised west, stopping to take pictures of the harbor boats at Pass Christian before driving over the bridge to Bay St. Louis.

Rosetta seemed almost too much car for the narrow street skirting the bluff that overlooked the bay. I debated whether to return to my favorite lunch spot and endure an emotional fistfight with the memories of Leni lurking there or take the easy route and grab a bite at another hangout known more for its festive atmosphere than its food. I was still wrestling with myself when I spotted it up ahead—the red T-bird parked in front of the bank.

The spaces next to it were taken, so I parked Rosetta just

around the corner and grabbed my camera out of the glove compartment.

Slowly circling the car, I took a few shots as I checked out the flawless paint job, the polished chrome, the shoot-down-the-road styling that earned it the nickname "Bullet Bird." This model had just a hint of fins, low and understated, a faint memory of the metal sails that soared off cars made just a few years earlier. The driver had put the top down, so I got to see the interior, which looked like it came straight off the '62 showroom floor, just like the rest of the car. As much as I wanted to climb behind the wheel, I took care to maintain a respectful distance. Car guys are usually flattered by the ogling of strangers, but don't you even think about touching their baby.

You had to wonder about the driver of a car like this. I assumed it was a guy, given the absence of anything remotely girlie inside. What if he was somebody Charly knew when she lived down here? The year of the car would be about right. Maybe it belonged to one of the airmen she and Mama had dated. What if he was here—right here—maybe depositing his paycheck in the bank and still holding on to the car he had back then? What if he remembered them?

"Looking to buy my ride?"

I jumped at the sound of a male voice, not just because it startled me but because I recognized it.

Slowly turning around, I stared, stupefied, at Cole Donovan standing on the steps of the bank. He didn't recognize me at first.

Finally, I found my voice. "If you think I'd give two cents for this clunker, you've spent way too much time out in the sun on that surfboard of yours." I kept a straight face as long as I could, which wasn't long at all.

"*Edie?*" His eyes opened wide as he hurried down the steps to me. When he was an arm's length away, he abruptly stopped and said, "Hey."

"Hey yourself."

We both laughed, and then he put his arms around me, not so much hugging me as holding me close the way he used to. He smelled like sandalwood.

"I can't believe you're here," he said, his face against my hair. When he finally let go, too soon for me, he took a step back and stared as if he were checking the twenty-something in front of him against the teenager of his memory. "What are you doing in Bay St. Louis?"

"Just taking an afternoon ramble. I quit my job not long ago. Punk's putting up with me till I can figure out what's next."

I had so many butterflies in my stomach that I was afraid they might lift me clean off the ground and hurl me headfirst into the bay. Cole looked almost the same, just more mature and muscular. "Filled out," as Punk would say. He had short hair now, but it was the same sun-kissed blond.

I was staring. I should be talking.

"What about you?" I asked. "What are you doing down here?"

"Stopping for lunch on my way back from New Orleans. I've moved back to Biloxi. An old Air Force buddy who works at the bank lets me park here."

"Let me guess—because the spaces are wider and offer more protection for your paint job?"

Cole smiled at me. "Of course."

Oh my goodness, that smile—full lips and a dimple on the right side. It still made me go weak at the knees.

"Since you trashed my '62, what are you driving that's so bloomin' hot?"

I fished the Impala keys out of my pocket and jingled them. "The name's Rosetta. Punk gave her to me. Read 'em and weep."

"Okay, you win." He started laughing but then abruptly stopped. "Wait, if you're driving Rosetta, does that mean your Pop . . . ?"

"He passed a few years ago. Punk says she doesn't want to keep Rosetta hidden away anymore. But to tell you the truth, I still feel like I need to ask Pop's permission to crank her. He sure loved that car."

Cole reached out and touched my hand. "I'm sorry. I really am. I know you guys were close. I thought a lot of him myself."

The air around us felt suddenly heavy, and I desperately wanted to lighten it before I got all weepy and ruined everything.

Cole seemed to feel it too. He shifted his weight a couple of times, and I knew he was looking for a way out of this sad conversation. He rubbed the back of his neck and said, "I think he'd be proud to know I still put Tabasco on everything."

We were laughing again at the memory of Pop introducing a California boy to Louisiana's signature condiment. That seemed like such a long time ago.

"You'll be pleased to hear that Punk still makes a mean gumbo, and you have a standing invitation to douse it with hot sauce."

"Your grandmother's gumbo is one of the best things I ever ate in my whole life. Speaking of gluttony, I was just about to head over and grab a burger—maybe watch a train or two go by." He put his hands in his pockets and ran his foot back and forth over a stray rock in the street. "Any chance you might come with me?"

I had to squint, looking up at him in the early afternoon sun. I hoped my voice sounded remotely steady when I answered, "A girl's gotta eat."

"She does indeed." He nodded toward our favorite spot. "Shall we?"

My heart jumped into my throat, just as it had a decade ago. It was plain silly, but I didn't care.

We crossed the street together and got a table at the edge of the deck so we could sit across from each other and look out at the bay. The waiter took our order, then disappeared into the kitchen.

Cole rested his elbows on the table, his hands lying flat against it. No wedding ring, hallelujah. *I am completely hopeless.*

"Since the last time I saw you, I have successfully acquired and consistently maintained my driver's license," I said.

"I remember. We left in August, and you were turning sixteen that September. Pass on the first try?"

"Of course."

"Well done."

"I trust you're equally accomplished?"

"Hardly."

"Where did you go from here, Cole?"

"Mostly I've been flying," he said. "I joined the ROTC in college, then went into officers' training with the Air Force when I graduated. Made it through advanced flight school and flew fighter jets. A few years in, we had a shortage of C-130 pilots, so I retrained and started flying those. Then I came stateside to train other pilots. And all that worked out because now I'm in the reserves, and I get to fly with the 53rd Weather Recon." He looked out at the bay sparkling under a warm sun. "Man, I'm glad to be back in Biloxi. I

74

transferred here from Little Rock, and all those mountains were too much for a beach bum like me."

It took me a minute to process what he'd just said. I leaned forward in my chair. "Wait a minute. Back up. First you were a fighter pilot, then you flew a C-130 so well they had you teaching other pilots, and now you're an honest-to-goodness hurricane hunter. But all you can say about your military career is that it's good to be back in Biloxi because you're not a mountain guy?"

He put his hands up. "It's not that dramatic."

"Are you or are you not a bona fide hurricane hunter?"

He did the "so-so" hand wave in midair. "Sometimes. And sometimes I'll just fly the crew that takes routine readings for the National Hurricane Center in Miami."

"I would kill to take pictures from inside the eye."

"I knew it." Cole lightly slapped the table. "I knew you'd end up getting into photography, as much as you loved taking pictures on Horn."

"I'm not exactly there yet. Took a long detour, but I'm hoping. I thought you wanted to become a commercial pilot after the Air Force—fly Delta or American all over the place?"

"I thought so too," he said. "But I got pretty attached to the military. It's like having a big family. You remember how I grew up, just Dad and me, right?"

"I remember." Of course I did. I remembered everything he ever said or did. The way his fingers curled when he rested his hands on his lap, the slight change in the timbre of his voice when we were alone together—every last subtlety had been etched in my memory, unaltered, for a decade.

"Once I got used to living in a whole community of people who looked out for each other, the idea of sleeping in hotels and flying planeloads of strangers to their vacations and business meetings didn't appeal too much."

"I can see that. You probably know this already, but folks down here love Keesler. The base is a big part of the community, so you can expect a warm welcome, even for a California surfer dude such as yourself."

Cole nodded and took a sip of his Coke. "I'll try to keep the hang-tens to a minimum."

I was trying very hard not to stare at his hands resting on the table. After all this time, I still remembered their touch, their warmth, their strength, more than I cared to admit. "Tell me about the T-bird."

"It was Dad's. He left it in California the summer we lived here. Always promised me I could have it if I got through flight school, and he kept his word. Her name is Chi-Chi, by the way."

I laughed and rolled my eyes. "You have *got* to be kidding me."

"Nope," Cole said. "Dad named her back in '62, and it seemed wrong somehow to change it. I just had her painted and put in a new engine. But that's boring car stuff. Tell me about your photography. Are you working anywhere right now?"

"I just got a part-time job at an antique gallery in Biloxi—starting next Tuesday—mostly to get myself out of Punk's hair. She's been looking after me for too long now, and I decided enough already. The antique dealer received an amazing donation of Hurricane Camille photography, and he's hired me to research and catalog the images so he can exhibit them somehow. Just thinking about working with the kind of pictures you see once and never forget—I guess it reminded me of how much I always wanted to shoot something that matters. Something that lasts."

We continued catching up until our waiter returned, and we had to sit back in our chairs to make room for him to deliver our food and drinks. Without realizing it, we had both moved closer, propping our elbows on the table and leaning in to talk like we did years ago.

I could have predicted that Cole was about to reach for the saltshaker. He never saw a French fry he didn't want to drown in Morton's. He was doing it right now.

"You're gonna have to stop that one of these days," I said, "now that you're, you know, knocking on thirty."

"Hey now!" He took a bite of his fries. "I want to see the exhibit when it's ready. Will you keep me posted?"

"Sure."

"My Uncle Joe—the one I was visiting in New Orleans— he's a Camille survivor, but he never talks about it. It's the same with his Vietnam tour. I guess he just keeps all the hard stuff to himself. He's been helping me with the car since I moved back."

We took the first bite of our burgers. Cole reached for extra napkins as the juice came pouring out, dripping down his hands. "That's the best cheeseburger on the planet," he said when he finally got his sandwich under control.

"I think it's the toasty bun that really makes a difference," I said, dabbing my chin with a napkin. "That and the juicy beef."

"Agreed. And the fresh lettuce and tomato. And the pickles and the homemade sauce. Look, here comes a train." He pointed to the tracks over the water, and we both watched as a freight train chugged across.

When the caboose finally passed, I turned and saw Cole looking at me. "How many cars?" he asked.

"What makes you think—"

He raised an eyebrow.

"Thirty-two," I said.

He grinned at me and took another sip of his Coke. "If you ever stop counting train cars, the world will stop turning."

"Okay then," I said. "You keep salting your fries, I'll keep counting train cars, and all will be well."

I had so many questions, and none of them had anything to do with trains or French fries. I wanted to know why a dream summer had to end. I wanted to know how you can kiss somebody like you'll never let them go and then just walk away. I still remembered that kiss. Did he? I think that's what I wanted to know most of all.

He ran his fingers through his hair a few times, something he used to do when he was anxious. "Edie . . . there's something I need to tell you. I've wanted to for a long time, but I didn't know if I had the right. Or if you'd want to hear it."

I couldn't say anything. It was all I could do to breathe in and out.

"My dad pressured me to stop writing to you when we went back to California."

My stomach turned a nauseating flip. "He didn't like me?"

Cole shook his head. "Just the opposite. He liked you very much, and he could see how serious I was getting. He told me I was way too young for that, and if I gave in to my emotions, I'd probably never become a pilot. He said I'd become a husband and a father before I was twenty, and those were critical training years I'd never get back. I listened. I wish I hadn't. Even at seventeen I should've had the gumption to believe I could do both—that we could do both."

He looked so miserable that I couldn't bring myself to tell him just how painful it was for me to lose him all those years ago. "I vote we don't kick our teenage selves in the teeth," I said. "Maybe they didn't get it exactly right, but they tried."

"You're kind to say that." He fidgeted with his wristwatch, then stopped and looked up at me. "But then, you always were—kind, I mean. And I can't blame it all on my dad. When I got back to California, all my friends were bragging about how many girls they'd dated over the summer. I only wanted one. I guess that scared me to death." Cole was looking at me the way he used to when we swam together in the gulf and took moonlit walks on the beach. It still made my heart pound. "So many times, I thought about reaching out to your grandparents to find out where you were, but I guess I was too scared of how they might react. Where have you been, Edie? Where did your road take you?"

I remembered now one of the many things that drew me to Cole. He listened to me like I was the most interesting person in the universe. "I went to New York by way of Auburn. Got my degree in graphic design because that was the artsiest pursuit I could think of that sounded employable. Then I moved to New York with my best friend."

"Leni, right?"

I couldn't believe he remembered her name after all this time. "That's right. We shared what had to be the tiniest apartment in the East Village and worked for the same ad agency. Leni was a copywriter who wanted to write novels. I was a graphic designer who wanted to take pictures. We were poor as Job's turkey, but we had so much fun—two Alabama girls unleashed on New York."

"What made you go there? Had you been before?"

I had a sudden mental image of Leni clenching the steering wheel as I struggled to decipher a New York street map. "We didn't have sense enough to realize it *might* be a good idea

79

to actually see a city," I said, "before we packed everything we owned into a rental van and moved there."

I loved the sound of Cole's laugh as he admitted, "Made a few of those rash decisions myself."

Remembering our first day as official residents of the city, I pictured Leni and me linking arms and skipping like school-girls down a sidewalk in Central Park. "You don't know how much of New York you've absorbed from the movies till you get up there. That whole first month, every time we'd see a landmark or a famous street sign, we'd point to it all wide-eyed, then look at each other and say it out loud: 'Madison Avenue! Bleecker Street!'"

Cole grabbed the saltshaker again. "So it's safe to say nobody mistook you for locals?"

"Not a chance. I remember the first time Leni and I went to a Broadway show, we got all gussied up. We're talking pageant hair and cocktail dresses, high heels and Silk Reflections— they're the Cadillac of pantyhose, in case you didn't know."

"I didn't."

"Well, now you do."

Cole frowned. "Could you explain 'pageant hair'?"

"I keep forgetting you didn't grow up down here. Pageant hair is long and poufy, with lots of drama and enough Aqua Net hairspray to withstand a fifty-knot gale."

"Got it."

"Anyway, after all that, we ended up sitting in a sea of tourists dressed in blue jeans and Reeboks."

"Not exactly a red-carpet situation?"

"No, definitely not. Leni said we looked like a couple of Miss Alabama wannabes who got lost en route to the runway and stumbled into the bleachers at the state playoffs." We shared a good laugh, a real one, and I realized this was the first time I had been able to do that while talking about my friend. "I was so proud of myself when I successfully hailed a cab to get us home, but then I got flustered trying to pay the guy. Later on, Leni figured out that I'd tipped him forty percent. No wonder he smiled so big when he said, 'Yous twos have a good night.'"

We kept swapping stories until Cole asked, "What brought you back here to Mississippi?" He shooed away a bee that had flown in and buzzed over our table.

Suddenly I felt like fifteen-year-old me talking to seventeen-year-old him. I took a deep breath to summon my courage. "Leni died, Cole. In March. And I just didn't . . . I couldn't stay in New York anymore."

He reached across the table and held both of my hands. "I don't know what to say, Edie. I'm so sorry. You two grew up together, right?"

I nodded but couldn't find my voice just yet. We sat there, silently looking at each other.

Finally he asked, "Do you think they still have Otis on the jukebox?"

As much as I felt like crying, I couldn't help but smile at the mention of Otis Redding, one of our all-time favorites. "I know for a fact they do."

Cole stood and pulled me up. Together we went to the jukebox that had been occupying the same spot here as long as anybody could remember. He dropped in a quarter and pushed J12. Just as we had done as teenagers, we both shuddered at the brassy intro that had never, in our opinion, made sense for "Try a Little Tenderness."

Cole slipped one arm around my waist and took my hand. I wrapped my arm around his shoulder. A breeze blew in from the water, and I could hear a train coming across the tracks. This time I didn't turn to count the cars. After all these years, the least—and best—two teenage sweethearts could offer each other was a warm hand to hold, a forgiving spirit, and the tender connection we had taken for granted when we were too young to know it was one of a kind.

*ten*

COCO'S GARDEN WAS SO EXOTIC—or maybe eccentric—that I would not be surprised to see a Bengal tiger come striding out of the gardenia bushes. Surrounded by stucco walls painted a deep salmon, the garden was like a colorful burst of fireworks more at home in Guadalajara than Gulfport.

Banana plants, palms, and black bamboo towered over borders of Mexican heather, bougainvillea, and sea lavender, with Meyer lemon trees in each corner. Bright-colored, waist-high ceramic containers held orange tropical hibiscus, red and yellow roses, bird-of-paradise, and sweet potato vine. One foliage plant that Coco called "dinosaur food" had leaves at least six feet wide, and she had four or five of them, along with a ten-foot, show-stopping dragon fruit cactus. Coco's plantings were so dense that the brick paths winding through her garden had dramatically narrowed in spots, leaving barely enough room for one person to squeeze between all the leaves, vines, and blooms.

But plants were only part of it. Coco had done her own spin on garden art—everything from a vintage baby's bathtub filled with multicolored blown-glass globes to several fountains and an assortment of children's chairs painted red, purple, and orange. A copper cat adorned the entry gate. Somehow, in the midst of all that, Coco still had managed to save room for a cypress table and chairs, plus enough tiki torches to light a casino.

"That was a good supper, Coco," Cookie said. "It's been a while since I've had Bill's eggplant."

Coco, who was pouring us all goblets of her "special garden punch," did not cook after breakfast. Ever. Whenever she had supper guests, she called up her favorite chef in Gulfport, gave him a head count, and asked him to make one of his signature dishes, which he boxed up for her. Tonight, he had prepared one of his best-loved recipes, an eggplant dish with shrimp, crab, and Parmesan cheese.

I took a sip of punch and felt a warm tingle as it went down, even though the drink was chilled. "Miss Coco, what's *in* this?"

She winked at me as she filled Charly's glass. "Let's just say you'll sleep good." Coco poured herself some punch and took a seat. Pierre, who had patiently waited next to her chair, hopped onto her lap. "This wasn't a bad idea, Punk. Answering those infernal questions is a lot more fun over food."

My grandmother had hit upon the notion of turning *Confessions* into a supper club. At each gathering, our host would draw one question from a basket, which we would all answer. We had also agreed to forgo recording our answers in the book. As Coco put it, "Why leave behind all that evidence?"

"So, Edie," Sugar said, clapping her hands together, "we hear you've been reunited with a certain young man! Tell us all about it."

"Not much to tell just yet, Miss Sugar." I knew I was doing that goofy smile women do when somebody asks them about a new romance. "But it was pretty amazing to see him again."

"She's blushing!" Sugar said. "Oh, how *mahvelous*!"

"Let her alone, Shug," Coco said. "You're embarrassing the daylights out of her."

"Oh, phooey." Sugar waved her hand in the air.

"He called last night," Charly said, winking at me.

"She was all smiles afterward," Punk added.

"If y'all will excuse me," I said, "I have to go dig a hole and crawl into it." Everybody laughed as I covered my face with my hands.

"Now, can we trust him?" Sugar asked. "I understand he hurt our girl once. We don't want that to happen again."

"I'll interrogate him over a bowl of gumbo at my earliest opportunity," Punk said. "But I never thought Cole was a cad. He was just confused—his father's doing, from what I could gather."

"How's his bod holding up?" Coco asked with a wink.

"Miss Coco!" My face must've turned bloodred as all the women died laughing.

"Don't worry, Edie, I'll change the subject," Charly said. "Miss Coco, how long did it take you to plant a garden like this?"

"You're no fun," Coco said. "Here I am trying to steer the conversation to pecs and glutes, and you want to bore me to death with petunias and geraniums!"

"Oh, hush!" Punk couldn't keep a straight face as she reprimanded her friend.

"But to answer your question," Coco said to Charly, "I'm *still* planting this garden. Every time I think I'm through, something I don't want to think about will land in my head, and I'll have to start planting again."

"When did you start it?" Charly asked.

Coco kept her eyes on Pierre. "The day I put Hudie in the home."

Charly looked horrified. "I'm so sorry. I didn't mean to bring up—"

Coco looked up and smiled at her. "Nothing wrong with your question, kiddo. Not your fault it has a depressing answer. I needed something to quiet my nerves before I went back to that empty house, so I stopped by a nursery out on Highway 49 and bought my first dinosaur food."

Hudie was Coco's husband, who'd had a stroke when he was in his late sixties. Punk told me that Coco insisted on taking care of him herself, but as his condition worsened and his mind deteriorated, he became more than she could handle. Their son and Hudie's doctors insisted on a nursing home, where he died two years later.

Bless Punk, she deftly shifted the conversation away from Coco's heartbreak and back to her garden. "You used to bring back plants from all your trips, didn't you?" she asked.

Coco took a sip of punch and nodded. "Sure did—mine and everybody else's. The bird-of-paradise and palms came from Islamorada. Got my yellow roses in San Antonio. Sugar brought me three camellias from Charleston. Cookie and Grady got me those azaleas in Augusta. I've got one for every time they went to the Masters. Plants last longer than postcards. And you don't have to worry about which drawer to stick 'em in."

"I like that," Charly said. "Even a long trip's over before you know it. Must be nice to have a living scrapbook to remind you of your rambles."

"I suspect you've got a touch of wanderlust yourself," Coco said with a wink.

Charly winked back at her. "I do. Did you do all the planting yourself?"

"Sure did." Pierre stood up in Coco's lap and made a couple of turns before settling into his chosen position. "I drew up a plan on a piece of notebook paper—looked like the work of a third grader—and hired a fella from Moss Point to break the ground and build the walls and paths. Then I got busy. Every time I'd catch myself dwelling on Hudie, I'd go to a nursery." She looked around her jungle of a garden and sighed. "I guess I dwelled on him a lot."

"That's alright, sister," Sugar said. "You transformed your grief into a lovely tapestry."

Coco grinned at Sugar, who was looking around at the crazy quilt of color. "Not exactly Bellingrath, is it, Shug?"

"I think it's every bit as beautiful," Sugar assured her. "And entirely original."

"Has gardening always been your balm of choice, Miss Coco?" Charly asked her.

Coco gave Pierre a scratch behind his ears. "Anybody who grew up in Louisiana knows how to grow stuff. I didn't have any particular interest in it when I was young. But once I realized how well it could occupy my mind during the day and exhaust my body into sleeping at night, I was hooked."

"Maybe I should try it," Charly said.

"All I can tell you is don't go near dinosaur food unless you're serious," Coco advised. "It leads to the hard stuff like hydrangeas and gardenias."

"Y'all only saw a little bit of her garden library when you came in the house," Cookie told us. "Those flower books are stacked everywhere, even inside her oven."

"Well, I never turn it on since Francis bought me that toaster," Coco said. "Might as well put it to work as a storage facility."

Punk passed the basket of questions to the head of the table. "Speaking of work, shall we get to it?"

Coco stroked Pierre's silvery fur with one hand as she drew a question. "Here goes nothing." She looked at the slip of paper in her hand. "Egad, this one's grim: What is your deepest regret?" She answered her own question. "I deeply regret that last bite of eggplant. I'm full as a tick in a blood bank."

"Seriously?" Cookie pressed her. "Your biggest regret in life is too much eggplant?"

Coco waved a dismissive hand at her sister. "Of course not. But I have so many. It's like being forced to choose a dog when you're a cat person. Every barkin' one of 'em's just as bad a choice as the other."

"Alright then," Cookie said. "I guess it's my turn. My biggest regret is anything and everything I missed doing with Grady because of some silly business I thought was so all-fired important at the time. I'm telling you what, everything I do now has to pass the six-months-to-live test."

"What's that, Miss Cookie?" Charly asked.

"Say you want to spend the day at the beach, but you feel like you need to clean out the garage instead. If you found out you had just six months to live, would you be saying to yourself, 'I sure wish I'd kept a cleaner garage'? No. You'd be saying, 'I sure wish I'd spent more afternoons on that beautiful beach.'"

Charly smiled and nodded. "You're absolutely right."

Coco kept petting Pierre. "Guess you're up next, Punk."

My grandmother took a sip of her garden punch, then

answered, "I definitely regret those dreadful white loafers I ordered from a catalog last summer. Coco said they made me look like Jerry Lee Lewis. But I guess we're supposed to go deeper than that." She thought for a minute. "More than anything, I guess I regret that I didn't spend my whole life here. I never knew what I was missing till we came to this old coast and built a house right on the water. We were always near it in Louisiana, but that's different from being able to look out your window and see the gulf any hour of the day."

"You regret everything about those years in Houma?" Coco asked.

Punk smiled and shook her head. "No, not everything. I never would've met y'all if I hadn't lived there. And I never would've met Cap. He was such a Louisiana boy."

Pop's given name was Nathan, but when he first came home from the Pacific, where he captained a PT boat, Punk said he went through a bossy spell. She started answering his commands with a salute, followed by "Aye, aye, Cap!" if she was willing to comply or "Don't count on it, Cap!" if she wasn't. Pop soon figured out that he was in Punk's navy now.

"Sister?" Coco said. "You up to it?"

Sugar sighed and shook her head. "You all know mine. Do I have to say it?"

Coco looked down at Pierre. "No need, Shug."

I saw Charly frown and realized nobody had ever told her about Sugar, who was still a newlywed when her first husband was killed at Pearl Harbor. She still called him "my beautiful boy." Then she married a much older man named Harlan Sykes, whom she never talked about. All Punk ever told me was that Sugar left him within a few months of their courthouse wedding, and then a year or so later he "had the good grace to die." She didn't remarry until years later, when she met Wade Vansant, a wealthy developer who treated her like a queen.

"Edie, I guess it's your turn," Coco said.

"I think y'all know my answer already," I said. "But I promise no more wallowing and crying. I'm starting to get on my own nerves. I'll just say I regret that I couldn't do enough. That's all."

"No, sweet girl." Punk reached over and laid her hand on my arm. "You regret there was *nothing* you could do because *nothing* would have been enough."

I managed a smile for my grandmother.

"Well, Charlotte, it's up to you," Coco said.

She stared at Coco before giving her answer. "I regret . . . that I can't seem to stop looking for what I'm looking for even though I know I'll never find it. I tell myself I'm done with it, but deep down I know I'm not. And I don't think I ever will be. Sometimes that makes it hard to get up in the morning."

"What is it that you're searching for, honey?" Cookie asked.

"An answer, I guess."

"Do you want to tell us about it?" Punk asked.

Charly shook her head as she absently braided a strand of her long red hair. "Not right now if that's okay."

"Well, this puts an extra dollop of grease in the skillet!" Coco exclaimed. "I didn't know we could have a *secret* regret. I've got one of those too, and here it is: I regret that I couldn't say yes."

"To what?" Cookie asked.

"Or whom?" Sugar suggested.

Coco leaned back in her chair. "That's for Pierre to know and y'all to find out."

# eleven

"SWEET GIRL, CAN YOU GET THE BACK DOOR?" Punk
was calling to me in her "I'm right in the middle of something" voice. I abandoned my feather duster in the living
room and headed for the kitchen, where I found my grandmother spreading Cool Whip over a Mudpie. "I just heard
the bell," she said as she carefully tucked the white fluff into
all four corners of her layered creation.

"Got it!" I grabbed a dish towel to wipe my hands and
hurried onto the porch to find Cole standing behind a cooler
resting on the top step.

"Hey," I said. "What brings you to our back door?"

He had one hand on his hip and the other on the doorframe. "Today's catch. Can you give me a hand?"

I held the door for him as he carried the cooler onto the
porch.

"Got something for Miss Punk," he said.

"She's mid-Mudpie. Hold on just a second."

She was sliding her dessert into the fridge when I stuck my
head in the kitchen door. "Got a minute, Punk? You have a
visitor. And he comes bearing gifts."

Punk came onto the porch and for a moment just stood there, staring at Cole. Then she held her arms out to him and said, "Welcome back, honey." He put his arms around her and surrendered to the oxygen deprivation of a Punk hug. When they finally let go and took a step back, she ran her fingers through his short hair. "Bless those military barbers."

Cole laughed. "I'm sorry you had to endure my surfer phase, Miss Punk. It won't happen again."

"I have no doubt," Punk said, still staring at him. "You've matured, Cole. I think you're a foot taller. And you're all filled out. The military has done right by you."

"Their cooking can't compare to yours," he said.

"Well, of course not." She laid her hands on his shoulders and gave them a squeeze.

"I brought you something." Cole opened the cooler to reveal a ton of freshly shucked shrimp and oysters, divided into clear plastic bags that probably held about a pound each, all packed on ice.

"Oh, dear heaven!" Punk bent over the cooler, studying her catch. "These are beautiful, Cole. Where did you get them?"

"A buddy on base has an uncle who's a waterman. These came straight off his boat."

Punk looked up at him. "They came out of the gulf shucked, did they?"

"No, ma'am, I handled that," Cole said. "I left some of the oysters whole in case you want to roast them. They're on the bottom."

"Well, bless your heart, that was a ton of work!" she said as she gave him another hug. "Let's make good use of them. I've got a pot of grits on the stove already. We'll throw in a few shrimp and have some breakfast. Any takers?"

"Always," I said.

"What about you, Cole? Oh, don't even answer. Of course you'll stay." Punk grabbed a bag of shrimp from the cooler and hurried off to the kitchen.

"Prepare yourself for an interrogation disguised as breakfast," I said to Cole. "But don't worry. The food will distract you from the soul-baring."

In no time, Punk had taken one of the humblest dishes in the South and transformed it into something sublime. "We won't bother with setting the table," she said. "There's a nice breeze this morning, so we can eat on the porch. I'll let y'all fix your coffee and dish up your grits. I'll bring the French bread." She gave Cole a wink and a nudge. "And the Tabasco."

Of course Punk would've remembered how much pride Pop took in introducing my golden boy to Tabasco sauce. First, he had Cole sprinkle the hot pepper sauce into his gumbo. Then he persuaded him to put it on po'boys and vegetables, fried catfish and muffalettas. I think Pop's shining moment came when he saw Cole shake Tabasco into a bag of popcorn. "I never thought of that!" my grandfather exclaimed, slapping Cole on the back. "It's genius! And to think a California boy came up with it all on his own."

Once we settled ourselves around the table and dug in, I saw Cole take his first bite, close his eyes, and lean back in his chair, just as I had done when I had my first gumbo after coming home to Punk.

"I had forgotten just how amazing this is," he said with a sigh, which clearly delighted Punk.

She tugged a piece of French bread from the crusty loaf she'd brought to the table and handed it to him. "Now, Cole," she began.

"Here we go," I said, winking at him. "Want me to hook up the hot lights, Punk?"

She swatted me with her napkin before giving him her full attention. "Tell me everything, honey, right from the beginning. Where have you been and what have you been doing since we last saw you?"

He told her all about his education and military career, much as he had explained it to me, though Punk required far more detail. Satisfied with his professional life, she turned to the personal. "And how is your father, Cole?"

"He's well. Retired from the Air Force and working for a charter company. He remarried during my junior year in college. They bought a new house and had a couple of kids together."

Punk laid a hand on his arm. "I remember that your mother had passed the year before you came here."

"Yes, ma'am. I guess my dad thought he needed to stay single till I left home. After he married, I still visited him sometimes on the weekends and school breaks, but I don't know—just never felt like home once he had a new family. The Air Force became my family."

"That sounds lonely," Punk said.

Cole frowned and shook his head. "It really wasn't. I always felt so much pressure from my dad. 'Don't do this or you'll never be a pilot. Don't do that or you'll ruin your chance at flight school.' I know he had my best interests at heart, but it was a lot. Once I made it into the cockpit and started living on base, all that pressure went away. I could just blend in with the other pilots. Nobody had any more or less at stake than I did from day to day, and we were all there to help each other through."

"Well, you'll always have a place at my table," Punk said.

He laid his hand over hers. "I'll bet you say that to all the flyboys."

Punk laughed and took a sip of her coffee. "Only those willing to shuck a tubful of crustaceans for me."

Cole blew on a steaming spoonful of shrimp and grits and took a bite.

"So your father married, but what about you?" Punk asked.

I felt like I'd just been gut-punched, not because I was embarrassed but because I was terrified of the answer. Punk had asked the question I hadn't dared, choosing instead to be satisfied with the absence of a wedding ring.

"No, ma'am, not me," he said. "I was too serious about flying to get serious about anything else, I guess." He glanced up at me. "Maybe I just haven't been in the right place for that to happen."

Was I holding my breath? I think I must've been because I exhaled enough air to push Pop's boat away from the dock.

"Well, you're far from over the hill," Punk went on. "Plenty of time for wherever life takes you."

He tapped his bowl with his spoon. "Do you think it might take me back here the next time you make shrimp and grits? Or—dare to dream—gumbo?"

Punk grabbed his hand and kissed it. "Count on it, honey! Count on it."

# twelve

**I LOVE IT WHEN A PLAN FALLS APART** and one of the tumbling pieces knocks you into something far better. When that happens, the trick is to be with somebody who recognizes serendipity when he sees it.

Cole had invited me out for sunset po'boys at a waterfront spot in Biloxi, but on the way there, we passed the mall, where we saw, to our surprise and delight, the parking lot covered with carnival rides. What had been an asphalt prairie just yesterday was now aglow with the rainbow lights of a Ferris wheel, merry-go-round, and midway. An arched sign over the entrance read "Suncoast Fair." When we first spotted all that color flashing against the night sky, we gasped like a couple of twelve-year-olds and immediately shouted, "*Roustabout!*"

As teenagers, we had both loved Elvis movies in a "they're so corny they're brilliant" kind of way. One rainy morning, we had stayed in, watching E try to save the carnival in *Roustabout.* When the weather finally cleared and Pop drove us all up the beach for burgers, this very traveling fair had appeared in Biloxi. Somehow Cole persuaded Pop to let him take me. He borrowed his dad's car, picked me up like a real date, and we had the night all to ourselves—well, until my curfew, at least. Now here we were again.

Cole turned into the mall entrance so fast that I didn't know how he kept all four wheels on the ground. Once we parked, he bought us a roll of tickets at a booth near the entrance, and we stood there together, taking it in.

"It's not Disney, but it's ours," he said as he surveyed the spectacle.

"I think it's better than Disney," I countered. "A theme park is so predictable. You know it'll always be there. Once you pay a fortune to get in, you can ride anything you want as many times as you're willing to stand in line. But nobody knows *when* this little fair might pop up. And who can say whether we'll get our fill of the Scrambler before our tickets run out or the whole shebang moves to the next town?"

"Let's not forget the unsurpassed dining options," Cole said. "Got your hot dogs, your corn dogs, your chili dogs . . ."

"Your popcorn, your cotton candy, your funnel cakes," I added.

"Now for the tough decision." Cole frowned and put his hands on his hips. "Eat first or ride first?"

"Seriously, old man?" I took off running toward the Scrambler, with Cole catching up in just a few strides. We were still laughing when we reached the front of the line, handed over our tickets, and selected a car.

I paused before climbing in. "Slammer or slammee?"

We both knew that, depending upon your seat position in this particular ride, you would either be endlessly slamming into your companion or getting slammed *by* them.

Cole took a step back, mouth agape, feigning offense at

the question. "Slammee, of course. It's the only honorable choice."

He helped me in and climbed up beside me before the carny closed and locked the security bar across us. Soon we heard the all clear and began to move.

Given its name and pattern of motion, I'm guessing the Scrambler was inspired by old-school eggbeaters, with clusters of four or five cars each spinning together in their own circle, while all the clusters simultaneously spun around in a much bigger circle. We felt as if we were being hurled out toward the crowd then yanked back in toward the center again and again. Every time we whirled out, I slammed into Cole, laughing my head off, till finally he shouted over the noise, "Enough, lady!" and put his arms around me so the ride couldn't keep slinging me back and forth across the seat.

Spinning round and round, in and out, with Cole holding me steady, I leaned back against him, looked up at the flashing carnival lights, and felt for a moment like I was in one of those old movie scenes where the main character begins dreaming. The picture suddenly dissolves into wavy distortion as harp music plays. Once everything slowly comes back into focus, you realize the dreamer has traveled back in time. I wouldn't have been surprised if this old ride suddenly stopped and two lovestruck teenagers, not a couple of twentysomethings, stepped out of our car.

Eventually, the ride did stop. And in a way, I got my dream sequence when Cole looked down at me and asked, "Didn't we ride the Ferris wheel next?"

"Yes, we did." Few things warm your heart like knowing that you have a place in someone else's, that they still cherish the memories you share.

The carny came by to hurry us out of our seat so more riders could board. Cole held my hand to help me down. Once we were on the ground, he didn't let go but laced his fingers through mine. We took our time strolling to the Ferris wheel, positioned at the back edge of the parking lot as always so that a ride to the top offered panoramic views of the carnival lights, Beach Boulevard, and the gulf. A kid could sprint there in a minute flat, but for two adults in no hurry to arrive, it was a slow journey.

As we walked together, I felt a shift, the kind of change you sense when you're standing outside on a summer day just before a storm blows in. One minute it's hot and sunny. Your view is clear to the horizon. But suddenly you become aware that a transformation is taking place. Seeping through the weight of hot, humid air is a lightness, then a cooling, then a darkening. Clouds wrap around the sun, and you can't read the sky as well as before. That's what was happening now. I felt a change in the weather—in our weather, Cole's and mine. The slightest movement of his fingers against mine as he held my hand, a tiny tightening or softening of his grip— I felt it all, amplified so that it blocked out everything else, one sense drowning out all the others, the touch of a hand silencing the blare of a calliope.

"Edie? You with me?"

Cole spoke softly and gently squeezed my hand. I didn't even realize we had stopped walking. He laid his hands on my shoulders and turned me to face him, looking down at me the way he used to before a kiss, his eyes soft, his lips slightly parted.

"I'm with you," I said. But I didn't sound like myself. My voice seemed to be coming from down in a well, speaking on its own, without any direction from me.

Cole brushed my hair away from my face. "You look scared."

"I feel scared."

"Of what?"

"I'm afraid of what might happen next. Even more afraid of what might not."

He bent down and softly kissed me. "Nothing to be scared of, Edie. Not this time." He nodded toward the glittering lights against the night sky. "What do you say? Should we take another turn on the old wheel?"

I looked up at all those colors chasing away the darkness, then wrapped my arms around Cole, who held me tight. "Yes," I said. "Let's take another turn. Let's see how high we can go."

*thirteen*

**"EXCITED ABOUT YOUR FIRST DAY?"** Punk was standing at the stove, turning French toast in a cast-iron skillet.

"I am," I said. "It's something different anyway. And it'll at least make me feel useful. Speaking of which, want me to take some of that to the table?"

She handed me the plated toast and a small bottle of cane syrup while she brought a plateful of bacon and fresh orange juice. We heard the doorbell.

"I'll get it!" Charly had just made it downstairs and answered the door. She came to the table carrying a gorgeous bouquet of flowers—roses, peonies, and freesia. "These are for you, chouchou!"

"For *me*? Nobody except Punk and Mama has sent me flowers in years."

Charly set the flowers on the table, and I read the card. I felt the heat rush to my cheeks and my heart jump into my throat.

*Knock 'em dead on your first day.*

*Cole*

Charly squealed and hugged me. "They're from him, aren't they?"

"Yes!" I couldn't help the stupid smile stretching my whole face into unnatural proportions.

"Oh, sweet girl! I'm so happy for you." Punk gave me a hug.

"Baby steps," I said. "I don't want to get my hopes up too high."

"On the other hand," Charly said, "you don't want to fire-hose them." She kissed me on the forehead and went to the kitchen to get her coffee. "Y'all need to start waking me up so I can help fix breakfast," she said as she sat down. "I always miss the labor."

"Doesn't seem fair for you to help cook our breakfast since you drink yours," Punk said. "Besides, I want you to enjoy your visit and get some rest."

"I'm definitely doing that," Charly said. "For months, I felt so tired all the time, but I could never sleep more than four or five hours a night. Here I seem to be sleeping as much as Libba and I did when we were teenagers, remember?"

"I do," Punk said. "I'd have to drag both of you out of bed for church when you slept over on Saturday nights."

"Must be the salt air," Charly said.

"Want some juice?" I filled a small glass next to my coffee cup.

"No thanks." She lifted her cup. "I'll stick to the rocket fuel."

Punk and I dug in while Charly picked up yesterday's paper still sitting on the table. "Well, it looks like the mysterious light has made another appearance. Did y'all see this?"

"I did." I took a sip of my juice.

"You know, I've gotten to the point where I hardly ever

read the newspaper anymore," Punk said. "It's always full of things to worry me, and if I can't do anything about them, I'd rather not know. I guess I'm just too lazy to cancel my subscription. What does it say about the light, Charlotte?"

She finished skimming the article. "Not much. About the same information as before—a bright, glowing light on the eastern tip of the island. Vanished within a few seconds. Nobody saw it but shrimpers out in the gulf. No explanation of its origins."

"Think it's some kind of phosphorescence?" I asked Punk.

"Could be." She frowned as she thought it over. "But I think shrimpers would recognize that kind of light. It sounds like they're seeing something they've never seen before. At least it gives everybody something to talk about at Nonnie's."

Charly was fidgeting with her cup instead of drinking her coffee, something she didn't ordinarily do. "Miss Punk, could I ask you about Miss Sugar's regret? I promise it won't hurt my feelings if you say no."

"I don't mind if you ask, honey. And I'll answer as well as I can." Punk drizzled syrup on her toast and took a bite.

"Outside of your family—Libba in particular—I never told much of anybody about the skeletons in my closet," Charly said. "I guess I thought if I did, they'd think I was a train wreck."

Punk added an extra drop or two of syrup. "You have never been a train wreck, Charlotte. It breaks my heart that you had to live through one as a child, but you've never been one."

Charly's eyes misted, but she didn't cry. "I guess it's hard for me to believe somebody like Miss Sugar has secrets too— bad ones, I mean. I think of her as the queen of the coast—

the big house, the fancy clothes, all her charity events and parties. But it wasn't always like that, was it?"

Punk shook her head. "No, it wasn't."

"Do you think she'd mind if you told me—told Edie and me—what happened? I'm not even sure why I want to know, but I do. At least I think I do."

"I don't believe she would mind if I told you," Punk said, "but she would never want you to ask *her* about it. Agreed?"

Charly and I both promised.

"This calls for coffee." Punk went to the kitchen and brought the pot to freshen our cups, then took her seat. "You can't imagine how popular Sugar was back in Louisiana when we were all young girls. Everybody loved her. She was sweet and charming and so pretty. She could sing like Judy Garland and play anything on the piano by ear. Graceful on the dance floor. For her talent in the Miss Louisiana pageant, she performed 'Somewhere Over the Rainbow,' accompanying herself on a Steinway grand. It was the first time she'd ever touched a piano like that. She always practiced on an old upright her sweet daddy bought her at a church auction. I'm here to tell you, Sugar brought the house down. Not one dry eye. Everybody in that audience was spellbound, and when Sugar sang the last note, I thought the applause would never stop."

"She must've really been something," I said.

"She was." Punk smiled and took a bite of bacon.

"Did she and Miss Coco spat the way they do now?" I asked.

Punk rolled her eyes. "Worse! Believe it or not, they've mellowed with age. But here's the thing: Coco would wrestle a bear for Sugar."

"I guess I could see that," Charly said.

"Sugar might get on her last nerve," Punk said, "but Coco will defend her against all comers—will and has."

"Are we talking about Harlan Sykes?" I asked.

Punk nodded and took a long sip of her coffee. "Before Harlan ruined everything, though, there was Robert Ardoin—Robbie—the one Sugar calls her beautiful boy. And he was that alright. But there was more to him than good looks. Robbie had a lot of character. And such a kind heart. Y'all both would've liked him."

"Where did they meet?" Charly asked.

"At a music festival. Sugar was in Lafayette, making an appearance as Miss Louisiana. Robbie introduced himself while she was signing autographs and proposed to her a week later."

"But was she allowed to keep her title after she got married?" Charly asked.

Punk shook her head. "No. That's why you've never heard her talk about the Miss America pageant."

I suddenly remembered a long-forgotten conversation with Sugar. "Years ago, I asked her about it, and she just laughed and said she didn't win, place, or show."

"She never got to compete," Punk corrected me. "The rest is history—literally. Europe was at war. America was getting pulled in. Robbie enlisted in the Navy and qualified for officers' training. Got stationed in Hawaii. Sugar was giddy about going with him. She wrote me that she was determined to turn their tiny base housing into a little slice of paradise." Punk shook her head sadly. "But then Pearl Harbor happened, Robbie's ship was destroyed, and that was the end of Sugar's beautiful boy. She flew back on the plane that brought his body home. She told me one time that her Miss Louisiana title was the only thing in her life that had belonged to her and her alone because she earned it all by herself. But she traded her crown for a wedding ring and then walked straight from the altar to the funeral home."

"Is this too hard for you, Miss Punk?" Charly asked.

Punk shook her head and shrugged. "Lots of things in life are hard. But you and Edie need to know, I think. It'll help you understand."

"You sure, Punk?" I was getting worried about her.

"I'm alright, sweet girl." She sat silently for a moment, her hands wrapped around her coffee cup. "The truly sad thing is that while Robbie made Sugar happier than she'd ever been, losing him set her up for the misery of Harlan Sykes."

Punk didn't so much say his name as spit it out, and it seemed to leave a bad taste in her mouth.

"He was older and had flatfoot, so he couldn't be drafted," she went on. "For Sugar, that meant she wouldn't have to worry about the war taking him. And he was a successful businessman, or so he claimed, so she thought she was safe. Nothing could've been further from the truth. Coco saw straight through him and threatened to kidnap Sugar to keep her from marrying him. But Sugar felt like she was a burden to her parents, moving back home after Robbie died. She wanted to be married and settled like her sisters. Harlan took full advantage of that."

"He changed after they married?" Charly asked.

"No, just showed his true colors," Punk said. "Turned out to be everything Coco predicted and then some. But he underestimated Sugar. He thought he could bully her into hiding the bruises and keeping quiet. Well, he thought wrong. She might've been willing to put up with his verbal abuse, but the first time he hit her, she went straight to Coco."

"And Miss Coco could never be bullied," I said.

"That's right. Harlan showed up at her kitchen door looking for Sugar. Hudie was overseas like all the other men. Harlan threatened to make Coco sorry if she didn't let him in. Coco says to this day she's never felt the kind of strength she had right then—like some powerful surge shot through her body. She grabbed a ladder-back chair with one hand and smashed it on the kitchen table, then used one of the legs like a billy club to thrash Harlan—chased him all the way off her back porch and into his car, whipping him with every step, and then she cracked his windshield for good measure. She said he left skid marks trying to get away from her."

"But did he come back?" Charly asked.

Punk shook her head. "No. The minute Coco saw his taillights speeding away, she called every police chief from Lake Charles to Pascagoula and told them what happened. She also promised a cash reward to any officer who could find a reason to arrest Harlan—anywhere, anytime, for anything. That snake spent so many days in local jails that when he finally got out the last time, he left for good. I can't say I shed a tear when we read in the paper that he'd been killed outside some honky-tonk in Memphis. And I'll tell you something else. Every single night I have to ask God to forgive me for the way I still feel about that man. If there's anything that might keep me out of heaven, it's the way I despise Harlan Sykes—even the memory of him."

"How awful for Miss Sugar," said Charly.

"I feel so sorry for her," I said.

"That's alright," Punk told us. "You can feel sorry for her. But you should feel proud of her too—proud of the courage it took for Sugar to get herself out of there and tell the truth about what happened. Can you imagine how humiliated and terrified she must've been? Not all bruises are physical. Matter of fact, some of the worst ones aren't."

The three of us grew quiet. I could hear the ticking of the kitchen clock and the seabirds calling outside.

Punk stretched out her arms to take both Charly and me by the hand. "What I hope you two will remember about Sugar's regret is that there's usually a reason why people are the way they are. Some might look at Sugar and think she's just a frivolous, rich old woman with no idea how the world really works. But that's not true. She knows exactly what can happen in this life. She gets a lot of flak for all the care she takes with appearances, but I think beauty is important to her because she's endured such ugliness. For her, keeping her hair done and wearing nice clothes and living in a lovely home—those aren't about personal vanity. They're about creating a beautiful world for herself and everybody in her orbit. It's her way of keeping the ugliness at bay, for all of us, not just for herself."

I got up and hugged my grandmother. "Love you, Punk."

"I love you too, sweet girl." She kissed me on the cheek. "Now get to work before Jason has to fire you on your first day."

*fourteen*

**I TOLD JASON I HAD DECIDED** to get serious about my own photography, and he offered me a table in front of The Trove for a merchants' walk that was coming up. He said the best exhibits tell a story, and I decided my story would be this coast. Ever since, I had been a little obsessed, pestering Charly and the Ten Spots to let me take environmental portraits of them, along with the ones I had shot of shrimpers and oystermen and anybody else who looked Mississippi-to-the-core. I had photographed landscapes and seascapes and probably every bird on Horn.

Now Cole was coming with me to the island for a sunset shoot. I packed us a picnic supper and cooler before running upstairs to collect my equipment.

"Edie!" Punk called up to me as I was double-checking my camera bag. "Cole's here."

Popping my sunglasses on top of my head, I threw the strap over my shoulder, then grabbed a quilt and a couple of beach towels before starting down. "I didn't hear the T-bird, Punk."

She stood at the foot of the stairs, resting one hand on the rail. "He didn't bring it. Come and look."

I joined Punk on the back porch just in time to see Cole finish securing a seaplane to Pop's dock and cross the backyard.

"That's what I'd call a ride," my grandmother said as he came up the steps and onto the screened porch.

Cole smiled and kissed both of us on the cheek. "I decided to bring some wings—if Edie trusts me to fly her to Horn."

Punk reached up and patted his cheek. "Don't get any blood on her, dear, or you'll have me to deal with."

"Yes, ma'am," he said with a quick salute.

"Is that your plane?" she asked.

"I just leased it for a month to see if the fun of flying it would be worth the poverty of owning it. I'll be living on peanut butter if I decide to keep it."

"No need for that," Punk said, patting him on the back. "You'll never starve as long as I own a gumbo pot. Now, you two get out of my house. If there's anything I can't stand, it's pleasant young people underfoot."

I hugged her goodbye. "I guess you should look for us when you hear a splash, Punk."

At the dock, Cole tucked my beach gear into the tight rear seats and helped me in, then handed me my camera bag. "Got the new lens?"

"Check."

I had never been inside the cockpit of a plane before. The instrument panel looked daunting, but Cole seemed unfazed by it. He helped me buckle up and put on a headset before cranking the engine. The propeller began to spin. Soon we were gliding across the water, picking up speed, and lifting off.

"I have an incredible urge to giggle like a teenybopper," I said into the mic on my headset.

"Go right ahead." Cole smiled at me. I couldn't get over how relaxed and completely natural he seemed flying. But then, he had always been like that with everything, from windsurfing to waterskiing. No reason flying should be any different, I guess.

We kept climbing until it felt like we were at just the right altitude to pull one of those signs advertising all-you-can-eat shrimp at Captain Bob's or five-dollar frozen libations at Coconut Willy's, a perennial summertime sales pitch to sunbathers up and down the beach.

When I could see Horn in the distance, I pulled out my camera and attached the new zoom lens I had just bought. Cole banked right so we could circle back and fly directly over the length of it, west to east, then he dropped altitude for an incredible view of the island—inland lagoons and pines, gray-gold waters of the Mississippi Sound spilling into the blues of the open gulf. Aiming out the window of the plane, I took shot after shot. I kept turning back to Cole to see if he saw what I did. I wasn't disappointed. We always got Horn the same way.

"Anchor on the eastern end?" he asked.

"Perfect." I kept shooting as he brought the plane down and landed on the surface of the water. "You're very good at this flying business," I said, motioning to all the instruments and dials in the cockpit.

"You're very good at this shooting business." He mimicked my hand motion toward the camera. I had shown him the sunset shots I took from the western end of Horn just a few days ago, and he asked if he could get several of them enlarged so he could frame them. As much as I wanted to make my living as a photographer, the truth is that a *New York Times* assignment couldn't have excited me any more than Cole's admiration for my work.

I packed up my bag and got ready to wade as we drifted toward shore. The sun was warm, the sky clear blue. I carried

my camera equipment, while Cole insisted on getting everything else. Already the sun was transforming Horn, its yellow
light of day melting into gold as sunset approached.

He began setting up camp at one of the best spots on
Horn, the island's narrow eastern tip. Look out at the water
from here and you feel as if you're part of the gulf—wrapped
by it, not just looking at it.

I tried to help, but he shooed me away. "Go do your thing.
I'll try to make sure we don't get chilly after dark."

Right now this whole island was pure magic. Water and
sky, sand and pines were all washed in the golden light of
late afternoon. I fired off so many shots I thought my camera
might explode. And then I faced the water, trying to capture
the feeling of standing here on this particular spot, watching
the Mississippi Sound find its way around the tip of Horn
and reunite with the gulf, like a couple of long-lost cousins
embracing each other at a family reunion.

Finally, I turned to Cole. So many times, I had pictured
him just like this—khaki shorts and a T-shirt, tanned skin,
blond hair tousled by the wind—a sun-kissed dream framed
in white sand and blue water.

It was the grown-up Cole I had found in Bay St. Louis.
Even at the fair, reliving youthful memories together, I still
saw him as the self-possessed adult he had become. But here
on this wilderness beach, building a fire in the sand, he was
the golden boy of my memory. Quietly I raised my camera.
Cole on his knees, laying a fire. *Click.* Cole looking over his
shoulder to catch a heron in flight. *Click.* Cole turning to see
my camera aimed right at him and giving me the "Seriously,
Edie?" look. *Click.* Cole shaking his head and smiling up at
me. *Click, click, click, click, click.*

I turned back to the water and left him in peace, knowing

that my camera had just revealed something I couldn't see on my own. Of course he was handsome. That was obvious. But I had worked in advertising in New York City. I had seen lots of pretty boys from modeling agencies, specimens of physical perfection that I forgot about as soon as their shoots were over. What set Cole apart went beyond his looks. It was a light, a center of warmth and wonder that shone from inside him. That's what I had seen but couldn't name as a teenage girl. That's what I had never been able to forget, no matter how many times I told myself I had outgrown the memory of my dream boy and our idyllic summer.

Sunset was coming fast. Cole lit the fire, and I joined him on my quilt, which he had spread over the sand. We could use the beach towels as windbreakers if we needed to.

The view from here never got old. "It's like riding a magic carpet," I said. "I feel like we're floating across the gulf, and any minute now we might bump into Cancun or Cuba—a geographically unsound notion, I realize."

Cole lightly ran his finger across my forehead. "I'm glad to see your imagination's still firing."

"Hope I have a little more control over it than I used to."

"I don't. I've always loved watching it roam loose." He stretched out his legs and leaned back on his elbows. "Wouldn't it be great to live here? Right here?"

I tilted my head back and closed my eyes. "The best. I don't think I'd ever get tired of it. Or bored with it."

I opened my eyes to see Cole looking at me. "Do you remember the first time we met?" he asked.

I pulled my knees to my chest and hugged them. "Of course. I was smitten with you, and you were smitten with Pop's boat."

"Only till you showed up," he corrected.

"Okay, we'll go with that."

He raised up and sat cross-legged. "That summer was the best one of my whole life, Edie. I know I'm not a geezer, and it's not like I'm looking back on eighty years or anything, but . . ." He looked out at the water, then at me. "It really was something, our summer."

"Yes, it was." I drew a tree in the sand with my fingertip. "Sometimes, after I stopped hearing from you, I wondered if I'd imagined the whole thing."

Cole reached over and drew a bird in my tree. "Me too. I can't remember any other time when I've looked forward to every single day the way I did back then."

I wondered whether his memory had clung to the same images as mine. Long days under a sun so bright it made the whole gulf look diamond dusted. Romantic nights in the moonlight, a gulf wind whispering in the live oaks.

We were quiet, just breathing in the salt air and feeling the breeze on our faces.

"Cole," I said, "there's something I need to say, but I don't want it to ruin everything."

He looked at me, his face serious. "You're entitled to tell me how awful I was to desert you."

I shook my head. "I never thought you were awful. I just need to know you won't kiss me goodbye and ride off into the sunset again, that whatever happens, we'll figure it out together, even if it's hard. Deal?"

He shook his head. "Not a deal, a promise." He slipped his arm around my waist, held my face in his hand, and gave me the kind of kiss that I'd still be daydreaming about when I was rocking my grandchildren.

"This is what I've missed the most," I said as he put his arms around me and I rested my head on his shoulder.

"What?"

"Being with somebody who's so easy to be with. Talking without trying. Not talking and not trying."

He kissed me again and tightened his arms around me. Together, we watched the sky turn shades of soft coral and pink before it faded into an inky canvas for the moon.

When I was a kid, Pop told me the old maritime legend of Sirens whose song lured ships to the rocks and sailors to their death. The warmth and light I saw in Cole was my own personal Siren's song, drawing me to him once again. But I didn't believe he intended to dash me against the rocks. He hadn't meant to then and he didn't mean to now.

*fifteen*

**MY ASSIGNMENT AT THE TROVE WAS A GIFT.** Following Jason upstairs, I found, spread across the reading table and spilling out of several cardboard boxes on the floor, incredible images taken during the aftermath of Hurricane Camille.

"Jason, where on earth did you get these?"

"I suppose you would call him my director—an investor in the community who prefers to remain unseen."

We stood looking at the pictures fanned out on the table. "That storm touched everybody," I said. "Old folks and teen-agers, mansions and beach shacks, even churches. It's just unbelievable."

Jason reached out and tapped one of the photographs with his finger. It was a black-and-white shot of a young couple standing in front of the storm-blasted remains of a church. The man held a little boy who looked two or three years old. The woman cradled an infant. The couple didn't look a day over twenty. A minister faced them, holding a Bible in one hand with the other raised high above the young family.

"Looks like a baby dedication," I said. "Protestant, judging by the minister's clothes."

Jason stared at the picture. "Human beings never cease to amaze me. Their church is destroyed. Their *world* is destroyed. Yet they continue on as though it's a typical Sunday."

"I guess that's how the church keeps going, maybe not exactly as it did before, but somehow."

"Tell me something, Edie. Do you think it's these sacred rites—the baby dedications and baptisms and Holy Communion—that bring comfort to the faithful after a disaster like Camille?"

I looked at the picture again. "Yes and no. Doing something that makes you feel normal, like taking Communion, does help you get your footing when everything's turned upside down. But I'm not sure church rites actually give comfort so much as they remind us where to find it." I held up another photograph. "Look at this one."

Jason studied it over my shoulder. The photographer had captured an elderly woman sitting on an overturned bucket. She stared blankly into the distance as a toddler sat on the ground at her feet, playing with rubble. In her lap was a tattered grocery sack.

"I'll bet you that sack holds everything she owns," I said.

Jason nodded in agreement. "This world is such a transitory place. Anything from a house to a life can be taken in a blink."

"Are you going to sell the pictures?" I asked.

"No." He picked up an eight-by-ten of a Keesler airman carrying a frail old woman in his arms. "I didn't come here to profit from human misery."

He had cracked open a door, and I wanted to walk through. "Why did you come here, Jason—if you can tell me?"

117

He hesitated, taking time to digest my question, I guess. Then he answered, "I came because there was work to be done. And people—customers—to serve." Jason picked up another image, this one of a boy surrounded by debris, drinking from a broken water pipe. "Everyone should see these. But first we need to find out as much as we can about each one and organize the information somehow. From there, we can figure out how best to present them—share them with the community."

"Won't be easy," I said. "Decades have gone by. The anniversary of the storm comes in August, so that might be a good time to introduce the exhibit. Maybe if I organize the pictures in batches by location or subject matter or something, we can research them faster?"

"An excellent plan," he said, smiling at me. "I'm convinced I've chosen a fine guardian for this project. Is there anything you need to get started?"

I nodded toward the tea service. "No disrespect to the chamomile, but do you own a coffeepot?"

It was almost three o'clock when I heard familiar voices and went down the spiral staircase to find Punk introducing Charly to Jason. I got a kick out of the look on her face when she saw him for the first time—likely the same way I had looked at him. It's very hard not to gawk at Jason Toussaint.

"Hey, you two," I said.

Punk came over and hugged me. "How's the working girl?"

"Jason gave me a dream project that I'm just diving into."

"What's the project?" Charly asked as she joined us.

"All this incredible Camille photography that somebody

118

donated. I'm about to start researching and cataloging it. Want to see?"

Charly's face froze. "I think I'll go have a look at the garden you told me about."

"Everyone, make yourselves at home," Jason said. "I have some accounts to attend to."

"What's up with Charly?" I asked Punk as I led her upstairs.

"She was in Biloxi when the storm hit, honey. Your mama never told you?"

"No, ma'am."

"I don't know what happened to her during that hurricane, but she was never quite the same afterward. And she absolutely will not talk about it."

We went to my worktable and sat next to each other. "Do you think she told Mama anything about it?"

"Probably," Punk said as she fanned out a stack of pictures I was just about to work with. "But I never pressed Libba for answers. One of the things I admire about their friendship is their loyalty to each other." She held up an image of a teenage girl sitting on a pile of debris in the middle of a flattened neighborhood. "They were much younger than this when they first latched on to each other. Ever since then, your mama's been the only living soul that Charlotte trusts with her whole heart, and I'd never want to compromise that."

"Was it the storm that made her leave Biloxi for good?"

Punk frowned and crossed her arms on the table. "I'm not sure. She moved when Pop was still building our house— January of 1970, I think. We've kept in touch through letters and phone calls mostly. I've flown up to Asheville to see her a few times. I guess I want to make sure she knows I'm always here." Punk picked up a picture of seabirds perched on the ruins of a fishing pier after the storm. "Everybody needs a safe place to land, sweet girl, just like the cranes and the pelicans." She held up a black-and-white shot of a woman on her knees in front of a wrecked house, her expression frantic as she reached for one of the pictures scattered over her yard. "Can you even imagine? Such desperation to salvage any remnant of her life before that awful storm."

"Look at this one." I showed her a color photograph of a church congregation, all wearing their Sunday best. The parishioners sat outside in chairs arranged in rows, just as the pews had surely been aligned in their sanctuary before the hurricane destroyed it. They appeared to listen intently as a priest held Mass. Behind them lay the ruins of their church. In front of them, just beyond the priest, was a languid gulf, the same waters that, just days before, had risen up in a raging fury and ravaged their lives.

"Look at all that yellow," Punk said, pointing out some of the women in the picture. "So many sunny yellow church dresses trying their best to shine through disaster."

I smiled at my grandmother. "Maybe it's time I got myself a yellow dress."

We heard somebody running up the stairs and turned to see Charly, who stopped at the landing, breathing hard. "I think I'd like to get going," she said. "I'll call a taxi."

Punk put down the church picture. "Wait and I'll come with you."

"It's okay. You stay and visit with Edie." Charly looked rattled, still trying to catch her breath.

"Honey, what's the matter?" Punk went to her and took her hand.

"Nothing," Charly said. "I'm just—I'm just ready to go."

"Come on then." Punk put her arm around Charly. "I'm hindering Edie's work anyway. We'll leave together."

"Punk, should I come too?" I asked.

My grandmother shook her head. "We'll be fine. You finish your work, and the three of us will have a nice quiet supper together when you get home. We just need a little salt air to clear our heads."

The two of them left, and Jason soon came up the stairs. "What happened?" I asked him.

"I found Miss Moran in the garden," he said. "She seemed very upset and hurried away. Is she alright?"

"Not really." Lying to Jason would be impossible. He could look right through you. Sometimes I imagined he was reading my mind and comparing what he saw there to what he heard coming out of my mouth. I tried to make sure they matched. As Sugar said, "He's just the tiniest bit disconcerting."

"Why don't you go on home and see about her," Jason said. "The pictures aren't going anywhere. We have plenty of time to learn whatever they have to tell us."

———

By the time I cleaned up my worktable and got home, Charly had taken off for Horn. Punk said she'd asked to borrow the boat, which was always stocked with camping essentials, and headed out with a hastily packed cooler and knapsack.

"Why do you think she made such a quick getaway?" I asked as Punk and I had an early supper of grilled oysters and toasted French bread on the back porch.

She sighed as she lifted an oyster from its shell with a small three-pronged fork and dipped it in drawn butter. "It's her custom, I'm afraid. When the going gets tough, Charlotte gets going." She laid the oyster on a small piece of bread and ate it. Then she frowned and corrected herself. "I shouldn't have said it that way. Charlotte would never abandon someone she loves when they're in trouble. I just mean that when something becomes too overwhelming for *her*, she tends to seclude herself."

"You think she'll stay on Horn all night?" I looked at the shallow tray in front of me, where half shells rested on a bed of rock salt. I had forgotten the taste of oysters fresh from the docks, their natural flavor preserved by Punk's clean and simple preparation.

"Everything she needs is on the boat," my grandmother said. "At least, that's what she thinks. The truth is, Charlotte needs a lot more than a tent and lantern. I'll leave the radio on so she can call us if she runs into any trouble."

"You always leave your radio on," I said as I leaned over and kissed her cheek. "Figuratively speaking."

# sixteen

I WAS STILL LYING AWAKE AT ONE A.M. when I heard the distinctive sputter of Pop's boat in low idle, returning to its slip. Charly had come home. I guess my brain was determined to wait up for her even though my body wanted rest. I must've fallen asleep right after the squeak of cypress boards told me she was tiptoeing up the stairs. The next time I opened my eyes, I could see the soft light of early morning out my windows.

Voices drifted up the stairs. I climbed out of bed, grabbed a quick shower, and got dressed before joining the Ten Spots.

"There she is!" Sugar exclaimed as I came into the kitchen and began fixing my plate.

"Morning, ladies," I said. "Will I ever get up early enough to start breakfast with y'all?"

"Probably not," Punk said, stopping to hug me as she poured my coffee.

I sat down next to Coco's empty seat, facing the gulf. This group had observed the same seating pattern since I was a child: Punk at the head of the table, closest to the kitchen, with Sugar and Cookie on one side and Coco on the other. They were as predictable as high tide.

"We're just now taking our second lap around the biscuit pan," Cookie said. "You've got time to catch up, Edie."

Punk's biscuits were feather light. This morning, she had served them with sausage gravy, brown-sugared bacon, and scrambled eggs with cheddar.

"Punk, it's not even eight o'clock, and you've already got me reaching for my stretchy pants," I told her.

"I love cooking for you, so indulge me," she said. "We were just talking about the mystery light on Horn. No breakthrough theories so far. Coco sent word that she suspects gnomes."

"Where is she?" I asked.

"En route," Sugar said. "She had to wait on her morning grocery delivery."

"Can you believe that?" Cookie said. "I've seen her shovel dirt and pitch around twenty-five-pound bags of fertilizer in that garden of hers, but she has Rouses deliver her groceries because she says walking those aisles wears her out."

"She doesn't cook anything but breakfast," Sugar added, "and half the time she eats that here. Why, I'll bet she'd have room enough in her buggy for a week's worth of groceries plus two sailors in a fistfight."

We all heard Coco when she came through Punk's front door. "Y'all better not be talking about me!" she called out.

"Of course we're talking about you," Cookie said as Coco made her entrance. "You're the center of our universe."

"Pfft!" Coco pulled a cigarette from behind her ear and tossed it at her sister.

"Pull up a chair while I fix you a plate," Punk said.

Coco took her seat and settled in as Punk brought her breakfast to the table. She stared, eyes narrowed, at Sugar across the table. "What is that on your head?"

Sugar reached up and touched the wide band in her hair. "It's called a hair band, sister."

"Well, I know what it's called," Coco said, frowning. "But old women like us don't wear hair bands."

"We do if we have a flair for accessories," Sugar answered. The hair band looked great on her, and she knew it.

Coco shrugged and took a bite of her biscuit just as Charly came into the kitchen. She greeted everybody before pouring herself a cup of coffee and sitting next to me.

"I'd ask if you want breakfast, but I know better," Punk said, putting an arm around her shoulders.

Charly raised her cup to Punk. She took a sip and silently stared out at the flat waters just beginning to sparkle as the sun brightened. "Would y'all mind if I took my coffee for a walk on the beach?" she asked.

"Of course not, dear," Sugar said. "Go and give the pelicans our warmest regards."

The women were quiet as Charly went onto the screened porch and took the back steps down. We all watched her cross Punk's small backyard and head for the narrow strip of sand that borders the water there.

"A million miles away," Sugar said.

"Maybe two," Punk added.

Coco poured herself some orange juice. "What's going on?"

Punk shrugged. "We visited Edie at Jason's yesterday while she was researching some Camille photographs. Charlotte wouldn't look at the pictures, but I guess just talking about them stirred something up."

"Why?" Coco asked.

"She was here during the storm."

"I can see how something like that would leave scars," Cookie said.

125

"But you know what's weird?" I asked. "Charly's not afraid of storms, not at all. She loves them as much as I do. Wouldn't you think they'd upset her if it was a hurricane that traumatized her?"

"Kid's got a point." Coco took a big bite of her biscuit.

Punk went into the kitchen, came back with the coffeepot, and topped off everyone's cup. "It's hard to know how best to help Charlotte. On the one hand, I think she needs to talk about whatever happened—get it out. But on the other, she's so private that I know if I push, she won't feel safe here anymore. And I believe she needs a refuge."

Sugar took a sip of orange juice and blotted her mouth with a napkin. "I suppose we'll just have to be patient."

"Not my strong suit," Coco said. "I can see you're shocked."

# seventeen

**"COOKIE, THIS WAS AN EXCELLENT IDEA!"** Punk said as the other Ten Spots, Charly, and I boated across the Mississippi Sound.

"It's good to see the ole girl at sea again!" Cookie shouted over the engine noise.

Once upon a time, Cookie and Grady had been locally famous for their fantastic floating parties. They'd bought several pontoons over the years, each one bigger than the last. After Grady died, Cookie couldn't bring herself to part with their last boat, which they'd named *Cookie's Dough*, though she rarely took it out.

We weren't far from Horn Island, where we planned to watch the sunset and have dinner on board. Nobody saw the need to haul everything to the island and back when Cookie's pontoon was a twenty-nine-footer furnished like a front porch, with comfy chairs and a scattering of small tables for food and drink.

Cookie throttled down as we approached shore, slowly cruising around till we found the best sunset spot. She shut off the engine and dropped anchor before joining us.

Coco looked out at the water and took a deep breath.

"Now this is the life. You can keep the mountains. Give me the gulf any day of the week."

"Remember that time you and Grady took us out to Horn and we didn't realize it was Labor Day weekend?" Punk asked Cookie.

"If she doesn't remember it, I do!" Coco said. "We couldn't find a vacant wave to park on. Just a sea of bikinis and coolers."

"That reminds me," Cookie said. "Y'all aren't gonna believe this, but I saw Nonnie Tucker in a bikini yesterday."

Coco slapped both her legs. "Get out!"

Cookie raised her right hand. "If I'm lyin', may Ole Miss never beat the Tide again."

"Sister, are you *sure* it was Nonnie?" Sugar couldn't have looked more aghast if you'd told her Estée Lauder just went out of business.

"I'm absolutely sure," Cookie said. "She was wearing a red bikini and lounging on a bowrider driven by that fellow that just retired here from somewhere up in Wisconsin. They went right by my dock and waved. Nonnie was giggling like a schoolgirl, and I know good and well she's got frequent flier miles on her Medicare card."

"Did she at least have on a cover-up?" Sugar asked.

Cookie shook her head. "Nothing but sunglasses."

"Oh dear." Sugar shuddered at the thought of Nonnie in her brazen red bikini. "How did she look?"

"About like I would," Cookie said. "At our age, there's not much that doesn't look better covered up."

"I hope to goodness she got a pedicure," Sugar said.

"What good would that do?" Cookie asked.

"Well, it would at least draw the eye down."

"Who's the fellow from Wisconsin?" Punk asked. "I don't believe I know him."

"Neither do I," Sugar said.

"Coco knows who I'm talking about." Cookie pointed at her older sister.

Coco reached down and scratched Pierre, who was lounging on the boat deck next to her chair. "I've tried to tell y'all Nonnie's a few Lincoln Logs shy of a cabin, and this just proves it. All you've got to do is watch that man walk, and you can see he's got a bad hip. If Nonnie doesn't look out, she'll wake up one morning and find herself putting his food in a blender on her way to fetch his walker. And let's hope he keeps fresh tennis balls on it. Nothing turns me off quicker than a walker with dirty old Wilsons scuffin' along. Even an old coot should have some pride."

There was a split second of silence before everybody burst out laughing.

"Oh, I had forgotten how much fun we used to have on your boat, Cookie!" Sugar clapped her hands together. "I vote we do this a lot more often!"

"I'll second," Punk said.

Cookie smiled and looked around at the group. "I sure miss Grady and our party boat days—the way we used to bring all kinds of people together. I think it would make him happy to see her on the water again, especially in such fine company. Everybody hungry?"

"Starving," Coco said. "I got busy in my garden and forgot to eat lunch."

Cookie had prepared boxed suppers for us with shrimp po'boys, potato salad, and coleslaw. "Grab whatever you'd like to drink out of that red cooler over there," she said as she handed us each a box. "Coco, I put a little container of crabmeat in your box for Pierre. There's a water bowl in the cooler for him too."

"Pierre thanks you for your hospitality," Coco said as we got our drinks and settled in, devouring our suppers and enjoying the gulf breeze.

"This is delicious, Cookie," Punk said. "I've always loved your potato salad."

Cookie smiled. "Glad you like it. And I'm glad my feeble old brain still remembers how to make it."

"Your brain's not feeble, Miss Cookie," I said. "Not the way you can handle a boat and fry shrimp."

Cookie grinned and pointed at me. "I knew I liked you for some reason."

We chatted and finished our supper, the sun gradually washing the sky in pinkish-blue and coral before sinking into the water.

Punk looked out at the horizon and sighed. "There is nothing more beautiful than a gulf sunset. Nothing in the whole wide world."

"You won't get any argument from me," said Charly, setting her almost-empty dinner box on the boat deck and leaning back in her chair. "Nothing feels better either. The air gets so cool and light. When Libba and I spent our last summer here together, we loved staying out in the sun all day, then coming in, cleaning up, putting on our long cotton sundresses and floppy straw hats, and having supper at one of the restaurants with a deck facing the water." She smiled at the memory. "I never could tan worth a flip, but I'd at least get a little glow going. I thought it made me look bohemian, like one of those hippie girls from San Francisco."

Sugar blotted a cookie crumb from her mouth and took a sip of chilled sparkling water. "I know *exactly* what you mean, Charlotte. There's something about a day at the beach that makes a girl feel transformed. The sun and the water and the salt air—it changes you inside and out. Makes you feel . . . unbound. And a sun-kissed complexion *really* sets off your jewelry, silver and gold most especially."

Coco looked at her sister and shook her head. "Only you would think of the sun as a cosmetic, Shug."

We watched a big fishing boat with three outboards heading toward Biloxi. The men on board tipped their fishing caps to us. "Afternoon, ladies!" they shouted. We all waved back.

"I wish you'd look at the size of that rig," Cookie said. "I'll bet you they've been fishing since way before daylight. Makes me jealous. I used to love getting on the water before dawn with Grady. Speaking of dawn, y'all want me to get going with our question before sunset turns into sunrise?"

"Proceed," Coco said. Pierre hopped onto her lap, made a few full turns till he decided on the perfect position, and curled up for a nap.

Cookie picked up the small basket next to her chair and drew out a question. "When were you the happiest?"

"Oh my, that's interesting," Sugar said.

"Want to answer first?" Cookie asked her.

Sugar closed her eyes and clasped her hands together. "Let me think for a minute. It was May . . . no, June. I was happiest on the first Saturday in June of 1950." She smiled and opened her eyes.

"What happened on that date, Miss Sugar?" I was intrigued with the specificity of her choice.

"It was my fourth date with Wade. On our *first* date, he had taken me out to dinner and then to Coop's Ice Cream Parlor, where I ordered a chocolate sundae but asked them to hold the walnuts. I've never cared for them. On our *fourth* date, we went back to Coop's and I ordered a chocolate sundae but forgot to tell them no walnuts. Wade stopped the waiter before he could get away and asked him to leave them off."

I waited for more to the story, but it never came. "Miss Sugar, I'm gonna need more information," I told her, which made everybody laugh.

"Well, don't you see?" she said. "A whole month had passed between our first date and our fourth, but he remembered something as trivial as the way I like my chocolate sundaes. That's when I knew I wanted to marry him. That's when I knew the waiting was over."

"The waiting?" Now Sugar had Charly's attention.

"You know, dear," Sugar said, "that feeling you get when you sense that you aren't where you're meant to be, with the person you're meant to be with. You're waiting, but you have no idea for whom or for how long. Does that make sense?"

"It makes a ton of sense," Charly said.

"What about you, Coco?" Cookie asked.

Coco looked down at Pierre and scratched his neck. "I'd have to say I'm the happiest right now. Good food. Good company. Exceptional cat. No more hard decisions to make. No more wondering how it's all gonna turn out. I'm telling you what, youth is overrated. It's nothing but a fishbowl full of question marks. You dive in and start pitchin' 'em over the side one by one as you find the answers, till one day you realize you've finally tossed enough of 'em to see out. I like the clear view from here."

"How about you, Punk?" Cookie asked.

She smiled and looked out at the water. "The first time Cap and I walked together on Horn. Right away, both of us breathed differently. I felt more hopeful than I had in years."

"That surprises me," Coco said. "I expected you to say

you were happiest when you met Nathan or when you married him."

Punk shook her head. "I didn't know what was at stake back then. I didn't know how hard we'd have to work for a life together—or that the life we built would absolutely be worth all the struggles. In the beginning, I didn't appreciate the cost or the reward of standing by someone you love the way I loved Cap. But that day on Horn, it all came together. I could look back over all we'd been through and look ahead to a happy future together. I could see it all from that island."

"Well, my answer's short and sweet," Cookie said. "The day I married Grady. Y'all knew that already. Edie, honey?"

I couldn't help smiling as I thought about my answer. "Can I name two? I don't think I can pick between them."

"Well, I don't see why not," Cookie said. "My boat, my rules."

"One of mine, y'all can guess—my summer with Cole. The other happened when Leni and I were near the end of our senior year at Auburn. We were giddy with plans for the future. Both of us wanted to work in publishing, so we were hoping to get jobs and live together in a big city—maybe Chicago, maybe New York or Los Angeles—anyplace exciting and glamorous."

Sugar closed her eyes and smiled. "I remember dreams like that. The kind you have when you're young."

"It was spring quarter," I went on, "and we were walking home from somewhere after dark. I don't even remember where we'd been. The two of us were standing at Toomer's Corner, waiting for the light to change, when a Greyhound bus pulled up to the curb, stopped, and opened its door. We looked up at the destination sign above the windshield. It said 'New York City.' We both gasped and said, 'It's a sign!'"

"Oh my goodness, I can just see you two," Punk said.

"We laughed and planned all the way back to our tiny apartment. Anything seemed possible that night. Absolutely anything. Trouble was, we were so focused on the good that we completely ignored the bad—possibilities, I mean. I've been kicking myself about that, but now—I don't know—maybe a touch of oblivion isn't such a bad thing. You might never leave the house if you saw everything that's coming."

"Oh, Edie, honey, you have many more days filled with possibility," Sugar said. "Even in the longest, darkest tunnel, there's always a little ray of hope glowing in the distance."

"Could be hope, could be a freight train with bad brakes," Coco said.

"Charlotte, honey?" Cookie prompted. "I guess that leaves you. When were you the happiest?"

Charly looked around at everybody like a poker player in a cowboy movie, debating whether to bluff or lay all her cards on the table. Finally, she said, "I was the happiest on August 17, 1969."

I couldn't believe what I was hearing. "But that was the night—"

"Of Camille," Charly finished for me. She reached into a small beach bag next to her chair and pulled out a portrait, probably five-by-seven, backed with cardboard and wrapped in cellophane. She handed it to me. Done in pen-and-ink, it was a very good likeness—professional even—of a handsome guy, probably in his twenties, with kind eyes and an arresting smile.

"Who's this?" I studied the drawing before passing it on to Punk.

"I wish I knew," Charly said. "You have no idea how hard I've tried to find out."

"He's *very* handsome," Sugar said as she and Cookie looked at the portrait together. They passed it on to Coco.

"He's a looker alright," she agreed.

"Who—I mean how—" I didn't even know what to ask.

"I found him and lost him during the storm," Charly explained. "All I have are his first name—Connor—and that drawing. I've held on to both since I was eighteen years old."

"Where did the drawing come from, dear?" Sugar asked as Coco passed it back to Charly.

"I had an artist friend in Bay St. Louis, a serious painter who made extra money doing portraits of hotel guests at the Broadwater. I asked her to draw him, based on my description. She sketched till we got the details right and then drew this pen-and-ink. I have to say, she captured him. As well as anybody could anyway."

"Okay, Charly," I said. "Spill."

# eighteen

**CHARLY SAT BACK IN HER CHAIR,** watching a couple of dolphins play in the surf, as the rest of us waited for her to tell us why the happiest moment of her life happened during a deadly hurricane.

"The water was so angry that day," she finally said, turning her attention back to us. "Hard to imagine now. The morning of the storm—Sunday—the sky was actually clear, but it was a weird color. It sort of—I don't know—glowed. All day long, civil defense was going door to door, telling everybody to get out. When I told them I wasn't leaving, they asked for the name and phone number of my next of kin."

"Were they just trying to scare you into evacuating?" I asked.

"That's what I thought at first. Turns out they were serious. As the day wore on, the wind kept picking up, and we'd have bouts of heavy rain. Huge waves crashed against the old seawall. I saw young people in the water, jumping the breakers. I guess they'd never seen anything like that before."

"Do you mean to tell me they were out in that gulf with a *hurricane* coming in?" Sugar said. "What on earth were they thinking?"

"Youth," Charly said with a shrug. "They weren't thinking at all."

"What did you do that day, with a storm approaching?" Punk asked.

Charly pulled her feet up into her chair. "Maxine was trying to save her equipment at the beauty shops. I found out, after I went to work for her, that she owned two. That Sunday morning, she hired a few teenage boys to load up all the dryer chairs and other heavy stuff, and she put me in charge of the Biloxi move while she handled Gulfport. She had a brother who lived further inland, a few blocks behind the railroad tracks. Since they run parallel to the water and the railroad bed is pretty high, Maxine thought it would dam the storm surge and keep her equipment dry."

"I've heard about that," Punk said. "Simple cottages on the back side of the tracks fared better than some of the mansions on the front side."

"Well, by the time we got everything loaded and moved, it was late afternoon and we were all exhausted. Traffic was insane. Seems like there was a wreck or something on 49. It was bumper to bumper as far as you could see in any direction."

"So you were trapped?" I asked.

"Yes, but I didn't see it that way at the time," Charly explained. "I just thought it would be too much trouble to leave—and too expensive. Landfall predictions were iffy back then, so I didn't think anyplace on the coast would necessarily be safer than where I was. I didn't have any friends living inland, so I'd have to foot the bill for a hotel, which I couldn't afford, even if I could get there somehow in all that traffic. When I was a kid, Mama always left it to me to batten down the hatches during hurricanes, so I knew what to do. I guess I thought I could ride it out."

"Were you still living with Louella?" Punk asked.

"I was, but her son Rooney up in Jackson made her evacuate. He came down here and got her."

"Oh, that's right," Punk said. "I had forgotten."

Charly stretched out her legs and was silent for so long that I thought I might die of curiosity. Finally, I said, "If you don't tell us the rest, I think I might have to jump overboard and drown myself before my curiosity kills me."

"It's just that I feel so stupid." She turned to me. "Don't ever be stupid like me."

"Charly, you're one of the smartest people I know." It was true. She had worked her way through college doing hair at a place called the Curly-Que, which was a beauty shop and barbecue joint under the same roof.

"Would a smart person keep believing in something that's just not possible?" she countered. "I tell myself I gave up on it a long time ago, but if I'm honest, I know I didn't. And that's just plain stupid."

"Not necessarily," Sugar argued. "We all know what it's like to harbor a secret hurt or hope. Every woman alive has done it."

"Sugar's right," Punk said to Charly, "and for the record, I'm with Edie. You're not stupid and never have been."

"But back to the storm," Coco said. "Louella went home with Rooney, but you stayed behind?"

"That's right. They both tried to get me to go with them, but I felt like I owed it to Maxine to help save her equipment."

"So that left you alone in Louella's house during the storm?" Punk asked.

Charly shook her head. "Not alone."

"Tell us about him," Coco said. "You'll feel better, and we

won't strip the gears in what's left of our old brains trying to figure it out for ourselves."

Charly smiled at Coco. "One of the teenagers Maxine hired to help me in Biloxi looked like a linebacker, but the other one was a little on the scrawny side. I had my doubts about whether he'd be able to lift his share of a dryer chair, so I grabbed part of his side to help him. Just as we were hoisting it into Maxine's pickup, he lost his grip, which caught the linebacker off guard, and the chair was about to fall on me." She pointed to the drawing. "That's when Connor showed up out of nowhere. Must've been six two or three. Military build. Blond hair and the kindest brown eyes I ever saw. Of course, I didn't notice all that at first. All I had time to think about was that he'd just saved me from the funeral home."

"Was he an airman?" Punk asked.

"No, ma'am, but he had an older brother who was career Air Force. Connor had been drafted when he was eighteen and served his hitch in the Army. He came down here to interview for med school at Tulane but decided to detour through Biloxi and talk to some of the guys at Keesler to see if any of them had come across his brother in Vietnam. The family hadn't heard from him in a while."

"So he wasn't from here?" Cookie asked.

"No, ma'am. He never named his actual hometown. When I asked him where he was from, he said he grew up 'east of Podunk and west of Nowhere.' We laughed about it. I wish to goodness we hadn't. I wish I'd made him tell me where he was from, but it didn't seem so important just then. The most likely area is West Tennessee. Could also be Mississippi or Arkansas or even north Alabama, though."

"Why there?" Coco asked.

"I said something about Christmas—how I'd be glad when

it got here because that would mean hurricane season was over—and he said he'd never forget the window displays in Memphis, where his family went Christmas shopping every year. He said they'd always go to the Peabody Hotel to see the big Christmas tree and the live ducks in the lobby fountain. I just figured that if they did their shopping in Memphis but lived in the middle of nowhere . . ."

"He was probably from a rural area someplace within an hour or two of the city," Coco agreed. "What happened after he saved you from death by beauty appliance?"

"He stayed and helped with everything else. The teenagers took off the minute I paid them. We hadn't eaten lunch, and everything was closed because of the hurricane, so I invited Connor back to the house and fixed us an early supper."

Charly had the dreamiest expression on her face, half smiling, a faraway look in her eyes, like she wasn't on this boat with us anymore.

"My whole life, I'd never talked to any guy like that. I'd never had a guy *listen* the way he did. There was no chitchat. No awkward laughter to fill the empty spaces. We just sort of—I don't know—flowed together like a couple of old river currents. I told him all about my sordid childhood and how I finally found a home in Biloxi." She gathered her hair over one shoulder and began slowly twisting it. "He told me what happened to him in Vietnam and how he had struggled to feel at home anywhere since he came back. He said he felt at home with me. I sure felt at home with him. I fell in love, plain and simple. Right then and there."

"Charly, this is just so . . ."

"Unlike me?"

I smiled and nodded. "Yes! Love at first sight is Mama's territory. You're supposed to be the logical one."

"Well, chouchou, what can I tell you? It happens."

"Of course it does," Sugar agreed.

"I'm glad," I said to Charly. "I mean I'm glad to know it can. And I'm glad it happened for you."

"My timing, of course, was terrible," she said. "He had just given me one of those kisses you remember till the day you die when the lights went out and the wind blew Louella's front door into the staircase."

"I guess you weren't paying any attention to the storm outside, what with all the fireworks inside?" Sugar grinned and winked at Charly.

"I guess not," she answered. "By then it was probably eight or nine o'clock. The wind—oh my gosh, there's no way to describe that awful sound—part roar, part shriek. It was deafening. When the door came off, the water came in. And it wasn't rain. It was surf. Louella's porch was whitecapping."

"Dear heaven," Punk said, shaking her head. "I've been through hurricanes, including Audrey, but nothing like that."

"Nobody had been through one like Camille," Charly said. "We dragged Louella's table next to the staircase, just past the spot where the front door had jammed it, and climbed on top. Connor lifted me over the railing and then climbed up behind me. We had just made it to the top of the stairs when most of the roof blew off, and we knew we had to get out of the house."

"I just can't believe it," I said. "I mean I can't believe I didn't know this about you."

"You couldn't know, sweetie. I've never talked about it, except to your mama, of course."

"What happened when the roof went?" Cookie asked. "What did you do?"

141

Charly took a deep breath. "With the roof gone, the upstairs walls started tearing away. The water was only a foot below the upstairs floor, which was open to the storm on one side. The wind was so loud, we had to yell to hear each other. It was pitch-black inside and out, but when lightning flashed, we could see Louella's live oak just a few yards away. We decided that if we could reach one of the limbs, we could climb up and ride out the storm in that big tree. Connor kicked a tall footboard loose from one of the beds and put it flat on the floor. We lay across it like a couple of surfers ready to paddle out, kissed each other for luck, and held on for dear life. Once the water got high enough, it washed us out into the storm."

Punk got up and put her arms around Charly, hugging her tight. "I just needed to do that," she said. Then she went back to her chair and sat down. "Go ahead, honey."

"You can probably guess what happened next," Charly said. "There's no swimming in a hurricane, not with any direction, anyway. All you can do is try to keep your head above the water and grab whatever floats by—or whatever *you* float by—that might help you survive. That storm threw us together and then blew us apart. It yanked Louella's footboard right out of our hands and sent us flailing in opposite directions. Within seconds, I couldn't hear Connor calling my name anymore. I was just swirling in a dark void with that horrible roar."

"What saved you?" Sugar asked.

"It seemed like forever before I finally landed in a tree—not Louella's but one a few blocks away. I didn't know that at the time, of course. I had no idea where I was. I just grabbed on to a limb and managed to climb and claw my way close to the trunk, where the branches could protect me

142

a little bit. When the storm finally passed, the whole coast was wrecked. I got picked up by the Seabees and taken to a mobile triage unit, which sent me to the hospital in Pensacola because the one here was already full. And I never saw Connor again."

"Were you badly hurt, Charlotte?" Punk asked.

"I had a bump on the head and an infection from a big gash on my back, but those were treatable."

"I guess you started looking for him when you were well enough?" Cookie asked.

Charly nodded. "I did. But I had been in the hospital for a week and had no idea where he was. Even family members who got separated during that storm had trouble finding each other, so you can imagine what it was like for two people who had just met and didn't know each other's last names. Except for the lighthouse, precious few landmarks held up to the wind and the water. The streets were torn up. Louella's whole block was gone. *Most* blocks near the water were gone. The beauty shop and everything around it got wiped out. There was nothing to navigate by, so unless you knew this area really well, half the time you couldn't tell where you were, once you lost sight of the lighthouse."

"Did you ask around Keesler—maybe some of the flyboys' hangouts?" Coco asked.

Charly nodded. "I did. All the hangouts were either flooded or obliterated, and civilians with no reason to be on base weren't allowed anywhere near Keesler right after the hurricane because it had flooded too. I tried asking some of the airmen who were helping clear debris. But you know military guys. They're tight. They see a desperate girl asking around about a guy she knows only by his first name . . ."

Punk took a sip of her coffee. "I saw the same thing happen

143

while Cap was overseas—frantic girls hovering around the base and searching the train station."

Charly held up the portrait and stared at it. "They thought I meant to cause him trouble, so if any of them did know Connor, they wouldn't tell me anything."

"It's all just so . . . so *tragic*," Sugar said. "How long did you search for him, dear?"

"Every waking minute for a few months after the storm," Charly said. "But I soon realized I'd go completely crazy if I kept that up. I had searched everywhere I could. During the first few weeks after Camille, I'd take a book and a quilt and spend a couple of hours every afternoon sitting near the lighthouse, just hoping Connor would think to look there since it was the one landmark that hadn't moved. But he never came."

"I'm sure if he didn't it's because he couldn't," Punk said. "From what you've told us, something kept him away or he would've been there."

"I checked the death rolls every day. No Connors, thank heaven. There were lists of the missing too, but since I had no idea who he had met at Keesler or how well he knew them, I didn't know if anybody would've reported him missing. Or if he *was* missing. Or injured or unconscious or swept away somewhere with no memory of me. Then again, maybe he was fine and just didn't care to find me. Is that possible? Something that meant everything to me maybe meant nothing to him at all?"

"Not from what you've told us about him, honey," Sugar said. "He sounds much too special for that."

"I hope you're right, Miss Sugar," Charly said. "But for whatever reason, Connor was lost, probably forever. And so was I. Even when I tried as hard as I could to focus on someone who was actually there, right in front of me, I could still see Connor out of the corner of my eye. Once you know what's possible, it's hard to settle for what's just available."

"Well, this is tragic," Sugar repeated, "absolutely tragic."

"See what you've done, Charlotte?" Coco said with a grin. "You've made Sugar clutch her pearls." She dramatically mimicked the grip her sister had on the short strand she was wearing.

We all laughed, even Charly. I guess it was from the tension Coco had released.

"I can't help it!" Sugar said when she stopped laughing. "When I'm upset, I need to grab hold of something!"

"Charlotte, how long did you stay down here after the storm?" Cookie asked.

"Not long. By the end of the year, I knew I had to make a change. I had gotten interested in architecture—preservation, in particular, since I had seen so many beautiful homes destroyed. I started applying to schools, got a scholarship to Auburn, and left Biloxi the day after Christmas."

"Left and never came back," Coco said.

"That's right," Charly said, "except to visit Miss Punk. But now listen, I don't want y'all to go throwing me a pity party. I've had a good life. I really have. Even thought I'd found someone I could be happy with a couple of times. But in the end, well, I couldn't settle for less. And I didn't think it would be fair to the other person if I did. I just had to accept that my life would be about my work, my friends, and my travels, not marriage and a family. And that's that."

"What was it about Jason's store that brought all this back, Charly?" I asked.

She stared at the portrait before answering. "I felt him. I

felt Connor in the garden, or at least I thought I did. And it was so *real*."

"Were you by the fountain?"

"Yes. Why?"

"Because I got a really strong feeling about Leni there." I turned to Punk. "It was the first time y'all took me to The Trove. I just got this powerful sense of her—and about her. It was like I suddenly knew she belongs someplace else now."

"What happened after that—right after that?" Charly asked.

"Jason showed up."

"Same here," she said. "I was looking at my own reflection in the water, and then there he was—Connor. Not literally, of course. I just suddenly felt the way I did when we were together. It was so strong that I turned around to see if he was standing behind me. Instead, I found Jason."

"Well, that's odd," Punk said. "A simple coincidence, I'm sure, but odd just the same."

"Did Connor seem—feel—different?" I asked Charly.

She shook her head. "No, he was the same. I mean, I *felt* the same. And it brought back the same old question I've wrestled with over the years."

"What's that, dear?" Sugar asked.

"Whether it was the actual Connor I was in love with or just the idea of him," Charly said. "Did I really meet someone that special, or was he just a nice guy I built into this dream soulmate in my mind? That's what I've always wondered. But when I was at the fountain, the Connor I sensed or felt or remembered—whatever you want to call it—he was everything I remembered him to be. And now I have to start all over."

146

"Doing what, honey?" Punk asked.

"Forgetting. I have to remember how to forget. Or at least try to. I can't keep doing this."

"Wouldn't it be better to let us help you remember?" Sugar asked.

"How?"

"Well, now that we know about your Connor, maybe we can help. Maybe if you go over some details with us, we'll spot something."

"Shug's right," Coco said. "Let us in on whatever you don't mind telling us, and maybe we'll catch something you missed. Fresh eyes and all that. Fresh eyes with cataracts."

Pierre hopped out of Coco's lap and scratched his neck, then stretched out at her feet. That cat had to be three feet long, nose to tail.

"Let's start with where he might be from," Coco suggested. "We know he lived in the middle of nowhere but close enough to Memphis to Christmas shop and sightsee there every year. Right off the bat, I'd say we can rule out north Alabama. People up there would handle their Christmas to-doing in Huntsville or Birmingham."

"You're right," I said.

"As for Mississippi," Coco went on, "we know for sure that he wasn't from the coast."

"We can rule out the Delta too," Sugar said. "Delta people are very proud of their land and culture. If Connor had been from there, he would've said so. And he would've promised to take you there so you could see what you've been missing."

"I think if he'd been from central Mississippi, his family would've shopped in Jackson instead of driving all the way to Memphis," Punk suggested. "Northeast Mississippi has Tupelo. That just leaves the northwest corner that might gravitate to Memphis—the Delta too, of course, but as Sugar said, anybody from the Delta will usually say so."

"What about Arkansas and Tennessee?" Charly asked. "What do y'all think about them?"

Pierre sat up and looked around at all of us, then lay back down, resting his head on Coco's foot, which made her smile. "Hudie had family in Arkansas," she recalled. "People up there always struck me as the small-town, outdoorsy type, not too inclined to big, bustling cities. They've got enough nice towns and Little Rock, of course, to do them fine for Christmas. But I imagine those who live just over the river from Memphis probably go there to shop and see the sights."

"And Tennessee?" Charly asked.

"Grady had an Army buddy in Nashville," Cookie said, "and he always said Tennessee is really three states—the east, the west, and the middle. Anybody who didn't live in the western section would likely do their Christmas shopping in Nashville or Chattanooga or Knoxville—maybe even the Smokies—but probably not Memphis." She stood up and retrieved a big tin of homemade cookies. "All this Sherlockin' is making me hungry. Pass these around while I pour us some of Coco's garden punch."

"See?" Coco said to Charly. "We've already made progress."

Charly smiled at her. "I have to admit, it's nice not to feel so alone in this."

"That's what we're here for," Coco said. "Support. And a boat ride. And maybe a little fueled-up punch, but only for medicinal purposes."

# nineteen

**"DON'T YOU WORRY,** Edie dear, I'm sure I've got the very thing—something *gaw-uh-geous*!" Sugar led me into the biggest walk-in closet I had ever seen. It might well qualify as a drive-through.

"We'll wait out here," Punk said as she and the other Ten Spots made themselves comfortable in Sugar's palatial master suite. Our host began rifling through racks of dresses lining one whole side of her closet. The opposite wall held pants, skirts, and tops, while the back was floor-to-ceiling shoes. Cabinets in the center stored Sugar's lingerie and accessories. Everything was organized by color.

Cole had called and asked me to dinner at the most romantic restaurant on the coast. He said we'd get all gussied up, pageant hair optional. I warned him that it was way too hot for Silk Reflections.

Sugar said that she and I were "proportionally twins" and insisted on outfitting me.

"Miss Sugar, I don't know about this. Your clothes are so nice, and it would be just like me to spill something on myself."

She waved away my objections and kept making selections. "If you spill something, you spill something. It's just a dress, honey. Besides, I'm going to gift you whatever we pick out as a little memento of this *very* special date. I don't want you worrying about a dress when you should be focused on hooking Cole and reeling him in. Now then, come out here to my mirror."

She carried out four dresses, which she draped over an armchair next to a gilded three-way mirror. First she chose a yellow wrap dress and held it up to me. She briefly studied the effect but then frowned and shook her head. "No, I don't think so. Ladies?"

I turned around so they could see.

"Too *Rebecca of Sunnybrook Farm*," Coco said. "The boy's got hormones. I say we fire 'em up and put 'em to work for Edie."

"My sister the vamp," Cookie said.

"Now this one I would call a daring choice, but it's not completely beyond the pale for a restaurant as elegant as The Oaks." Sugar held up a black sequined number with a feather boa.

"Miss Sugar, it's beautiful, but I don't think I have the chutzpah to pull off this much glam."

Sugar laughed and threw the boa around her neck. "Well, I do!"

Maybe I'd grow bolder with age, but I was definitely not in Sugar's league just yet.

"Here's the one, Edie," she said. "I feel it in my bones." The outfit she held in front of me was drop-dead gorgeous— a sleeveless, midi-length dress in peacock blue with a V-neck in front and back. Clean lines, no fuss, dreamy silk chiffon fabric.

"Oh, Miss Sugar." I couldn't stop staring at the dress. "It's beautiful."

"That's the one alright," Punk agreed.

Coco popped a cigarette between her lips. "Gets my vote."

"Mine too," Cookie said.

"Step into the closet and put it on, dear," Sugar said. "Show us how fabulous you look in it."

I obeyed and had an instant Cinderella moment when I zipped the dress and stood before the mirror in Sugar's closet. Then I stepped into the bedroom and enjoyed the Ten Spots' collective gasps. I could only hope for the same reaction from Cole.

"Perfect," Punk said. "Does she need a wrap, Sugar, in case it gets breezy?"

Sugar took off the boa and tossed it at Punk. "Well, of course not! If she has a wrap, he'll have no reason to put his dinner jacket around her, thereby getting close enough to become intoxicated with her perfume. That reminds me, Edie, be sure to spritz a little Chanel in your hair."

"Miss Sugar, you're entirely devious," I said.

She giggled and winked at me.

"What about jewelry, Shug?" Coco asked her.

"Of course, Edie can accessorize however she likes, but this neckline creates a lovely visual journey from the face to the décolletage. A necklace would only insert an unfortunate speed bump. I recommend chandelier earrings and nothing more. Maybe a bracelet, but that's *suhtainly* all. Naturally, Edie dear, I think your hair should be up to show off your lovely back, but I'd keep it loose, low, and romantic—a tempting tendril here and there—nothing high and stiff. That's not you. As for shoes, you've always demonstrated some flair in that arena. I'll bet you have a classic pump or strappy sandal in your repertoire. Black or silver would be just right."

"I've got both."

Sugar gave me a thumbs-up. "That's my girl. I'll send you home with a clutch to match each so you don't have to decide before you see them with the dress. What do you think?"

I laughed and kissed her on the cheek. "Miss Sugar, I think whatever you think."

———

Cole picked me up in the T-bird and drove us to The Oaks, a gourmet restaurant housed in a regal two-hundred-year-old Greek Revival. Besides two formal dining rooms, the restaurant had a scattering of tables on the veranda and a very special one all by itself on the upper balcony. Ever since I was a little girl, I had wondered what it would feel like to sit at that balcony table.

Cole took my hand as we climbed the steps to the grand front entrance. He had worn military-crisp khakis and a navy jacket with a pale-blue dress shirt. No tie. He looked perfect—and perfectly himself, just like always.

Inside, a hostess greeted us and studied her reservation list as I looked around. This place oozed elegance—candlelight and starched white linens, Spode china and sterling silver everywhere. I breathed in the heady fragrance of roses from simple arrangements on each table. I had been here only once in my life, for Punk and Pop's fiftieth wedding anniversary.

"Right this way," the hostess said.

I was hoping we might get lucky enough for a table on the veranda, but as we made our way to the sweeping staircase, I realized Cole had managed something far better. I tried to maintain my composure when we started up, his hand against my back. On the second floor, we followed the hostess through an opulent sitting room, where she opened French doors onto the upper balcony with its solitary candlelit table. After pulling out my chair, she handed us our menus and a wine list, then promised that our waiter would be with us shortly.

I looked at Cole across the table. "Are we grown up enough to be here?"

He glanced around at the French doors, the candlelight, the silver on our table. "No. But maybe we can scarf down some quality bivalves before they figure that out."

We laughed together as we looked out from our private hideaway. A breeze stirred the four live oaks towering over the corners of the house, their mammoth branches reaching midway across the upper floor so that I could almost touch them as they swayed ever so slightly. They framed the gulf, lit by a full moon tonight.

"This is just . . . *magic*," I said. "What made you think of it?"

He ran his hand through his hair and leaned back in his chair. "I remembered how you used to look up at it when your Pop and Grady would drive us to Bay St. Louis for burgers. You could be mid-sentence, and you'd stop talking to look up here, after which you'd shake your head and say a long, wistful 'wow.'"

Even though I remembered the tiniest minutiae about Cole, it amazed me when he recalled things I had forgotten about myself. "Thank you—very much—for bringing me here. Now that I've seen it in person, I'll say an even bigger 'wow.'" I looked down at three couples making their way up the sidewalk to the front steps. "I have an incredible urge to yell down there, 'Hey, everybody, look at us!' Would that be frowned upon, do you think?"

153

"In that dress, you could absolutely pull it off," he said. "Just don't hang over the balcony when you do it. That might be crossing the line."

I couldn't stop smiling. "How on earth did you manage to book this table? I thought you had to know somebody who knows somebody to get it."

"That's true. And fortunately, I do—know somebody who knows somebody, that is."

A waiter appeared with crystal goblets of ice water, then stepped inside and came out again with two champagne coupes and a bottle of prosecco chilling in an ice bucket, which he set on a small iron stand next to our table. "Compliments of General Jeffries," he said as he poured two glasses and then recited tonight's featured specialties.

Cole ordered the fillet. I chose seared shrimp with a white wine butter sauce. We decided to split an appetizer of char-broiled oysters.

With our orders in, the waiter left, and Cole proposed a toast. "To pretending we know what we're doing."

I clinked glasses with him. "Cheers." We took a sip of the bubbly drink. "So who is General Jeffries?" I asked.

"Brigadier general, to be exact. He's my commander. His granddaughter's flight from North Carolina to Biloxi got canceled a few weeks ago, and she was going to miss her grandmother's seventieth birthday party. The general wasn't free to go, so he told me if I'd be willing to sacrifice my day off to fly up there and get her, he'd owe me one. I took him up on it. Managed to get myself an appointment on his calendar and told him I needed to plan a special date that might require a little string pulling. He made a phone call, and here we sit. No way would they have given this table to a lowly pilot like me."

"Who kept watch over the great state of Mississippi while you and the general scored my dream table?"

Cole frowned and ran his hand over his mouth. "I'm not sure. Guess the Coast Guard picked up the slack."

Our waiter delivered the most enticing platter of char-broiled oysters this side of Punk's grill and grated fresh Parmesan on top. "Enjoy," he said.

"Heavenly days, just take a deep breath over that platter." I was inhaling the aromas of saltwater and woodsmoke and freshly grated cheese.

"Breathe all you want, ma'am," Cole said. "I've got an oyster fork, and I'm not afraid to use it."

Each of us speared an oyster out of its shell and tasted the purest flavor of the gulf. In spontaneous unison, we both swallowed, leaned back in our chairs, and said, "Oh my gosh."

When we finally stopped laughing, Cole raised his glass again. "To oystermen."

I clicked mine against it. "To oystermen." We sipped the prosecco as we made short work of the half shells before us. "If we keep sipping this stuff," I said, "pretty soon we'll be toasting the cicadas."

"There are worse things to toast than the signature bug of the South," Cole argued.

"I believe you're thinking of the mosquito."

He pointed to a couple of strategically placed fans on the balcony. "Guess those are keeping them away. I thought I'd escape those things in desert countries, but no. Mosquitoes can find you there too."

We had one more toast—to mosquito repellent—before I asked about his active duty. "Is it something you can talk about? Because if you'd rather not . . ."

He dusted some rock salt off his hand and shook his head. "No, it's okay. With you anyway. I don't much like it when total strangers see me in a flight suit and ask something crazy like, 'How many kills, ace?' I usually just walk away, but what I want to say is, 'Why don't you ask me how many of our guys I safely landed in hot zones? Or how many times I was able to drop food and medical supplies to troops?' Nobody wants to hear about that."

"I do. You have so much to be proud of, Cole."

"I don't know if I'd call it pride so much as satisfaction. Or maybe gratification? Anyway, it meant something to me—being able to help. That's the part that really matters."

"What about the actual flying? Was it everything you thought it would be when you were younger?"

He looked out at the full moon as he thought about it. "Yes and no," he said, turning back to me. "I thought I'd be the most excited about the machine itself—feeling the engine power and learning to control it, executing all kinds of complicated maneuvers. But for me, the real excitement is where the plane can take you and what you can accomplish with it. That's why the 53rd Weather Recon appealed to me so much. How great would it be to help warn people about dangerous storms so they can get out of harm's way?"

"I'm a little jealous. I hope one day I can do something that matters, even if it's just inspiring people to stop and think."

"Edie, you're already doing that with the pictures you're shooting *and* the ones you're researching. You're going to tell some powerful stories."

"You really think so?"

He reached across the table and took my hand. "I know so."

156

"You sure about this?" Cole asked. He and I were standing in the only Gulfport souvenir shop that was open late.

"Positive," I said, looking through a rack of giant beach towels—more like beach sheets, they were so huge. I held up two. "Palm trees or seahorses?"

"Definitely seahorses," he said.

I nodded in agreement. "Always a stylish choice. And it's on sale for twelve dollars."

After dinner, Cole had asked where I wanted to go next—a fancy wine bar, a club with live music and dancing . . . I picked the beach.

We bought our towel and then drove west for a bit, out of the casino traffic and onto a quiet stretch of sand near Pass Christian. We took our shoes off and walked down to the water's edge, then spread our beach towel just far enough away from the surf to keep us dry.

"Here, you probably need this more than I do." Cole took off his jacket and put it around me. Of course I giggled out loud. Of course I did.

"What?" He grinned as he held the jacket around me by its lapels.

"While Miss Sugar was outfitting me for our big date, Punk asked her if I would need a wrap. And Sugar said no because if I had one with me, then you'd have no reason to put your jacket around me and get intoxicated by the perfume she made me spray in my hair."

Cole smiled down at me. "Here's to intoxication." He curled one arm around my waist and slipped his hand against my neck, pulling me close against him. I forgot all about Sugar and her perfume and everything else in the world except Cole's deep kiss, the warmth of his touch, and the hope that I would never stop feeling this way, ever.

*twenty*

**IT WAS A WEDNESDAY MORNING** when I opened the door at The Trove and found Jason standing behind the front counter, going through receipts.

"Welcome back," he said as he looked up. "How was Hattiesburg?"

"Productive." I held the door open with my foot as I attempted to drag in a box filled with transcripts. I had heard a radio spot about a collection at Southern Miss—interviews with Camille survivors, recorded ten years after the storm. Jason let me spend a day over there to see what I could find out.

"Let me help you." He hurried from behind the counter, picked up the box, and carried it upstairs. Nothing ever seemed heavy to him, be it a tea service or a crateful of research. Yet another Jason quirk.

He set the box on the table for me, and I opened it to show him the fruits of my labor. "You can buy photocopies of the interview transcripts for little or nothing, so I got quite a few."

"Money well spent, I imagine," he said.

"I've been sorting the images geographically, at least as many as I could, with so few landmarks left after Camille," I explained. "If I can find connections between, say, the Pass Christian images and survivor accounts from there, maybe I'll learn something? Maybe find out if there are still survivors there who could fill in the gaps?"

Jason smiled at me and nodded. "Excellent idea. You are tenacious in the best sense of the word, Edie. I'm very lucky to have your help. And I believe you'll find I've learned to make a respectable pot of coffee." He nodded to the coffee-maker still dripping and hissing.

I had to laugh at the refined tea connoisseur stooping to brew me a pot of Folgers. "It's good to know we're both trainable."

The afternoon brought a heavy rain, which I've always loved. Makes it easier to think. And the Camille interviews had given me plenty to think about. I sat at my worktable rereading them and making notes while Jason arranged a collection of Mississippi history books on the shelves in front of me.

"Got time for a little theology?" I asked him.

"Always." He kept his eyes on his work.

"Do you think God still appears to people—here on earth, I mean?"

"I do, though sometimes not how they expect."

"What do you mean?"

He dusted the cover of a yellow volume as big as a phone book and gave it a prominent spot on the center shelf. "I mean there needn't be a pillar of fire or a burning bush or a booming voice from the heavens for God to make his presence known. He can do it invisibly, silently. He can send messengers."

"You mean like angels?"

"Yes. Prophets too. Human beings tend to want things done their way, but that's not necessarily God's way, in my humble opinion." Jason took a step back to evaluate the book display before sitting down at the table with me. "May I ask what prompted your question?"

"Several things, I guess. But mostly this." I tapped my pen on the transcript I was reading. "A woman says she prayed so hard during the storm that she thought she saw Jesus. That's what got her through. Do you think it's true—that she really saw him?"

"It's possible."

"Or did she just want to see him so badly that she hallucinated?"

"I'm not sure it matters whether he manifested physically—that is, literally came to earth—or appeared only in her mind. Either way, his image brought her the comfort and courage that helped her survive. Either way, he materialized for her because of her faith in him." He leaned back in his chair and gave me what I had come to call The Stare. "Something else is bothering you."

I matched his gaze as best I could. "Are you dissecting my brain when you look at me like that?"

Jason laughed and covered his eyes with his hand. "I apologize. I'm told I have a bad habit of staring when I'm thinking. But your brain is intact. I promise."

I panned the half-moon of transcripts around me. "I guess reading all of these stories, memories of real people who lived through a disaster . . . I don't know. It's got me thinking. Punk says that if someone you love is very sick and can't get any better, there comes a time when the best you can do for them is pray that God will be merciful and end their suffering. I guess I have a hard time seeing mercy in some of these stories."

"Why?"

I pointed to one of the transcripts on my left. "This family—the parents, maternal grandparents, and four little kids—they all lived together in a small house a few blocks off the beach. Hardworking. Not very well-off. They didn't evacuate because the grandparents refused to leave. They had built the house themselves and lived there all their lives. They wanted to defend it against looters after the storm."

"Possessions before people?" Jason asked.

"The house was all they had, I guess. When it splintered, the grandparents were swept away, along with the two grandchildren they held. The parents managed to hold on to the other two children and jump onto a mattress as it floated out. Before it could get saturated and sink, they moved onto a wooden church door that had wedged between two trees. It held them steady through the storm."

"You don't see mercy in the church door?" Jason asked.

"Yes, but there's more. When the hurricane passed, the mother realized that the toddler in her arms, the baby of the family, was very still. She examined the little boy and saw that something sharp in all the debris had severed the artery in his leg, but in the howling wind, his mother never knew it. She couldn't hear the baby cry. And even if she had, she couldn't have done anything about it."

Jason got up and poured a cup of coffee for me and some tea for himself. "These are difficult stories, aren't they?" he said as he sat back down.

"Yes." The coffee smelled strong, just the way I like it. "But

I think this one gives me the most trouble. It just seems cruel that the mother managed to save her child from an obvious threat only to lose him to one she never saw coming."

Jason slowly turned his teacup between his hands. I could hear the fragile china rubbing against the heavy wood table. "Maybe you're looking for mercy in the wrong place."

"Where should I be looking?"

"Don't you imagine any mother would rather hold her baby to the very end than have him ripped from her arms?" Jason asked. "Wouldn't she have more peace knowing he had died and gone to be with God than forever wondering if he were lost, if he had suffered, if he had been taken by someone who might abuse him?"

I clamped my eyes shut and shook my head in frustration. "But why did she have to lose the baby at all?"

"I've not been given all the answers, Edie. I would never claim otherwise. But I do know that people can create some impossible choices for themselves because their knowledge is based on what they see or have seen—even what they feel and what they want to believe—but they don't realize how limited their vision is."

"In other words, we don't know what we don't know?" I asked.

"Exactly. The grandparents couldn't imagine any storm stronger than the ones they had lived through, but Camille was exactly that—stronger than anything they had ever seen. And because they didn't understand what was coming, they risked lives—their own and others'—to try and save *things*. And why? Because they couldn't see that the home they loved was not the house they lived in but the people who lived in the house. That left their daughter and her husband with an impossible decision—abandon their elders or endanger their children. What happened to the child who lived?"

"He's a missionary."

Jason took a long sip of tea. "Interesting. And the parents?"

"The mother died from an infection soon after the storm. The father lives with the son and his family in Argentina. He gave the interview by phone. He said it comforted him to know that his wife was in heaven with their other children and her parents. He also said he thanked God every night that he had not been left alone in the world but had been able to raise his son. And he said his surviving son has told him many times that he wouldn't be able to serve if his father wasn't there to help watch over his wife and children."

"So . . . mercy?" Jason asked.

I thought about it and nodded. "I guess so. Yes. Mercy."

"Would you like to tell me about Leni?"

I felt the bottom drop out of my stomach. "H-how did you know about her?" I must've looked unnerved because Jason put his hands up as if to stop where my mind was going.

"I didn't read your mind. I don't think you realize that you said the name out loud at the fountain that first day you came here with your grandmother and her friends. I walked into the garden and found you sitting by the fountain. You said 'Leni,' and you looked upset. That's when I realized I was intruding and let you know I was there. It seemed obvious that whoever Leni was, he or she mattered to you. If you'd rather not talk about it, I completely respect your privacy."

I didn't remember saying Leni's name out loud, but I didn't remember *not* saying it either.

"Leni was my best friend," I said. "More than that. More like a sister, a soulmate. We grew up together in Birmingham."

Again with The Stare. "You said 'was.'"

"That's right. She died in the spring."

"I'm very sorry, Edie. Was it sudden?"

"Yes and no," I said. "Her illness came out of nowhere, but she was sick for a year before she died."

"And you saw no mercy."

"It just seemed like every break in the sickness—sometimes several weeks when Leni would feel strong and happy—would be followed by a fresh wave of misery. The treatment made her feel worse than the disease. It was all so . . . relentless."

"Were you with her the whole time?"

"We shared an apartment in New York. Both of us got jobs up there after college. Whenever she was in the hospital, I'd stay as much as I could, especially on weekends, so her mom could get some rest. Her dad died when she was little, and she didn't have any brothers or sisters, so it was just the two of them. I think that's why it was hard for Leni to be honest with her mom about what she was going through."

"How so?"

"Sometimes she just needed to laugh at her situation—break the tension, you know? She knew it would upset her mom, but she could do it with me."

Jason frowned as he lightly drummed his fingers against the table. He looked confused—a rarity. "I'm not sure I understand. She wanted to laugh at death?"

I took a second to think about it. "No, not exactly. More like laughing at the situations that present themselves when people believe you have a terminal illness. You know what I mean?"

"I don't believe I do."

I had the perfect example. "I remember one time when this church group visited Leni in the hospital, and nobody was with her except me. It wasn't even her church—just a group of well-intentioned but clueless strangers. They brought her a book called *The End of Life's Journey*."

"People who didn't even know Leni brought her such a book?"

"They did. I think they were handing them out to all the patients on her hallway. The expression on her face when she saw it . . . not sad or distraught but . . . resigned, I guess you'd say. Resigned to enduring this kind of thing at the hands of people who meant well but had no idea what it felt like to be her."

Jason leaned forward and rested his elbows on the table. "How did she respond?"

"When the church group left, she looked down at the book and said, 'Why didn't they just call it *You Are DYING*?' And I said, 'Subtitled *Read Fast!*' We both laughed so hard we couldn't breathe. I know we were whistling in the dark and other people would think we were weird or crass or whatever, but it made her feel better—like it was still us against the world and all its craziness."

"How long was she in the hospital?"

"She was in and out the year she was sick, probably five or six times—before the last time, I mean."

"Who was with her then—during the last time?"

"Just me." I took a long, deep breath and let it out. "Leni had been home for a week and was feeling great, so her mom flew back to Birmingham to check on the house, pay some bills . . . But then an infection came on really fast. By the time her mom could get a flight back to New York, Leni was unconscious. She died a few days later. They never got to say goodbye. That's where I struggle, I guess. I just don't see any mercy in that. I've tried and tried, but I can't find it."

"Did you look in the mirror?"

"What?"

"Don't you think it was merciful for Leni to have a friend who could fill a special need, one particular to her, like finding a way to laugh when the natural impulse of most people would be to cry?"

"Maybe."

"Isn't the unconditional love of a friend a gift of mercy for any human being? Leni's unconditional love for you—the ability to remember it and carry it with you always—wasn't that a gift of mercy? A mercy you didn't even know you would need until she was gone?" Jason leaned back in his chair. His voice was kind and soothing when he asked me, "Now who's staring, Edie?"

# twenty-one

**"MIND IF I ASK YOU SOMETHING?"**

Charly had just come into Punk's backyard, where I was using a chamois to dry Rosetta after giving her a bumper-to-bumper handwashing. Pop never could abide water spots. He said they were a slap in the face to the entire city of Detroit.

Charly held up a glass of iced tea. "I brought a bribe."

"Accepted." At five thirty in the afternoon, it was hot and muggy outside, and I welcomed anything on ice.

We sat down in a porch swing hanging from a live oak in Punk's backyard and sipped our tea. "You must really be hot," I said, "to trade your usual rocket fuel for tea."

She smiled and nodded. "I guess I've been in the mountains too long—lost my humidity tolerance. Now the heat just makes me feel tired." She ran her icy glass across her forehead. I did the same. There's no quicker way to cool off when you don't have time to jump in the nearest body of water or douse yourself with a garden hose.

"What's up?" I felt the blessed cool of a gulf breeze on my face.

"How well do you know Jason?"

"Not as well as he seems to know me."

"How so?"

I took a sip of tea and ran the glass across my forehead again, then waited for the breeze to hit it. "He has a knack for showing up when something major's going on in my head—like the time I sensed Leni at the fountain. But I don't know anything about him, not really. He doesn't have a Mississippi accent or any accent, now that I think about it, and I have no idea where he's from. He's obviously well educated, but I don't have a clue where he went to school."

"Have you ever asked him?"

"No. To tell you the truth, I don't think he welcomes personal questions."

Charly looked out at the water. "You're probably right about that."

"I did ask him what brought him here, and he seemed startled by the question, maybe even a little uncomfortable."

"Did he answer you?"

"He said he came because there was work to be done and customers he could help. He didn't volunteer any more than that."

Charly watched a butterfly briefly light on her knee and then fly away. "He's a puzzle alright."

"You know what else, though? I trust him. For whatever reason, I just feel like I can. It reminds me of the first time Mama and Daddy let Seth take me out for a brother-sister movie night without them. I didn't have to ask him if he'd look out for me. I knew he would. It's the same with Jason, which makes no sense, given that he's virtually a stranger and definitely not family. Why the questions?"

"I had a dream about him, and it rattled me."

"What happened?"

Charly turned to face me, resting her arm on the back of the swing. "I was standing by the lighthouse on a bright, sunny morning. There wasn't a single car on Beach Boulevard and not a soul in sight. As I looked out at the water, I noticed a long pier I'd never seen before, jutting straight out in front of the lighthouse. I decided to take a walk on it. Once I was so far out that I could barely see the beach, a dense fog appeared out of nowhere and covered everything. I could only see a few inches in front of me. But way off in the distance, I could make out this amazing light—silver white, gleaming through the fog. I was scared, clutching the railing because I was terrified a misstep would send me into the gulf, but I kept walking."

"I hate dreams like that—just close enough to possible to scare the daylights out of you," I said.

"The water started rising and getting rough, crashing over the railing of the pier. I was terrified, but something told me if I could just get to that light . . . No matter how far I walked, though, I never could reach it. Then it disappeared, and Jason was standing right in front of me. He stared at me for a few seconds, then looked over his shoulder and motioned to someone I couldn't see. Out of the fog came Connor. Jason turned to me and said, 'He's lost, but you can find him.' That's when I woke up."

I set down my tea glass and ran my hand over my arm. "Goose bumps."

"I know. It's weird, right?" Charly didn't cry, but she looked like she needed to. "I know it was just a crazy dream. But it was so vivid. Do you think it means anything?" As soon as the words were out, she covered her face with her hands. "How stupid can one woman be?" Her voice was muffled by her hands. I reached over and pulled them away. She looked exhausted and desolate, her face drawn, her eyes misty. "I wish this would just . . . end," she said.

I put my arms around her. "You're not stupid, chouchou. Anybody would be shaken up by a dream like that. And anybody would wonder if it meant something."

She went limp, her voice muffled as she rested her head on my shoulder. "Sorry for all my drama, chouchou. You know I love you more than Mudpie, don't you?"

I squeezed my arms a little tighter for a second. "And I love you more than gumbo, chouchou."

After a while, Charly sat up and silently stared at me until she said, "There's something else, Edie. The light in my dream . . . it was the light on Horn. I've seen it for myself."

———

"Punk! Where are you?" I had Charly by the hand, and we were running through the house looking for my grand-mother.

"Up here!" she called from the top of the stairs.

The two of us barreled up there, struggling to catch our breath.

"Charly has something to tell you," I said between gasps. "Let's go to my room."

The three of us sat down on my bed, and Charly began telling Punk about the light. "I saw it around midnight, Miss Punk, when I was on Horn."

Punk put her hand to her mouth. "Charlotte, are you sure?"

"Very sure. I've never seen anything like it in my life. And I'm not one bit ashamed to admit that it scared me half to death."

"What caused it?" Punk asked. "Where was it coming from?"

"That I don't know," Charly said. "I had anchored about midway down the island, and the light was on the eastern tip. But it was unbelievable. The clearest, cleanest, most silver-white light you've ever seen. It lasted only for a few seconds, and then it was gone. I was way too scared to go looking for it on the island by myself at night. That's why I came back instead of camping overnight."

"Did you hear anything?" Punk asked.

Charly shook her head. "No, ma'am. But here's the strange thing. As much as it scared me, I want to see it again. There was something so beautiful and—I don't know—pure about it. Something hopeful. I feel like I need to see it again, just one more time so I can believe it's real."

# twenty-two

**"I SEE YOU AT MY TABLE,** but I don't believe you're here."

I looked up to see Punk smiling at me. I had been staring into space and poking aimlessly at my cheese grits. The other Ten Spots hadn't come today, and Charly was still asleep, so I had my grandmother all to myself. "I'm sorry my mind's drifting, Punk. It oughta be a crime to let food this good get cold."

"I'm not the least bit offended," she said, "just curious. Let me warm up your coffee." She took my cup to the kitchen and topped it till it steamed, then rejoined me at the table. "Are daydreams of a dashing pilot distracting you?"

"Normally, I'd say yes because I'm having trouble thinking about anything else. But this time it's one of the Camille pictures I can't seem to shake."

"Tell me about it."

"It's one of the few shots that has any identification written on the back. All it says is 'Biloxi, August 18, 1969,' so it was taken the day after the storm."

"What's the subject matter?" Punk refastened a small

seagull pin that had come loose from her blouse and then gave me her full attention.

I had stared at that picture so much that I could re-create it in my mind, every last inch of it. "There's a cluster of airmen, most of them wearing their fatigue pants and a white T-shirt or no shirt at all in the heat. They're sweaty and surrounded by debris. In the foreground, two airmen are carrying a man on a stretcher. He's young, about their age, and he looks military—the physique, the haircut—but he's wearing civilian clothes, or what's left of them anyway. He doesn't have on a shirt, so you can see that he has no dog tags, and he's wearing light-colored pants, not fatigues, but the leg of one has been cut or torn off at the knee and there's a blood-soaked bandage covering his calf. He has another bandage wrapped around his forehead. No shoes. He's slightly slumped over to one side—looks limp and unconscious, like he might not make it to wherever they're taking him. I want to cry every time I look at it."

Punk laid her hand over mine. "Why that one, sweet girl? Why that one more than the others?"

I had to think for a minute before I could answer. "The guy on the stretcher looks so alone, completely dependent on a group of airmen, but he's not one of them. The people who love him probably have no idea where he is or what's happened to him. He just looks forsaken. I think it might be the loneliest picture I've ever seen."

Punk took a long sip of orange juice and watched a pelican light on the swing in her backyard. Then she reached over and brushed my cheek with her hand. "That's what it was like for me when Pop was overseas. I could look past his smile when he sent me pictures. I could see the loneliness, even when he was surrounded by fellow sailors, some of them dear friends of his. There was a distance in his eyes that broke my heart. And I'll tell you something else. It followed him home and stayed for a long, long time."

"Did Pop have PTSD?"

"They didn't call it that back then, but yes. In the forties we called it shell shock. Your Pop fought it hard for the first ten years after he came home and still had to beat it back from time to time long after that. I remember how I had to be careful waking him—take my time and make sure I didn't startle him. He was sensitive to loud noises for the rest of his life. I think that's why he went into electrical engineering instead of civil like Grady and Hudie. He saw it as a quieter enterprise. But I've taken us off course. We were talking about you and your civilian—why he troubled you so much."

"Even though I couldn't clearly see his face, something about him looked—I don't know—kind. Like he would never hurt a soul, but the storm had hurt him. Badly. It just seemed unfair, I guess."

"Now you're getting into why bad things happen to good people. I don't have the answer to that one, honey. Sometimes I think it's the wrong question. Maybe instead we should ask what we can do to help good people when bad things happen to them."

I smiled at my grandmother and nodded. "Maybe so. Can we talk about Pop some more?"

"Of course."

"What was it like when he first came home?"

Punk sighed and shook her head. "Hard. Very hard. Nightmares, night sweats. Always on edge. A car could backfire or a neighbor could drop the lid to their garbage can and he'd duck and cover. It embarrassed him to death. Made him feel ashamed."

"Why? He couldn't help it."

"Exactly. But he thought he *should* be able to. He thought he should be strong enough to overcome it. I never would've told you this while he was alive, but there were times I feared for his life, times I feared he might take his own life. I wore out my knees praying for him back then."

"He didn't hurt himself, so your prayers were answered, right?"

"In time. I had some lessons to learn first, like patience and compassion—the limitless kind, which I'd never been called on to offer before. It took a lot to stay, Edie. Those first ten years after the war were mighty rough."

"A lot of people would've quit after one hard year."

"I loved your Pop very much. Cap was a wonderful man—kind and loving and strong, so courageous. He just had the misfortune to come up against something he couldn't fight on his own."

"Did he try therapy?"

"Our generation wasn't big on that. There was such a stigma attached to it. But eventually, I just felt this powerful . . . internal push, I guess you'd say. Call it a divine skillet to the head. I grew convinced, maybe even convicted, that Cap needed to find other veterans he could talk to. So that's what I did. I found a group of war vets who met for coffee every Saturday morning at a little café not far from our house. Your Pop started going—reluctantly at first—and then he got to the point where he couldn't wait for Saturday mornings to roll around. That was a turning point. It really was. You have to remember, he was a young man back then—not much older than you are right now—but he had already fought a war, married, earned his degree, then Libba came along in '51 . . . It was a lot."

"It was a lot for you too."

"Yes, it was."

I knew she must be tired of questions. But I had one more. "Punk, I'm surprised that y'all moved here when you did. You'd gone through so much to try and get over the war, but then you moved to a place that looked like it had been bombed after Camille."

She smiled and nodded. "We did. And I had my doubts about it, believe me—at least until I saw Horn for the first time. But your Pop had reached a point where he said he was tired of running from his war. That's what he called the nightmares and all the rest of it—his war. When Hudie told him about plans for Camille recovery and the government contracts that were paying more money than any of us had ever seen, he decided the thing to do was face his war head-on—move right into the path of destruction. 'Once more unto the breach,' I guess."

"It must've worked. I mean, you've stayed all these years."

"You remember that famous line of FDR's—'The only thing we have to fear is fear itself'?"

"Drilled into me by every high school history teacher I ever had."

"Well, that's what Mississippi did for Pop. He would always carry remnants of the terrible fear instilled in him by the war, but after a few years here, he wasn't afraid of it anymore. He didn't fear the fear. He knew it couldn't hurt him, couldn't control him. All the time he spent rebuilding what Camille destroyed—that showed him he could still exert some control over the chaos instead of being helplessly buffeted by it. And those serene, flat waters were better for him than any tranquilizer. He could take his boat out and fish or just paddle the marshes and bayous. It quieted his mind. Mississippi set your Pop free, Edie. Me too in the process."

"Oddly enough, I think I get that, which doesn't make much sense."

"Sure it does. We all have our battles, sweet girl. You've been trying your best to bravely soldier on. But you've been hit with the kind of grief that's powerful enough to pin you down just as surely as wartime gunfire. And you're no more invincible than your Pop was. Nobody is."

# twenty-three

**ON SUNDAY,** Charly and I went to church with the Ten
Spots. After lunch, the ladies had to make their monthly
goodie-basket deliveries to the community shut-ins—Coco
called them the Icy Hots—and Charly's friend in Bay St.
Louis had invited her to visit. Cole was on maneuvers with
the reserves. That gave me a rare afternoon left to my own
devices. And even though it was overcast outside, my own
devices inevitably took me straight to Pop's boat for a trip
to Horn.

Like every other vehicle my grandfather owned, his boat
was a classic, a 1960 Chris-Craft Sea Skiff that he bought
after he and Punk moved here. He liked to say he "bought
it from a little old lady who only drove it to church on Sun-
days." Punk named it *The Other Woman*, which she painted
on the stern, because she said she knew from the day Pop
bought it that the boat would give her serious competition
for his attention. I used to help him raise it out of the water
with the boat lift and wash it when I was little. Once I got
old enough, he'd let me take it out by myself on days when

Grady had "called a meeting with the grouper," which meant the two of them were going fishing on Grady's boat.

Despite all the clouds in the sky, I expected to see at least a scattering of boats around the island but found none. I dropped anchor toward the eastern end and waded ashore with my camera. Taking a deep breath of salty air, I stood on the sand and let the island wrap itself around me. The wind was warm and brisk, setting the palms and pines to swaying and sighing. Looping my camera strap around my neck, I began my ramble down the beach. I would need to keep a close eye on the weather, but so far so good.

When I spotted a great white heron wading in the surf, I moved in as close as I could and knelt in the sand, raising my camera. On the hunt for fish, the graceful bird danced a stealthy, slow-motion ballet in the shallow water, sometimes pausing with one foot in midair before planting it in the sand and diving down with its beak to make the catch.

I always had an ulterior motive when I shot on Horn. As much as I enjoyed taking the pictures themselves, I was hoping to inspire Punk to interpret some of them on canvas. I knew that one day I'd have a home of my own, and I wanted to fill it with Punk's seascapes. After Leni, I no longer assumed I'd outlive Punk or anybody else. But if I did, I wanted to be surrounded by her paintings, by her vision of this place we both loved so much.

Completely focused on the heron, I lost my balance and had to flail about to catch myself. The quick movement startled the bird. Just as it began flapping its wings to take flight, I saw a flash of light coming from the east, so fast that I thought I might've imagined it. On a sunny day, I might not have noticed it at all, but the sky overhead was gray. I rubbed my eyes and looked in the direction the light came from but saw nothing.

Walking down the beach, I rounded a slight curve on the shoreline and finally had a clear view of the eastern tip of the island, where the light had flashed. I saw a person sitting on the sand near the water. A person with no boat, sitting on an island with no bridge. Aiming my camera, I used the zoom lens to see if I could make anything out. What I saw through the lens was none other than Jason Toussaint, wearing joggers, sneakers, and a T-shirt, a far cry from his usual white shirts and dress pants.

"Afternoon!" I called out when I was a few yards away.

"Edie! Hello!" He waved to me as I walked over to him. "What brings you to Horn?"

"A boat. You?" I stood next to him and surveyed the empty shore.

"Fair question." He looked up at me, shading his eyes with his hand. Even with an overcast sky, the gray light was still bright. "Would you like to join me?"

I sat down next to him on the sand.

"I was dropped off," he explained.

"Oh." I waited for details, but of course got none. "Are they coming back?"

"Yes." He looked up at the clouds, now in constant motion, then out at the water, which was getting choppy. "Unfortunately, I doubt they'll arrive before I get wet."

"Want a ride?"

"I do indeed, thank you."

"We can radio whoever dropped you off."

"No need. If they don't see me on the beach where they left me, they'll move on."

"I have to say, Jason, you're remarkably calm for somebody stranded on an island with rain clouds threatening."

"I had a feeling help was on the way. And here you are."

He closed his eyes and tilted his head back. I had seen him do that before, and it made me wonder if Jason's ice-blue eyes let in so much sensory detail that he had to shut them now and again for his own protection. I imagined him taking a moment to absorb what was already there before still more came pouring in.

"How long have you been here?" I asked.

He shrugged. "A while."

"Need to get back right away?"

"No, not unless the weather drives us home."

I looked out at the water, wondering if I could see the exact spot where rivery waters of the Mississippi Sound converged with a blue gulf. "What made you choose this spot, Jason—this one in particular?"

He kept his gaze on the water. "I guess it reminds me a little bit of home."

"Oh." I knew I shouldn't ask, though I desperately wanted to.

He looked at me and smiled. "Edie, you're going to explode if you don't ask me where home is."

I laughed and nodded. "You're right. I probably will."

"Home is a long way from here. But it's beautiful—infinitely so. And it's utterly peaceful."

"Like Horn?"

"Yes, but much more so, if you can believe that."

"I think I'd like to see it one day."

"I expect you will."

I let it go at that. I never cared for people who kept pushing for more once you made it clear that you had revealed all you intended to. "Did you by any chance see a bright flash of light over here? Just a few minutes before I walked up?"

"No, why?"

"The local paper reported several sightings of one, always right here, always around midnight. I could've sworn I just saw it, but that doesn't really make sense. It never appears in the daytime, and you would've seen it too. Guess my eyes are playing tricks."

"It happens," he said. "Where do they think it's coming from?"

"Well, that's just it. Nobody knows. Most of the sightings have come from shrimpers in the gulf. They see it when they're out on their boats at night. They say this tip of the island glows brightly for a few seconds and then goes dark again. Charly saw it when she was over here to camp one night, but the light scared her so bad that she left and came home."

"What's frightening about it?"

"Apparently, it looks different from anything else—any other kind of light, I mean. Just extremely clear and bright. Sort of silver white."

"That sounds more inspiring than frightening."

"I guess it's just so different from anything anybody's ever seen. And they can't find the source."

"That's something I've always found puzzling," he said, frowning as he turned to face me. "Why do people have such an aversion to mystery? Why can't they just accept that an inexplicable wonder has occurred and appreciate it for what it is, as it is?"

"You mean like this?" I traced a Hebrew letter in the sand, one from the message I had found there on Horn. "I've stared at my pictures of that message so much that I can duplicate it. But there's a difference between copying something and understanding it."

"True."

"You've helped me with that, Jason—helped me see that just because I don't understand something, that doesn't make it any less real. Not necessarily anyway. And just because the reason for something isn't obvious, that doesn't mean there isn't one."

"Not necessarily anyway?"

"Not necessarily. Hey, look." I pointed to the longest, whitest feather I'd ever seen, floating in the water. I got up and retrieved it when the surf pushed it in. "I've never seen one like this before." I ran my finger along the edge of the snowy barbs. "Look how big it is. And so white. Where do you think it came from?"

Jason studied the feather as I sat down next to him. "Could be a great egret, I suppose. Or maybe a heron or white ibis. But from the size of it, I'd suspect a white pelican."

"I didn't know there was such a thing."

"Yes. They like to winter on the Gulf and the Pacific. Not a common sight in Mississippi this time of year, but they do exist. And their feathers are brilliant white."

I held the feather out so that it was outlined against the blue water. "What do you suppose the brown pelicans think of the white ones? Shun them? Fear them? Revere them?"

Jason looked at me and smiled. "I think the synapses in your brain fire in unusual directions."

I had to laugh. "In other words, you think I'm just the tiniest bit odd."

"I never said that."

The wind, stronger now, blew my hair away from my face. I closed my eyes and breathed in the island's salty scent.

"May I ask you a question, Edie? A personal one?"

I turned to look at him. "I've asked you a few, so fair's fair, I guess."

"Your family friend—Ms. Moran—is she alright, do you think?"

"Charly? As far as I know. Why?" I had the strangest feeling he was about to tell me something I already knew deep down. I just hadn't allowed it to bubble up to the surface.

Jason was looking at the water, which was growing choppier as the wind picked up. "It's difficult to explain, but sometimes I get a sense about people, or maybe I should say a sense *of* them." He turned back to me. "I've had a sense of her."

I began replaying conversations with Charly, remembering things she said and holding them up to the light of Jason's concern. *"It's a mighty empty feeling when you give up . . . Sometimes that makes it hard to get up in the morning."* Then I did that embarrassing thing I occasionally do—blurt something out without considering that the other person has no idea what was swirling in my head before I said it.

"Jason, do you know where Connor is? Can you find him?"

He looked completely confused, frowning and staring at me, no doubt trying to figure out what on earth I was talking about. "I don't know anyone by that name. Or where he might be. Why did you think I would?"

I shook my head. "Sorry. That must've sounded crazy. It's just that Connor immediately came to mind when you asked about Charly. He was the love of her life, and she lost him during Camille. The two of them had just met, in what I guess you'd call a love-at-first-sight experience, when they got washed out into the storm and separated. They didn't even know each other's last names and never found each other again."

"Never?"

"Never. And that loss, well, it left a hole in Charly's heart. She had a moment by your fountain when she sensed Connor, sort of the way I sensed Leni, but not quite the same. It stirred up a lot of old feelings she's tried to forget. And then she had a dream that upset her. You were in it."

"That's strange."

"I know. You and Connor were together. Charly dreamed that she was walking on a pier over the gulf. It suddenly got covered with fog, and the water grew rough. First the Horn Island light appeared, and then you. You brought Connor out of the fog and told Charly that he was lost but she could find him. Then she woke up. And if she ever finds out I told you, she'll never forgive me."

"She won't hear it from me," he said.

"What does it mean, Jason? Even if it's all just her imagination, why would she connect you with Connor and the Horn Island light? Do you see anything in the dream, something that might help you help Charly?"

He stared at the Hebrew letter I had drawn in the sand, retracing it with his finger before looking up at me. "If I can help her, I will. You have my promise. Right now, I don't understand it any more than you do. Things come to us when it's time, not necessarily when we want them to. No matter how desperately."

I looked out at the water, an infinite expanse between earth and sky, and hoped for the peace it always brought, but my mind felt as clouded as the gray sky overhead, my emotions stirred up like the choppy gulf waters surrounding us. I wanted to cry. Punk or Cole would've put their arms around me and held me tight. But I knew Jason wasn't made that way. Still, he could tell I was sinking.

"Some of us, Edie, were created to help," he said. "Others were called to it. That's a gift. But it's also a weight, isn't it?"

With my eyes stinging and my stomach in knots, all I could do was nod in agreement.

Jason looked up at the sky, and a raindrop landed on his cheek. "That's what I would call a hint—and not a subtle one." He stood and helped me up. "Let's get you home."

By the time we got back to Pop's boat, it was rocking in the choppy water now beginning to whitecap. A light but steady rain fell on us as we quickly waded out to it and climbed aboard. Jason pulled up the anchor while I cranked the engine, grateful for a covered helm to keep us mostly dry.

A dark wall cloud was dropping down on the horizon, with lightning flashing inside it. If I were safe in my room at Punk's, I would have loved every flash and rumble, but out here, with the wind and water getting angrier by the minute, I knew anything could happen, and I struggled to steady both my nerves and Pop's boat.

"Would you like to trade places, Edie?" Jason shouted over the noise of the storm and the engine.

"Yes!" I shouted back.

I knew I was in over my head and happily agreed to Jason's help. He took the helm and was able to work with the wind and the currents, keeping the boat steady as we rode the crests and troughs of wave after wave. It wasn't that late—maybe three o'clock—but the sky had darkened to twilight.

My one thought was that I hoped Punk was still visiting the Icy Hots and didn't realize I was on the water, or she'd be worried to death. Eventually, I had my answer as the mainland finally—mercifully—came into sight. I navigated as Jason steered us to Punk's dock, which was lit up like a Christmas tree. Sure enough, Punk was standing there, draped in a rain poncho and frantically waving at us.

Once the boat was in its slip, Punk tossed me the ropes

to secure it. That was when she spotted my relief captain. "Jason!" she exclaimed. "What on earth are you doing in that boat? You two come on inside!"

We hurried into the house just before the bottom fell out, with the hardest rain I've seen in years pelting Punk's roof.

"Y'all go to the living room while I get you some towels," she said.

Now that we were safe, I realized I was soaked and shivering. Our cold, wet clothes didn't seem to bother Jason at all.

"Here we go," Punk said. She handed each of us a big, thick towel to dry off with. "You two have a seat and I'll pour us some warm cider."

"Please don't go to any trouble," Jason said.

"No trouble at all."

I knew there was no stopping Punk when it came to hospitality. In a minute, she was back with a tray holding three steaming mugs.

"Now then," she said as she sat down. "Tell me what happened."

I caught her up on how I found Jason stranded on Horn and then how he got us both safely home.

"Well, that's just this side of a miracle," Punk said. "It's a thousand wonders you two crossed paths at just the right time."

"I'm really sorry I worried you, Punk," I said.

"That's alright, sweet girl. I'm very good at it. You're just helping me stay in practice."

"Is Charly back?"

"Not yet, honey."

"Look what washed up while we were on Horn, Punk." I showed her the white feather I had tucked into my windbreaker before we waded off the island and back onto the boat.

"Why, it's beautiful!" She took it and studied the shape and color.

I had a sip of cider. "Jason thinks it might be from a white pelican."

"I haven't seen one of those in years," Punk said, "but I'll never forget the one Pop and I spotted on Horn a long time ago. Wasn't anywhere near that big, though."

"Think you could be persuaded to paint it for me?" I took another sip of my cider and hoped for a yes.

"We'll see," Punk said.

"The needlepoint above your fireplace is very well done, Mrs. Cheramie," Jason said. "Is that your work?" He was looking at the first half of a verse from Hebrews: "Be not forgetful to entertain strangers."

"Thank you, Jason, and yes, that's my work from a hundred years ago," Punk said. "Or at least it seems that way."

"The other half of the verse is in the dining room," I said.

"'For thereby some have entertained angels unawares,'" Jason quoted.

"Excellent, Jason." Punk smiled. "It's good to meet a man who paid attention in Sunday school."

"I like the way Punk divided the verse," I said. "Makes you think about both parts a little differently."

"Do you still needlepoint?" Jason asked her.

"Rarely," Punk said. "I took it up when Libba—that's Edie's mother—first went away to college and I was feeling a little adrift in my empty nest. Now I'd rather spend my time painting seascapes—not like a real painter, of course. Just dabbling."

"She's completely wrong," I told him. "Her paintings are beautiful and soulful."

"I'd love to see some of your work sometime if you feel comfortable showing me," he said.

Punk shook her head and took a sip of cider. "I imagine you've seen many fine works of art in your line of work, Jason. I think I'd be embarrassed to show you an old woman's indulgence."

"I'm inclined to trust Edie's judgment on the quality of your work," he said. "But I'll not push. Just know my door is open."

"I appreciate that," Punk said.

As coastal storms can do, this one blew over as abruptly as it blew in. The rain was beginning to let up.

"Edie, if I could trouble you with one more ride, I suppose I should be going," Jason said.

"No trouble," I said.

"Won't you stay for supper, Jason?" Punk asked him.

"Thank you, but I'm afraid I need to get back."

"Do you live far from here?" Punk took our cider cups as we stood up to go.

"Actually, my car is at the gallery," Jason said. "I was catching up on a few things after lunch when I had an opportunity to go to Horn—which of course I took."

"Well, if you're enamored with Horn, you're among kindred spirits," Punk said. "I hope you'll come again, Jason. You're always welcome here."

He smiled at her. "I imagine everyone feels welcome in your home, Mrs. Cheramie, even relative strangers like me. And I thank you."

# twenty-four

NORA GILLIAM AND I SAT ACROSS from each other on her front porch in Gulfport, a few blocks north of the railroad tracks. "The hardest part," she was saying, "is when you realize that something you love means to kill you."

"Are you talking about the gulf, Mrs. Gilliam?"

As she slowly nodded, I noticed the furrowed brow, the misty eyes. Even her skin seemed to turn a shade paler as she talked about Camille. "I know it sounds silly. The water ain't got no feelin's or intentions. But I'm here to tell you, it sure seemed like them swells was comin' after me on purpose. Ain't that silly?"

I shook my head. "Not at all. I imagine anybody would feel that way."

Nora was forty when Camille hit. That would put her in her seventies now. I had found her picture in Jason's collection and matched it to one of the transcripts from Southern Miss.

She brushed away a tear before it could roll down her cheek. "Young girl like you prob'ly can't imagine crying over something that happened over thirty years ago. But if you'd

190

seen it and heard it, got beat up by it, nearly drowned in it, if you'd waked up on Deer Island with your clothes ripped off and mosquitoes 'bout to eat you alive, well . . ."

Tall and thin, Nora had a weathered face etched with lines of worry. Her polyester slacks and frayed cotton blouse looked like something from the thrift store, but I'd be willing to bet they were the best things she owned. Women like Nora always presented their best to company, no matter how humble their circumstances.

"I don't want you to feel any pressure, Mrs. Gilliam," I said. "We don't have to talk about Camille if you don't want to. You don't have to relive anything you'd rather forget."

She swatted at a fly buzzing around her rocking chair. "Maybe I ought to talk about it. Kept a lot to myself all these years. Might be a relief to tell somebody."

"I'd be honored to listen. But we can stop anytime you want." I pulled a recorder and notebook out of my tote bag. "Do you mind if I record us? Just so I don't miss anything?"

She shrugged. "Go on and do what you need to. And you can call me Nora."

I started the recorder and set it on the small table between our rocking chairs, then got ready to take notes for backup. "Alright, Nora, I believe you told the interviewer from Southern Miss that it was your husband's idea to stay?"

"That's right."

For a minute, I thought that was all she planned to give me. But then she said, "I'll bet you a lotta women died that night on accounta bein' married to men that thought they knew best. Anybody that stayed when they coulda got out—they didn't know best."

"Do you know—I mean, did your husband say why he wanted to stay?"

Nora nervously brushed at her slacks, though I didn't see anything there. "He'd just got him a real good job at the docks, loadin' and unloadin' trucks for Dole. He figured they'd be real shorthanded after a big storm, and he could pick up a lotta overtime. We had some bills." Nora paused and shook her head. "I tried to tell Cecil—that was my husband—but he wouldn't listen."

"Tried to tell him what?"

"What a hurricane can do. You have to understand, Cecil wasn't from here. He grew up in Tennessee. But I'm from Louisiana, raised in Cameron Parish, right where Audrey came through. I was a young woman back then, just widowed from my first husband. You don't forget a big storm like Audrey if you're lucky enough to survive it. I never wanted to live through another one of them things. So I begged and I pleaded and I hollered and I screamed, but nothin' would convince Cecil that a little overtime wasn't worth riskin' his life, not to mention mine. He absolutely would not leave. Told me them civil defense people was just bein' silly, gettin' ever'body all worked up."

I was writing so fast my hand started to cramp. "Did you ever consider leaving without him, Nora?"

"As his wife," she said, "I guess I thought I had a duty to stay with him. I'll tell you one thing, though. I'd never do it again. Any man got no better sense than to face down a hurricane can do it by hisself, far as I'm concerned. I know Cecil died for his mistake, and I hope he's restin' in peace, but I might as well tell you, I've had a real hard time forgivin' him for ever'thing he put me through, all because he thought he knew best."

192

"Can you tell me about that—what you went through during the storm? As much as you're comfortable with?"

"I'll try," she said.

In her interview with the university, Nora had given many personal details about her life—how she met her first husband, who was much older than she was and very kind, how he died from a heart attack the year before Hurricane Audrey, how she met Cecil Gilliam at a church social while visiting cousins in Gulfport and married him a few months later. But when it came to Camille, Nora revealed very little, and to the interviewer's credit, he didn't push her. Nora told him she saw Cecil die in the water. Then somehow she landed on Deer Island, was picked up by the Coast Guard, and had to stay in a shelter for weeks afterward. That was it. She gave no more details than that, even with gentle prompting from the interviewer.

I checked the tape recorder to make sure it was still working and then said, "Whenever you feel ready."

Nora looked toward the gulf, though we couldn't see it from her porch. "I knew we was gonna end up in it—all that angry water. Cecil kept saying no, that would never happen, but I knew it would. We lived three blocks off the beach in Biloxi. Had a one-story wooden house. Wasn't on pilings. I knew good and well the kinda wind and water they was predictin' from Camille would either blow us to kingdom come or wash us there. Still, I did what I could. Put a hatchet in the attic so we could cut a hole in the roof in case the floods stayed low enough for us to climb up on the roof and stay out of it. Filled up the bathtub with water. Put bat'ries in all the flashlights. Drug Cecil's bass boat around by the front porch and tied it to a post there. Used a long rope so it could rise with the water. Fried some fish for supper. I remember taking my time with it to make sure it was just right because I had a feelin' it'd be the last hot meal we had for a while. Maybe the last one, period."

"You knew Camille was going to be that bad?"

"I sure did. Lotta people down here said no, maybe it wouldn't even hit us, but I knew better. I could feel it. And I remembered the people in Louisiana that lived in two-story houses and thought they'd be fine because they'd just go upstairs if the water went to risin'. Never occurred to 'em that the wind and the water could knock the bottom floor right out from under 'em and then there they'd be. But that's exactly what Audrey did. And I knew that's what Camille had on her mind too."

A boy on a bicycle rode by and tossed a newspaper onto the sidewalk. "Mornin', Miss Nora!" he called.

"Mornin', Richie, honey!" she called back. She watched him toss his papers down the block and then hang a right, disappearing around the corner. She turned back to me. "Is it alright with you if I skip the part about Cecil dyin' and just tell you about myself?"

"Of course," I said.

"Good. I don't think I can tell that part. Sometimes I still have a hard time keepin' it outta my mind, and I'm afraid talkin' about it'll bring it way up to the top again."

"You don't have to talk about anything you don't want to," I reassured her.

"Could I have another look at that picture o' me you brung with you?"

"Sure." I handed her an eight-by-ten, black-and-white photograph of a woman sitting in a metal folding chair, leaning back to rest her head against the wall behind her. She wore what looked like a man's shirt over a one-piece bathing suit and held a Styrofoam cup in her hand. Her legs and feet were bare and covered with scratches. She looked exhausted in every way that you could be.

"I remember her," Nora said. "I don't feel like her anymore, but I remember her."

"Do you remember when this was taken, Nora? Do you remember where you were and what you were doing?"

"Like it was yesterday," she said. "That was prob'ly a coupla hours after I got picked up and brought to what they called a triage station. If you wasn't hurt bad, they'd clean you up and bandage your wounds and make sure you had something to eat and drink. Then you'd wait for a ride to one o' the shelters. That was one time civil defense didn't have to worry about people bringing too much stuff with 'em to the shelters. Most of us didn't have nothin' left to bring."

We both rocked quietly on the porch before she went on. "You've read that interview I did with the college, so you know I saw Cecil die. Guess I might as well go on and get it out. A big swell washed him into a downed power line that was still live, and it electrocuted him. There. That's out. I'll spare you what it looked like. Wish I could spare myself."

Nora closed her eyes tight for a few seconds before going on. "The truth is, I'm not real sure what all happened next. I remember a big pile of debris passing by me. When the lightning flashed, it looked like a ship on the water. Something about it reminded me of Noah's ark from the Bible. And I remember thinking to myself that if a ark could save people from a flood durin' Bible times, maybe it could save me from one now. So without thinkin' too much, I just grabbed ahold and climbed till I got close to the top and tucked myself into a little cubbyhole of sorts. That's the last thing I remember before I waked up on Deer Island the next day."

"And how did you know where you were?"

"I could tell by how close I was to the mainland. That was the only way. Just about everything on the beachfront was gone except for the lighthouse."

"What condition were you in when you first came to, Nora?" I was turning pages in my notebook every few seconds. I tend to write bigger and bigger when I'm really caught up in a story. I stopped the recorder, quickly flipped the tape, and made sure it was recording again.

"Well, it wasn't good, I can tell you that," she said. "The night Camille hit, I had slipped and put on my bathin' suit underneath my housedress right before supper. I didn't tell Cecil because I knew it'd just get him stirred up again. But it's a good thing I did that because whatever happened to me between climbing onto my ark and waking up on Deer Island tore my dress clean off. Whatever I was ridin' on musta fell apart in the gulf because the beach around me was bare as could be, except for the few of us that landed there."

"How many would you say?"

"Three that I saw, besides myself. I don't know if there was others on the southern shore. We was on the north, facin' Biloxi."

"Do you know who the others were?"

She shook her head. "It was strange after the storm. You'da thought four people stranded on a island together would get to know one another, make a plan—all that kinda thing. But lookin' back, I think we was all in shock. At first I thought we was all women. These two that kinda acted like sisters—prob'ly in their sixties—they come stumblin' outta the pine trees, clingin' to each other for dear life, and set down about thirty or forty yards up the beach from me. And then I realized there was a man among us."

Nora picked up two cardboard fans from the small table by her rocker and handed me one. "Sometimes," she said as she began to fan herself, "you can't help but wonder how come some of us live and some of us die. Here was four of us that lived when so many others died."

I fanned for a few seconds to let Nora know I appreciated her thoughtfulness, but I needed both hands to keep up with the recorder and my notebook, so I laid it on the floor beside my rocker. "Can you tell me about the man on the island, Nora? Did you find out who he was?"

She stopped fanning and shook her head. "Got no idea. I saw him come walkin' up the beach—staggerin's more like it. Blood had done soaked one leg of his britches. More blood dripped down on his foot. He had other wounds too, but it was that leg that had my attention. It was bad."

Right away, the troubling photograph I had told Punk about popped into my head. No doubt, Camille delivered many leg injuries as people fought their way through floating debris during the hurricane. Still, I couldn't help wondering if the man on Deer Island with Nora might have been my lonely civilian on the stretcher.

"Was he old or young, Miss Nora?"

"Young. Prob'ly in his twenties."

"What did he do? Did he see you?"

"He came right up to me and sorta fell down on the sand. Looked real confused. Asked me was I here to go swimmin'. That's the first time I give much thought to how I must look, sittin' there in my bathin' suit right after a hurricane. I told him what happened—stammered it out, really, since I could barely put a thought together, but I managed to make him understand how come I was in that suit. Right away, he took off his shirt and put it around me. I really appreciated it, too, because by then the mosquitoes was fierce."

"Did he tell you what happened to him?"

She shook her head. "He wasn't in no shape to talk. That's how come I 'preciated him givin' me his shirt so much. That fella couldn't think straight enough to carry on a conversation, but still he did me a kindness. That told me he must be kind down to the bone. Didn't even need to think about it."

"What did you do to get off the island?" I asked.

"First thing I did was try to get them other women to help me help *him*. But they was too busy cryin' and hand-wringin' and carryin' on. I want to tell you something, Edie, and you remember it. If you mean to survive a tough situation, your brain better keep a-workin'. Your body can be beat up and banged up, but as long as you can think, you got a chance. Them women wasn't thinkin'. So I left 'em to their hand-wringin'. I had things to do."

"To help the man, you mean?"

Nora nodded. "First I found a rip in his britches leg and used it to tear the bottom half off so I could see what I was dealin' with. Worst gash I ever saw on anybody. I helped him down to the water and got him to sit there and let the gulf wash that leg. My daddy taught me that saltwater can cauterize a wound like that sometimes. Keep you from bleedin' to death till you can get yourself to help. He taught me how to start a fire without no matches too, so I did that. By then, it was either start a fire or get carried off by the mosquitoes. That fire felt good. We was still freezin' from bein' in the water all night, and it was cool the mornin' after. But I knew it'd get hot before long, and we wouldn't be able to stand bein' so close to the flames. We let it keep the mosquitoes off as long as we could."

"How long were you there?"

"We was mighty lucky—no, blessed. We was mighty blessed. Judgin' by the sun, I guessed it was prob'ly around ten or eleven in the morning when a Coast Guard rescue boat spotted our fire and picked us up. Got them other women too. That nice fella was way worse off than me, so the medics went to workin' with him right off. Once we got back to Biloxi and they did some field dressin's on him, a coupla airmen carried him off on a stretcher—headed for a helicopter that was flyin' people to hospitals all over the place. Somebody drove me to a triage center, and that was that."

"You never saw him again?"

Nora shook her head. "You know, I always hated that I didn't give him his shirt back. I didn't even realize I still had it on till he was gone. Held on to it for the longest time, thinkin' maybe I'd get a chance to return it and thank him. But by and by, I put it in the church yard sale. I still remember it—blue and white plaid, the small kind o' pattern, not the big kind."

"You say you wish you could thank him, Nora, but it sounds to me like he has a lot to thank you for. You probably saved his life."

Nora stopped fanning and looked at me. "You really think so?"

"Of course." I picked up my fan and flapped it by my face to make a little breeze. Nora did the same.

"I reckon that's somethin' at least," she said.

I checked my watch. "Oh, Nora, I've taken up way too much of your time. I'm sorry. I didn't realize how long I'd been here."

She smiled and flapped her fan. "That's alright, Edie. I ain't got no jet plane to catch."

I laughed. "Me neither. Could I ask you one more question before I get out of your way?"

"Of course."

"This one's kind of personal. More for me than the Camille catalog. You see, I lost a dear friend this year. She passed in March."

Nora put her hand to her mouth and shook her head. "I'm so sorry, Edie."

"Thank you. It's just that I'm really struggling to understand why she's—that is, why—"

"Why she's gone and you're still here?" Nora asked.

"Yes," I said. "Why do I get to live and she doesn't?"

"I 'spect anybody that's ever outlived somebody they love has asked that very question, Edie. But you know that old hymn that says we'll understand it better by and by?"

"Yes, ma'am."

"I've come to believe that. In my lifetime, God has revealed the answers to many of my whys. Others, he's still keeping to hisself. Like that man on Deer Island. I can see now that we both landed there together so I could help him with his leg. But whether he lived or died, I don't know—nor the why in either direction. But God does. And he's revealed enough of his reasons for me to believe he's always got one."

I reached across the table and squeezed Nora's hand. "Thank you for that."

She smiled and fanned her face. "You call or stop by anytime, Edie. Today I welcomed a stranger. Next time, you'll be a friend."

# twenty-five

**I HAD JUST ARRIVED** at Sugar's Greek Revival on East Scenic Drive. The historic Italianate mansion was a wedding present from the third husband she had outlived—her beloved Wade Vansant.

"Miss Sugar, do you want me to take off my shoes?"

"I most *suhtainly* do not," she said as she hugged me at the door. Linking arms, we made our way to her sunroom, which overlooked the gulf from the highest ground in Pass Christian.

"I'll *nevah* understand people who put the condition of their *flo-uhs* above the comfort of their guests," Sugar was saying. "You'll *nevah* catch me with a bunch of barefoot souls wandering all over my home like they just lost their last dime at the casinah. Capisce?"

"Capisce, Miss Sugar," I said with renewed admiration for Miss Louisiana 1941. Unlike the rest of us, who confined ourselves to the accent we'd acquired in childhood or the non-accent we'd cultivated in college, Sugar felt no such compunction. At any given moment, she might channel Selma or Sicily. The choice was entirely hers, as far as she was concerned.

"Hey, y'all! Look who's here!" she exclaimed as she led me into her sunroom.

The two of us joined Charly and the other Ten Spots at a glass-topped wicker dining table. "How's everybody doing?" I asked as I took a seat next to Charly and Sugar excused herself to the kitchen.

"We're fine," Cookie said. "How's the job?"

"A lot more than I bargained for but in a good way."

Sugar returned to the sunroom, followed by Ora and Mattine, who had worked for her since she moved into this house. They carried in large serving trays and set them on stands near the table. We all knew we were in for some serious food. Sugar loves to cook. Over the years, she has scored recipes from some of the best restaurants on the Mississippi coast, as well as a few French Quarter stalwarts like Brennan's and Commander's. She pays Ora and Mattine to stay late and help with the serving and cleanup, but Sugar does the cooking herself. She offered thanks before inviting us all to commit gluttony.

First came meticulously sliced French bread, sparkling water infused with sliced lemons, limes, and oranges, and a salad of watermelon, heirloom tomatoes, red onion, and goat cheese.

"Sugar, this is delicious," Punk said after tasting her salad. "Is this a Commander's recipe?"

Sugar took a sip of sparkling water from a crystal goblet and shook her head. "No, this one came from my good friend Mary-Allen Sonnier. I *nevah* would've thought to put tomatoes and watermelon *togethah*, but I think it works."

"I'll say," Charly agreed. "Am I tasting mint?"

"Yes, dear," Sugar said. "Fresh mint and basil, plus honey and lime . . . and a little ginger, I think. I'll have to check the recipe. I've only made it this one time."

Punk winked at me across the table as the breadbasket went around, and she took out a piece of French bread cut into a precise square, the crust trimmed away. Beside each bread plate, Mattine had placed a little silver well of olive oil and cracked pepper for dipping.

I looked around the sunroom, with its sixteen-foot ceiling, soaring windows, and marble floor laid in a mosaic of forest green and white. Outside, the sunset cast rosy light through the windows. "I've always thought this room was just incredible, Miss Sugar," I said.

"Thank you, honey. As much as I loved the house when Wade surprised me with it, I thought it looked a little lopsided, the way his study protruded from the eastern side with nothing to balance it on the west. So I suggested we add a sunroom. We used to eat our breakfast out here every morning. I kept trying to sway the menu, but my Wade always wanted the same thing: Eggs Hussarde—that's a Brennan's recipe—with brown-sugared bacon and cheese grits—Gouda, not cheddar. That was his favorite."

"Where on earth did you find this marble?" Charly asked.

"Wade knew an Italian fella who lived in the Delta," Sugar explained. "His name was Giuseppe Giardina. Isn't that the most musical name you ever heard? Back in the old country, his people had been in the marble business for centuries. Giuseppe got the marble for us, and several of his Italian cousins laid the floor. Wade flew them over and we put them up in our guest house."

"So that's where you picked up 'capisce'?" I asked.

"Sí, mio caro," she said with a wink at me.

Ora and Mattine took our salad plates as we finished and soon returned from the kitchen with bowls of Commander's turtle soup with sherry. Then came trout amandine served with a sweet potato soufflé, fresh green beans cooked in bacon drippings, and Sugar's homemade dinner rolls brushed with melted butter.

"Have mercy, Sugar, you outdid yourself," Punk said.

Sugar laughed as she blotted her mouth with a starched white napkin. "Well, you know how much I love to play in the kitchen."

I was still curious about the Italian tile—and the Italians. "Miss Sugar, you said the men who laid your tile came over from Italy. Did they even speak English?"

"Not the first word. But do you know, one of them was curious about a lunch I prepared for everybody early on, so the two of us got in the kitchen and made up our own little sign language. Somehow we figured out how to share the recipe! Food is the universal language. I've always said so. Anyway, Luciano—that was his name, he was Giuseppe's uncle—Luciano taught me Italian and a bunch of his mama's recipes, and I taught him English and just about every famous dish in New Orleans!" Sugar laughed as she dipped a piece of bread into some olive oil and tapped it on the side of the silver well next to her bread plate.

"You did this while he was laying your floor?" I asked.

"Oh, no, dear," Sugar said. "I told Wade the cultural exchange was worth a fortune in and of itself and asked him to fly over another cousin to work on the floor so Luciano and I could continue our lessons." She grinned at me. "I presented this idea to Wade over a dinner of tagliatelle al ragù, served with a nice bottle of Sangiovese. Sometimes men need to be led." She popped the oil-soaked bread into her mouth and took a sip of wine. "Luciano ended up staying two years in our guest house and met his second wife in Bay St. Louis. He was a widower, bless his heart. They went back to Italy to open a restaurant, but we still write to each other."

The sky slowly dimmed as we finished our supper. Ora and Mattine swapped our empty dinner plates for crème brûlée and coffee.

Sugar loved candles and had scattered tealights down the center of a natural table runner made of moss and ivy. Pillar candles flickered from iron stands along the windowed walls. The darker the sky grew, the warmer the candlelight glowed. I could imagine travelers on Beach Boulevard speculating as to what those women were up to in the glass room of a grand house on the closest thing to a hill this beachfront could claim.

"Sugar, if we don't make our confession pretty soon, you're gonna have to call the fire department to pry me out of your house because I won't fit through the door," Cookie said, leaning back in her chair and taking a deep breath.

"I agree," Punk said. "I think I went up a pant size somewhere between the soup course and the crème brûlée."

"I can take a hint," said Sugar, laughing as Punk passed her the question basket. She closed her eyes, stirred the slips of paper with her hand, and drew one out. "What is your idea of misery?" Sugar slowly twirled the slip of paper between her manicured fingers as she thought it over. "I think," she finally said, "my idea of misery is being surrounded by ugliness, the way things were when all of us first moved here right after Camille. Just destruction and debris everywhere. So many lovely old homes and churches left in ruins. Nobody had the energy to think about how things looked or how they made you feel because they were too busy just getting by from one day to the next. Nothing but loss every direction you turned. That's my idea of misery. What about you, sister?"

Cookie sat with her hands wrapped around her coffee cup. "I guess I'd say being disengaged—you know, having nothing that interests you and nothing to look forward to."

"Remember how Hudie got there toward the end?" Coco asked Cookie, who nodded. "When he wasn't trying to escape the nursing home, he just stared out the window like he was on the lookout for somebody to come get him." Coco was quiet for a moment before she shook her head and waved her arms in the air. "Alright, y'all, that's enough. I want a different question. Does anybody object?"

Nobody did. I think we were all relieved.

"Good!" Sugar said. "Let me try again." She closed her eyes, dipped her hand into the basket, and fished out another slip of paper. "Oh my, this one's intriguing! What did you love best about the one you loved best?"

"Say that again?" Charly squinted and leaned forward in her chair, as if she might somehow read Sugar's words floating in the air and understand them better.

"It's almost like a riddle," Sugar said. "What did *you* love best . . . about the *one* you loved best?"

"I can answer," Cookie offered.

"Go ahead, sister," Sugar said.

"What I loved best about Grady is that he saw me."

Coco frowned at her sister. "*Saw* you?"

"That's right," Cookie said.

"That doesn't make sense, sister," Sugar said.

Coco agreed with her—a rarity. "Everybody who ever met you saw you."

"No, they didn't," Cookie insisted. "Sometimes even you didn't."

"I did too!"

"Did not."

206

"Cookie, you're just flat-out wrong." Coco reached down and picked up Pierre, lounging by her chair. The cat wiggled up to rest his head on her shoulder.

"Neither one of y'all knows what it's like to be the middle one," Cookie explained without any complaint or resentment in her voice. "Especially the middle girl. Coco was the oldest, the strong one, the force of nature. And Sugar, you were the pretty one, the talented one, the sister all the boys wanted to court. I got lost in the middle."

"We were never any more special than you were, sister." Sugar looked worried.

"I know," Cookie said, winking at her. "But my version of 'special' was like that trick ink the kids used to get at the dime store—invisible to the naked eye. Grady's the only one who could read it."

"I could read it," Coco insisted.

"Could not," Cookie said with a grin. "Did you know that I like Louis Armstrong better than Benny Goodman and Glenn Miller put together?"

"It's not like we go out dancing every night," Coco said. "I can't possibly know who you listen to."

"Or that I taught myself to play the guitar and learned Spanish while my boys were in elementary school, won eight golf tournaments with Grady, and got my diving certificate last year?"

"Why, sister, if I'd known you could play the guitar, I would've invited you to accompany me at all my charity events," Sugar said.

"I know." Cookie chuckled. "That's why I kept my mouth shut."

"Well, I feel like two cents minus a penny," Coco said. "I wish you'd spoken up seventy years ago."

207

"Don't be silly," Cookie said. "It's not your fault or Sugar's. You're who you are, and I'm who I am. I guess I'm just more—I don't know—under the radar than you two. But for whatever reason, I caught Grady's attention and held it, one hundred percent, without even trying. Right off, he could see me, and he never looked away. That's what I loved best about him."

"I have secrets too," Coco said with a sly smile. "Sometimes I tap dance on my back porch where nobody can see me."

"That's what you think," Cookie said. "I sell tickets. We all hide in the bushes." Everybody had a laugh, which we needed.

"Maybe I picked the wrong question," Sugar said. "We could be here all night."

"No, no, I can answer quickly," said Charly. "Miss Cookie loved being seen. I guess I loved being heard. That's what I loved best about Connor. He made me feel like what I said was important and interesting and worth paying attention to. That's all."

Sugar spoke up. "My answer is devotion. Wade was completely devoted to me, and that made it easy for me to be devoted to him. Plain and simple. Fine della storia."

"I think I'm ready now," Punk said. "What I loved best about Cap is that he needed me—me in particular. That was a powerful thing, given how strong and self-reliant he was. Somehow he always found ways to let me know that he couldn't make it without me. My whole life, nothing else ever made me feel so worthy."

"Of what?" Coco asked.

"Love, I guess," Punk said. "You remember Mama and Daddy, what they were like."

"Not exactly huggers, were they, my friend?" Coco said, her voice lacking its usual edge.

My grandmother shook her head. "No, they weren't."

"I guess I might as well get it over with," Coco said. "What I loved best about the one I loved best was his sense of adventure."

Sugar frowned at Coco. "Hudie had many fine qualities, sister, but I don't think I ever saw that side of him."

"I'm not talking about Hudie." Coco scratched Pierre's neck.

Charly and I looked at each other and then at Punk, the only one around the table who didn't seem surprised.

"Quit looking at me like I just grew an extra head," Coco said to Sugar and Cookie. "It was a lifetime ago. Your turn, Edie."

"Now you just hold on," Cookie said. "You can't drop something like that on us and head for the hills."

"Can too," Coco argued.

"Can *not*." Sugar joined the fray.

Cookie looked at Punk. "Aren't you gonna help us out here?"

Punk didn't answer, so Coco did. "She doesn't have to. She already knows. She's always known."

"Known *what*?" Sugar and Cookie said together. They both looked at Punk, but she shook her head.

"It's Coco's secret, Coco's business," she said.

"I never should've opened my mouth," Coco huffed.

"Maybe not, sister," Sugar said. "But you did."

Coco let out a long sigh and rested her cheek against Pierre's. "There's not much to it, really. It was the year Punk and I graduated high school and got jobs shucking shrimp and oysters in Cocodrie."

"I had forgotten about that," Cookie said. "Sugar and I were still in school."

"Aunt Pep and Uncle Otie lived down there with their family," Coco said. "They let Punk and me sleep on cots on their screened-in porch until it got too cold, and then we'd move the cots to the kitchen. Had to set 'em up every night and take 'em down every morning before breakfast got started. Remember, Punk?"

"I sure do."

"They charged us each seven dollars a month for room and board."

"That's right," Punk said. "Seven dollars plus any fresh seafood we could scrounge off the docks. They were good people. Your Aunt Pep was such a sweet lady. I still have a handkerchief she gave me for my seventeenth birthday. Pale blue with a white camellia she embroidered on it."

"Is that why you love white empress?" It had never occurred to me there was any special meaning behind Punk's affection for the blooming shrubs she had planted up and down her driveway.

"It is," she said. "Aunt Pep—she insisted I call her that, just like Coco—she was the first truly maternal woman I ever had in my life. I never knew my grandparents. And my own mother . . . Looking back on it, she was probably struggling with depression, but of course, I didn't understand that then. I just thought she didn't like being a mother. Or didn't like me. Aunt Pep had an overflow of love and affection for her children and both of us teenage girls crowding into her little house."

Pierre scrunched down into Coco's lap so that only his pointy ears were visible above the table. "If it hadn't been for her, I would've been a real mess," she said. "I was so young and dumb."

210

"Young, yes," Punk said, "and naive just like I was. But dumb, never a day in your life."

Coco shook her head. "You have no idea what you're in for at that age. You don't realize that you might have just one shot at it."

"At what?" Sugar asked.

"Happiness. The love of your life. The whole nine yards."

Sugar's voice quivered when she spoke. "This just makes me so . . . so sad, sister. To think you didn't have what we all thought you had."

Cookie chimed in, sounding a little like an attorney arguing her case. "But you took such wonderful care of Hudie. You fought tooth and nail against that nursing home."

"Hudie was always very good to me," Coco said. "And I really did love him, even more the day I buried him than the day I married him. But he wasn't the one that shot a lightning bolt through my heart, and I never wanted him to know that. He deserved so much better than second fiddle. I did my best to keep it from him. Always."

"Can you tell us who . . . that is . . . do you want to tell us . . . ?" Sugar's question evaporated, unfinished, above her well-appointed table.

"His name was Mack Fontenot," Coco said. "A shrimper from there in Cocodrie. He was working for one of the big shrimp companies out of New Orleans, saving up to buy his own trawler. We met at a fais-dodo. Aunt Pep and Uncle Otie used to take the whole family to the Saturday night dances every week. Mack asked me to waltz with him, and that was that. We had a summer together, but about the time we started talking marriage that fall, Mama got sick and Daddy asked me would I come back home and help. Mack wanted me to stay with him, and I wanted to, more than I ever wanted anything before or since. But I just couldn't do that to Mama and Daddy. So I said no."

"That was the 'no' in your regret, wasn't it?" Cookie asked. "You told us you regretted that you couldn't say yes."

Coco nodded. "That's right. But at the same time, I don't know how I could've done anything different. Mama was so sick during the months before she died. Daddy had to have some help so he could work and keep food on the table."

"Do you know what happened to Mack, Miss Coco?" I asked.

"Influenza, same as Mama. They had an outbreak on a big shrimper he was working. Most of the crew died, including Mack. Aunt Pep wrote and broke the news to me."

By the time Coco finished, all of us were sniffling and dabbing at our eyes with our napkins. We all felt the loss of what she might've had but didn't.

"Enough with the boo-hoo," Coco said. "That was a lifetime ago. Maybe I didn't have the life I dreamed of, but I've had a good one. Pass the Kleenex and get on with it."

"Edie, sweet girl?" Punk said. "I think you're the only one of us left."

Sugar clasped her hands together. "Yes, and we want an update since the riunione degli innamorati!"

I had to laugh. "Miss Sugar, that sounds like something I might need forgiveness for."

"Ha!" she said. "No need to be forgiven for amore!"

"So what do you love best, chouchou?" Charly asked with a smile.

I watched the candle flames flicker on the table as I thought about my answer. "When I first met Cole, I just loved looking at him—the golden-blond hair, eyes the same blue gray as the gulf, a smile that still knocks my knees out from under me . . . That sounds so shallow, but it's the truth."

"Nothing wrong with a little eye candy, darlin'," Cookie said.

"No, siree," Coco agreed. "I used to make a meatloaf that tasted way better than Sugar's, but it looked like a pile of mud so I never could get anybody to try it. It's the same with men."

"Coco, what on earth does that even mean?" Cookie said.

"Oh, don't be so dense," Coco answered. "It means we eat with our eyes first just like we romance with our eyes first. Simple." She motioned to me like a choir director cueing a reluctant soloist. "Go ahead, kiddo."

I knew this would be hard. "It wasn't *only* about his looks. Cole has always been kind and thoughtful. He has a great sense of humor. We like the same music, the same movies. But I could say the same thing about other guys I've dated. What stayed with me all these years is more than just the way he looked on the beach that summer."

I paused for a few seconds, and we all heard Pierre snoring, to Coco's obvious delight. "Don't take it personally, kiddo," she said. "I'm sure he's listening."

"There's a kind of light in Cole," I went on. "Or maybe you'd call it warmth. I'm not sure. But it's something inside that has nothing to do with how he looks."

"You have it too, chouchou," Charly said.

"She's absolutely right," Punk agreed.

"You really think so?" It would be nice to believe I had the same something special as Cole.

"Absolutely," Coco said as Sugar and Cookie nodded.

"I'm assuming he's an ottimo baciatore?" Sugar asked with a smile.

"What's that?" Cookie asked.

Sugar winked at me. "An *excellent* kisser."

"Sì, Miss Sugar, he's an ottimo baciatore."

Sugar clapped her hands together. "Bene!"

"Shug," Coco threatened, "if you don't quit speaking that Italian, I'm gonna strip off my clothes and run naked—make that *buck nekkid*—up Beach Boulevard, hollering, 'I'm Sugar Vansant's sister!'"

"That's enough to give me a migraine." Sugar laid her hand against her forehead. Then she grinned and added, "Probably give the seagulls a heart attack. I can see them right now, falling out of the sky. *Plop! Plop! Plop!*"

"I'm not sure I can move us past that one," Punk said as we all laughed, "but back to Edie. I've been thinking about what you said, sweet girl. And there's a lot to it. The first time I saw Cap, I thought he was the most handsome boy I had ever laid eyes on. I remember being fascinated with everything about him—his dark hair, his eyes, his strong hands—everything. But there was something else, something inside him."

Sugar took a sip of wine. "When you're young, you really don't know that you might be feeling something you'll never feel again—not in quite the same way, at least. You can love somebody with such abandon when you're young. No thought for how you'll pay the light bill or what will happen if one of you gets sick. Love is different when you're older. It's still wonderful, still special, even better in some ways. But it's not the same."

# twenty-six

**"I DON'T THINK I'VE EVER MET** anybody like him,"Cole whispered as we sat down at my worktable upstairs. I had just introduced him to Jason. Like the rest of us, Cole found himself grappling for words after that initial encounter.

"I know," I whispered back. "But the more you're around him, the more you'll like him." I started speaking normally again. "Want some coffee or tea?"

"No thanks. I shouldn't stay that long. Might get in your way. I just wanted to get some idea of what the storm was like. I wonder if I'll ever fly into one like that."

"Selfishly, I hope not, much as you probably want to."

He smiled at me. "I do. But I'm glad you don't want me to, if that makes any sense."

I showed him one of the church pictures. "Look at the congregation." I pointed to the parishioners seated in folding chairs outside the ruins of their church. "Punk noticed all the yellow dresses. I mean, look at them. This was taken the week after the storm. Their whole community is wrecked, but they're wearing their Sunday best. Most of the women have on heels. Somebody even managed to drag a piano out there to sing by."

"Unbelievable. Oh, wow, look at this." Cole picked up a shot of a priest sitting in a straight-back chair with his back to the camera. In front of him lay the remains of his church. Next to him, a kneeling woman appeared to be offering her confession. Even though you couldn't see his face, the priest looked battered, slightly slumping in his chair. "He looks like it's all he can do to hold himself up, let alone anybody else," Cole said.

"Can you imagine what that must've been like," I said, "trying to keep a congregation together, surrounded by the ruins of your church?"

Cole looked through a stack of images I had been working on. "What about the one you were telling me about, the one of airmen carrying a civilian on a stretcher?"

"It's not here, unfortunately," I said. "Once I finish researching the ones Jason wants for the exhibit, I make backup copies of them, which I keep at Punk's, and then send the originals off to be enlarged and mounted. I can show it to you the next time you come over."

"And nobody knows who he is?"

"I managed to find one of the airmen who was carrying the man on the stretcher, but he never knew the civilian's name either. So unless somebody recognizes him from the exhibit, I guess he's just lost."

"It's hard for you, isn't it?" Cole said. "Taking in the stories of these people."

"Yes. And I know that sounds weird because they're total strangers."

"I don't think it's weird."

I smiled at him. "Thank you for that. It's just that the

priest looks so beaten down. The church members in their Sunday clothes—all those women in their hopeful yellow dresses—are they being brave or are they in shock and just can't accept what's all around them? And then the guy on the stretcher—he looks so desolate in the picture. I guess I was hoping for proof that he found his way home, back to his family."

Cole put his arm around me. "Try not to give up, Edie. Like you said, maybe somebody will recognize him at the exhibit. When is it, by the way, so I can make sure I'm not flying that day?"

"August 17. That's the anniversary of the storm. We'll definitely keep it open through the end of the month, and then Jason will decide what to do next. I think he's hoping the exhibit will find a permanent home."

"Well, I'm keeping you from your work," Cole said. I walked him to the top of the stairs, where he kissed me goodbye. "Is Miss Punk still willing to feed me tonight?"

"You're her new favorite." I smiled up at him. "Not something to be taken lightly."

# twenty-seven

PUNK SUGGESTED THAT WE MAKE our last confessions around her backyard firepit overlooking the water. In late July, the evening air was warm, but with the sun going down and a strong breeze blowing off the gulf, we welcomed the wraps she had draped over the Adirondacks ringing the pit. After supper, I lit the fire as Punk served her Liz Taylors.

"I don't think anything feels better than warm-in-cool," Sugar said as she snuggled into her wrap.

"What does that mean?" Coco asked as Pierre poked his head out of her wrap. She had put him in her lap, where he tucked himself in.

"This." Sugar tugged at her wrap. "Here we are, outside in the cool ocean breeze, but we've got our wraps and our toasty fire. Makes you feel so protected. I think it's divine."

"I like the opposite—cool in the heat," Cookie said. "Nothing like a cold dip when it's nine hundred degrees outside. Most liberating feeling in the world. You could be so hot and sweaty you can't breathe, but all you have to do is jump in the water and right away you're cool and clean, with enough energy to land a marlin."

"Well, I don't see any marlins around," Coco said, "so grab that infernal basket, Punk, and land us a question."

Punk picked up the basket and drew one out. "If not yourself, whom would you be? That's kind of interesting."

"Living or dead?" Coco asked.

"It doesn't say," Punk answered. "As your host, I declare it can be either. Why don't you start, Coco?"

"Ginger Rogers," she answered. "Always wanted to be a serious hoofer, and that girl had style. Never took any guff from Astaire."

"How about you, Edie?" Punk asked.

I took a few seconds to think it over. "I guess I'd like to be one of those early women photographers like Dorothea Lange or Margaret Bourke-White—the ones who took pictures that still move people."

"Don't you worry, sweet girl," Punk said. "You're just getting serious about it, but you've always had the talent."

"What about you, Punk?" I asked. "Who would you like to be?"

She didn't have to think long. "Marie Hull. Her paintings are so beautiful, and she seems to have loved nature and people as much as I do. It would be extraordinary to know what it's like to paint them the way she did."

"Cookie?" Sugar prompted her sister.

"Jacques Cousteau," Cookie said. "I'd like to see what it's like to captain the *Calypso* and explore the mighty deep. At least now I can dive and see a little bit of what's down there."

Sugar shook her head. "Not me. Just the thought of all those sea creatures makes me *shuddah*."

"Well, who would you like to be?" Cookie asked.

"Coco Chanel," Sugar said as she twirled a long strand of

beads around her neck. "She made women all over the world look a hundred percent better. Smell better too."

"Charlotte?" Punk said. "I guess that just leaves you."

Charly gathered her long hair into a ponytail and twisted it into a bun but had nothing to fasten it, so she just let it fall. "I think I'd like to be the hot dog boat captain on Captiva Island."

"The what, dear?" Sugar looked a little concerned, as if Charly's mental state had suddenly come into question.

"I saw him once on a work trip to Florida," Charly explained. "We'd been stuck in workshops and meetings most every day, but they finally gave us an afternoon off to enjoy the island. The ocean was calm and flat that day, just like here. I was sitting in a beach chair with my feet in the water when I saw this guy come slowly chugging along the shoreline in a snazzy fishing boat with a big sign on the side advertising fresh hot dogs and ice-cold drinks. People would just wade out to the boat, hand him money, and get their stuff."

"So . . . you'd like to enter the food service industry, dear?" Sugar was clearly struggling with this one.

Charly laughed. "It's not so much his line of work as his state of mind I'd like to claim, Miss Sugar. He looked so happy, that guy. Not a care in the world. Just loaded his boat with hot dogs and iced down some drinks in the morning, then cruised along that beautiful beach till the tourists bought everything he had to sell. His office attire was a bathing suit and a tank top. I could picture him diving off the boat and taking a cool dip whenever he got hot. He had a big smile and a dark tan. I can't imagine anybody with that smile and that tan ever being depressed. So that's who I'd like to be—captain of the hot dog boat on Captiva Island, happy and content with what I have and never wanting for more."

Sugar took a sip of her Liz Taylor. "Your answer raises another question."

"What's that, Miss Sugar?" Charly asked.

"Why isn't joy enough?"

"What do you mean, Shug?" Cookie asked.

"Well, I mean people seem to believe that joy alone is not enough, whether you're receiving it or giving it. Take Charlotte's boat captain. Happy as a clam. Not a care in the world. But I'd bet my house that somewhere in his life there's a mama or a daddy or a wife or a girlfriend telling him he needs to quit that nonsense and make something of himself."

"You're probably right," Punk agreed.

"It's the same with beauty and hospitality," Sugar went on. "People tell me they love coming to my house, and I believe them because I just about have to run them off with a stick whenever I host a dinner party or even a little backyard barbecue. And why is that? Why does it bring them joy to be there?"

"Because your home is lovely and you're a gracious, generous host," Punk said. "You make everybody feel welcome. And you feed us till we pop."

"Well, why isn't that enough for some people?" Sugar looked genuinely troubled by her own question. "Why aren't they satisfied that I've tried to create a place of beauty to share with them? But no. I'm always hearing from this one or that one how I need to open the house for tours or host big receptions to raise money for one cause or another because a place like this 'could do so much good.' I listened to them for a while, until somebody in one of their tour groups nearly set my silk sofa on fire with a cigarette."

"Some people were raised in a barn," Cookie said.

"They even try to make me feel guilty for living there,"

Sugar went on. "I've had people ask me whether it might be more responsible to donate my house to the city since a woman alone doesn't need all that space. No, I don't need it. But I enjoy it. And I adored the man who bought it for me. All of my best memories of Wade are there—the ones that wiped away all the bad ones. Why isn't that reason enough for me to keep it and share it as I see fit? I can write checks to charities I believe in as easily from my sunroom as I could from some condominium in a retirement community."

"You can, and I know for a fact that you do," Punk assured her. "Bringing joy and beauty into the world should be enough if that's where your gifts lie. Whatever anybody's gifts are—that's enough. *We're* enough."

# twenty-eight

**THE FRONT DOOR CHIMED,** but I didn't hear Jason call out his usual greeting, so I went downstairs to see who it was. Charly stood by the front counter.

"Hello, ma'am," I said from the stairs. "Could I interest you in a candelabra?"

Normally, that would've gotten a laugh, but not today. Charly hurried to me and pointed up. "Can I talk to you for a minute—up there?"

I led her to the second floor and fixed her a cup of coffee before we sat down across from each other at my worktable.

Charly leaned forward and whispered, "Is Jason here?"

I shrugged and whispered back, "I'm not sure. Could be in the garden, or he might've stepped out for a minute."

She sipped her coffee and kept her voice low. "You're going to think I'm a total flake. I'm beginning to think so myself. But I had another dream about him."

"Jason?"

She nodded. "Same lighthouse, same pier, same fog, same light. And same him. Only this time he was alone."

"What did he say?"

"He said, 'Go to Edie.' And then I woke up. You had already left for work."

"I came in early," I said. "With all the Camille interviews I've been doing, I feel like I'm running behind."

"Got any idea why he sent me here today?" she asked. She leaned back in her chair and covered her face with her hands. "Would you listen to me? It's like I've decided my dreams are telegrams from on high."

"Well, just in case they are, let me show you what I'm working on."

Charly glanced around the table. "Looks like you've got a system going."

"I'm organizing the pictures geographically as best I can. Then I use the survivor interviews I got in Hattiesburg and try to piece together more information about each image. Many of the survivors and their relatives still live around here, so I'm interviewing them as I find them."

"Is it working?" Charly asked.

"Pretty well," I said. "Most of the stacks around the table contain images and interviews from a particular town—Bay St. Louis, Pass Christian, and so on. The ones I'm double-checking this morning have all been identified—the location, at least some of the people in the picture, and the date when they were taken."

"Did you ever work for the military, chouchou?" Charly asked as she scanned all my carefully organized stacks and lists and printouts.

I shook my head. "No, I just inherited Daddy's organizational skills. This kind of thing makes Mama's head explode."

"Always has."

I pointed to a large red pocket folder. "Those are the ones Jason has already chosen for the exhibit. Once the mounted enlargements come in, I have them delivered to the library, and then I keep the originals here in that folder."

"Can I look?" she asked.

I slid the folder to her. Charly opened it and studied each picture—the boy drinking from a busted waterline, the priest hearing confession in front of a church turned to rubble, the woman on her knees, frantically salvaging a picture from her yard. Charly gasped when she came to the picture of a church congregation worshiping among the ruins. She pointed to a woman in the foreground. "I used to do her hair. That's Miss Mamie Jeffers."

I checked my notes. "You're right. She's one of the few people in this picture who was clear enough to identify."

Eventually, Charly came to the picture on the bottom of the stack, the solitary wounded civilian being carried on a stretcher by two airmen. She suddenly became very still. "Edie, who is this?" She spoke so softly that I could barely hear her.

"I still don't know. But something about that picture gets to me. I even talked to Punk about it. This is one of the few shots that had any information written on the back. None of the people were identified, but it was taken in Biloxi the day after the storm. I was able to track down one of the airmen carrying the stretcher. He never knew the wounded man's name, though. There's just something about that man on the stretcher. He looks so alone. Makes me want to help him somehow. I know that sounds ridiculous."

She kept her eyes on the picture. "It doesn't sound ridiculous at all. You don't know anything more about him?"

"Charly, you don't think this is Connor, do you?"

She looked up at me with a mix of fear and hope in her eyes, now wide and teary. "It could be. Do you know anything more? Anything at all?"

"I might know what happened to him before the picture was taken. Not long ago, I interviewed a survivor named Nora Gilliam. She washed up on Deer Island the night of the hurricane. The next morning, she woke up on the beach, along with three other people. Only one was a man. The way she described him, he sounded so much like the man in this picture—a young civilian who looked military and had a bad wound on his left leg. Nora tore his pants leg off and helped him soak his wound in saltwater to try and stop the bleeding. You can see that the guy in the picture is missing the bottom of his left pants leg. Nora said the mosquitoes were fierce on the island, and the man she helped, even though he was in shock, had the kindness to take off his shirt and wrap it around her. That man on the stretcher has no shirt."

"Did she by any chance say if it was blue and white—the shirt he gave her?" Charly brought the picture closer to her face.

I had that same knife-in-the-stomach feeling I used to get from memories of Leni right after she died. "Blue and white plaid, a small print."

Charly seemed to struggle to get the words out. "This . . . this Nora . . . did she know if he . . ."

"She didn't know what happened to him."

Charly laid the picture down. I reached over and took her hand.

"But listen, if this really is Connor, there's as much reason to believe he lived as to think he didn't make it. Nora said the last time she saw him, they were putting him on a helicopter and getting him to a hospital. She didn't have any idea which one because they were sending people all over the place as everything around here filled up. You said you were sent to Pensacola, right?"

"That's right."

"Maybe Connor was too. Or he could've gone to New Orleans—even Houston."

Charly spoke almost in a whisper. "Sometimes I feel like some terrible, cruel joke is being played on me. On my whole life."

"Why, Charly?"

She started to cry and wiped a tear from her cheek. "When I met Connor, I thought to myself, 'This is it. This is the reason I had to endure such an awful childhood, so I could appreciate someone like him.' But then he was taken away. The minute I believed I could have him, he was gone."

Charly cried harder, pausing now and then to collect herself. "It makes me feel—like I was born to be disappointed. And I don't know why. If he were just a long-ago crush, I would've gotten—I would've gotten past it a long time ago. But there was more to it than that. I always thought he was sent—sent especially for me. But then he got taken away. And I've tried and tried to figure it out. What did I do to deserve that?"

I gently squeezed her hand. "Nothing, Charly. You're a good person. You don't deserve to be punished any more than the rest of us. We're all 'short of the glory.' And I don't believe for a minute that you were born for disappointment. I just think, for whatever reason, this is when it's all supposed to come together. Maybe we can't see it right now, but I believe there's a reason."

She looked at me and made what must've been a bold effort to smile. I didn't talk anymore or ask her to. I just got up and went around the table to sit beside her, put my arms around her, and held her. That's what my mother would have done. Or Punk. It was what Leni always did.

# twenty-nine

**THE TEN SPOTS HAD NO SHAME.** As soon as the merchants' walk began, Punk and Coco showed up at my table and bought an armload. Then Coco loudly called out to Sugar and Cookie, who had positioned themselves across the street, "Hey, girls! Come over here! You won't *believe* this new photographer everybody's been talking about!" Once they had stirred up a crowd for me, they'd drift down the street for a while and then circle back to repeat the process. Punk said they got the idea from an episode of *I Love Lucy*.

"All of this your work?" A man in khakis and a red golf shirt held up one of the storm pictures I had asked my brother to mail me from home.

"Yes, sir, it is," I said. "I'm Edie Gardner."

"Do you have a card?"

I handed him one, hoping the ink didn't smear. I had forgotten to order them till the last minute.

"Here's mine." He took out his wallet and handed me a business card. He was editor of the local newspaper. "The bean counters over at the paper tell me they're finally getting off their checkbook and letting me hire a new photographer,

228

first of the year. I'm looking for somebody to shoot weather and maritime news. Your storm shots are good. So are your pictures from the docks. Interested?"

I was unprofessionally staring, mouth agape, until my brain finally started working again. "Yes, of course," I finally babbled. "I'm committed to the gallery until the end of the year, but after that I'll be looking."

"Her gallery hours are entirely flexible." I turned to see Jason standing behind me. "Should any opportunities arise, I'm sure we can adjust Edie's schedule to accommodate."

"It's settled then," the editor said. I could tell by his expression that he was staring at Jason over my shoulder. Even newspaper editors weren't immune. "Call me after the first, Miss Gardner, and we'll figure it all out. In the meantime, if you shoot something we can use, we'll pay you as a freelancer."

"Thank you. I'll be in touch."

I watched until he was out of sight and then turned to Jason. "I'm screaming on the inside. Also, I'm mentally jumping up and down. Thank you, Jason."

I gave him a quick hug, which of course caught him off guard. He smiled and said, "I think your talent had a lot more to do with your success than anything I did. Now back to work before your sales slump."

Around midnight, I woke to the sound of thunder. We couldn't have had a more perfectly sunny day for the merchants' walk, but now it was pouring outside. I grabbed a throw and took my usual spot on the window seat, wishing Cole were here to watch the storm with me. But he had gone home after I fell asleep on his shoulder, sitting on Punk's porch after supper.

I kept going over the day's events in my head, for once in a good way, because I wanted to remember them. The Ten Spots pulling a Lucy. People buying my pictures for the first time. Getting a job offer. Making Jason laugh. Jason, the unsolvable puzzle.

I pressed my palm against the windowpane, dry on this side, streaked with rain on the other, two sides almost touching but worlds apart. Three flashes of lightning briefly illuminated the horizon. Sea and sky, almost touching but worlds apart.

*Good night, Leni.*

# thirty

**THE NEXT MORNING,** I came downstairs to find the Ten Spots gathered at the table, deep in conversation, but not in the usual spirit. Their voices were hushed. Lots of furrowed brows on worried faces. It stopped me in my tracks. "Did something happen?"

Punk immediately got up and hugged me good morning. "No, dear. Everything's fine. That is, we hope so. You sit down while I get your breakfast, and we'll talk about it."

I greeted everybody and took my spot at the table as Punk returned from the kitchen with what she called her "Saturday special": Parmesan grits topped with andouille sausage and a poached egg, with little bowls of cane syrup for sausage dipping, something she picked up as a child in Louisiana and never gave up.

Just as I dipped my fork into the grits, I heard the seaplane outside.

"Oh, I hope you don't mind, dear," Punk said. "I invited Cole to breakfast after you fell asleep last night. Don't get up. I'll deliver him to you."

Punk waited for Cole on the back porch and ushered him

to the seat next to me. He greeted the other Ten Spots and said, "Am I the only guy you ladies invited?"

"Our annual male sacrifice," Coco said. "Guarantees a good crop." Everybody laughed—a good thing because they all looked like they needed to.

"But you're feeding me before you do me in?" Cole asked her with a grin.

"We're murderous, not uncivilized," Coco said.

Punk brought Cole his breakfast and coffee before taking her seat.

"Miss Punk, you know there's a weight limit for pilots," he said as he dug in.

"Fiddlesticks." She gave him a dismissive wave of her hand.

I speared a piece of sausage and took a bite before quizzing the Ten Spots. "What's up this morning, y'all? Everybody looked so worried when I came down."

"It's Charlotte," Punk said. "Maybe I'm just being a foolish old woman with nothing better to do, but I'm worried about her."

"Why?"

"Remember I told you she begged off the merchants' walk, said she felt a migraine coming on?"

"Yes, ma'am."

Punk wrapped her hands around her coffee cup. "Well, when I got home, I found a note from her. She said her headache had passed and her friend had invited her to Bay St. Louis. She said she'd catch a cab and probably stay overnight, maybe even a couple of days. She told me not to worry. I tried, but I've just got a bad feeling about this. I know Charlotte's not accustomed to answering to anybody, so it probably never occurred to her to call and let me know for sure that she was staying over."

"Even so," Sugar said, "as your guest, you'd think she would've let you know. It's so hard to plan a proper table if you have no idea who's coming."

Coco pierced her poached egg with her fork and stirred it into her grits. "It's not like she needs a reservation, Shug. This ain't the Ritz-Carlton."

"Should I be offended?" Punk winked at me.

"Oh, you know what I mean, Punk," Coco said. "Shug can't host a weenie roast without place cards. But Charlotte never eats a bite before lunch anyway, so if she makes it or she doesn't, I'd say you're prepared. She won't need anything more than a coffee cup."

Cole was watching them as if they were a flock of white pelicans he had stumbled upon. He leaned over and half whispered, "Is it always like this?"

"They aren't even wound up yet," I whispered back before taking a bite of my grits.

Cole glanced up and down the table, and I knew he was looking for the Tabasco. He put his hand over his heart when I found it hiding behind the juice pitcher and passed it to him.

"I think I might know why Charly's off, Punk," I said. "She came to visit me at the gallery. I showed her the pictures Jason has chosen for the exhibit so far, including the one of the man on the stretcher, the one I told you about." I turned to Cole. "It's the same one we were talking about."

"Who is the man on the stretcher, honey?" Sugar asked me.

I described the image and tried to explain why it made such an impression on me.

"What does that have to do with Charlotte, darlin'?" Cookie asked.

"She thought it might be, you know, *him*."

"Oh!" Sugar exclaimed. "Did it look like him to you, Edie? Like the drawing she showed us, I mean?"

I dipped a piece of andouille in syrup and let the excess drip off. "I could see a resemblance. But the angle of the photograph makes it hard to say for sure."

"Catch me up," Cole said. "Who is *him*?"

"A guy Charly met the night Camille hit Biloxi," I explained. "They made this incredible love-at-first-sight connection, and then the storm literally blew them apart. They never saw each other again."

"Now I really want to see that picture," Cole said. "Didn't you say you have a copy of it here?"

I smacked my forehead. "Where are my brain cells? Y'all excuse me for just a sec." Hurrying to my room, I found the photo and brought it down.

To my surprise, Cole studied it the same way Charly had, holding it close to his face, then farther away, as if he were trying to bring it into focus.

"That's unreal," he said.

I leaned over to look at the picture with him. "It's powerful, right?"

"It is . . . but that's not what I'm talking about. This guy looks an awful lot like my uncle, not the way he looks now but how he was in old pictures from Vietnam."

"You told me he was a Camille survivor," I said. "Do you really think this could be him?"

"It looks a lot like him, but you said this picture was taken in Biloxi. I always assumed Uncle Joe was in New Orleans when the storm hit since he's been down there so long, ever since med school, I think."

"Med school?" Punk sat up the way Pierre did when he

heard a dog bark in the neighborhood. I imagined her ears pricking up just like the cat's.

Looking around the table, I saw the Ten Spots casting glances at each other.

"Yes, ma'am. He went to Tulane after his Army hitch." Cole scrutinized the picture again. "Even the injuries match. My uncle's had trouble with his left leg ever since the storm. Dad told me he had several surgeries on it and did a ton of rehab. He still walks with a cane sometimes, mostly when he's tired. One of the few things he's ever volunteered about Camille was that he probably would've lost his leg if it weren't for an amazing doctor who treated him. That's what inspired him to go into orthopedics."

"Alright, you two, pass that picture around," Coco said. She and her sisters gathered around Punk's chair as Cole handed her the picture.

All the ladies shook their heads sadly. "Reminds me of my beautiful boy," Sugar said.

"All the beautiful boys," Punk added. "Such precious human life thrown into a maelstrom, be it a war or a hurricane."

"No telling what he's seen or how badly it rattled him," Coco said. She went onto the porch, where Pierre was lounging in his favorite chair, and stroked his head as if she needed a little comfort right now. She picked him up and brought him back to the table with her. Pierre sat on her lap, snuggled into the crook of her arm, and rested his head against her shoulder.

"Do y'all think the man in the picture could be sort of an everyman?" I asked. "People are drawn to it because they see something in it that reminds them of someone they care about?"

"Now that's interesting," Punk said.

"Y'all," Cookie said, "I think we might be hopping down a bunny trail."

"Cole, why don't you tell us a little more about your uncle?" Sugar suggested as everybody sat back down.

"I'm really just getting to know him." Cole sprinkled more Tabasco on his breakfast bowl. "Growing up in California, I only saw him a few times a year. Before this summer, we never lived close enough to spend much time together. He and my dad are originally from Arkansas. Dad's the oldest. Their family had a farm on the Mississippi River."

"This farm, dear, was it anywhere near Memphis?" Sugar asked.

"Yes, ma'am. About an hour or so away." This time Cole noticed the Ten Spots' group glance. "Am I missing something?"

"Yes, Cole," Punk said. "You're missing that we're a rude bunch of old birds. We're picking you for information and not sharing why. You say the man on the stretcher looks like your uncle. Charlotte thought he looked like her lost love. It's just odd that the two men have so much in common. They both grew up in the country but within an easy drive to Memphis. Both have a connection to Tulane and to medicine. Both got caught up in Camille. But as much as we'd like to help Charlotte, there's no getting around the obvious. One of these men is named Joe and the other is—"

"Connor?" Cole asked. You could've heard a pin drop.

"Yes," Punk finally said. "How did you know?"

"That's my Uncle Joe's real name. His legal name." Cole leaned back in his chair and looked out at the water.

"Are you okay?" I couldn't read his face. He didn't look happy, but he didn't look upset either. He was blank.

Cole ran his hand through his hair several times. "Just trying to sort this all out."

"Honey, how on earth did your uncle end up with two names?" Sugar wanted to know.

"My whole life," Cole said, "I never heard anybody call him anything but Joe. We were in California, so I only saw him when he visited us out there or when the extended family went home to Arkansas for Thanksgiving. Everybody called him Joe—my dad, my grandparents, aunts, uncles, cousins, neighbors—everybody."

"How did you find out that wasn't his name?" Sugar asked.

"When I first moved back here, I always met him for lunch at his house because he was helping me work on my car. But the last time, he asked me to pick him up at the hospital. I asked for Dr. Joe Donovan, but the receptionist told me there was nobody on staff by that name. I said there had to be some mistake because he'd spent his entire career there. That's when she asked me if Joe could be a nickname. She said their head orthopedic surgeon was a Dr. Connor Donovan."

"You took a chance that this doctor was your uncle?" Cookie asked.

"Yes, ma'am. I didn't really have much choice. Over lunch, he explained what happened. He and Dad had an Aunt Rosalie they were very close to—the family matriarch. Everybody loved her. When my uncle was born, she said he didn't look like a Connor to her. He looked like a Joe. She just started calling him that, and over time, everybody else did too. It wasn't until he got drafted and had to use his legal name that he decided to take it back. Now everybody in the family still calls him Joe, but everybody else in his life calls him Connor. I'm trying to make the switch, but it's not easy."

"And he's been in New Orleans all this time?" Coco asked.

"Yes, ma'am. He's been practicing there for years."

"I'm sorry we hit you with this out of the blue," Punk said.

"Actually, it explains some things," Cole said. "My uncle's always had gaps, a couple of stretches in his life that he just won't talk about. Vietnam for one. Camille was the other. Dad's always said Camille changed Uncle Joe—Uncle Connor—even more than the war did."

"How so, dear?" Sugar asked.

"According to Dad, my uncle's reaction to Vietnam was very much in character for him. He was always humble and didn't like to talk about himself, so it was no surprise that he never told the family what he did to earn all the medals he came home with. He never talked about his combat experience at all. But after Camille, Dad said it was like a light went out in him. He never married. Never had kids. Devoted himself to his work. And always changed the subject if anybody asked him about the hurricane."

Sugar clapped her hands together. "I knew it! I just knew they'd get back together somehow."

"Now, hold on," Coco said. "Let's make sure we get this right before we go running to Charlotte with the good news."

"Coco's right," Cookie said. "And as much as we care about her, Charlotte's not the only one to consider here. For all we know, Cole's uncle might not even remember the storm—or Charlotte. We can't just throw them into each other."

The phone rang.

"Keep your seat, Punk," I said. "I'll get it. You look like you might need a minute."

# thirty-one

**I SLOWLY SET THE RECEIVER BACK** in its cradle and stood by the phone cubby in Punk's hallway, collecting myself to deliver bad news to my grandmother.

"Who was it?" she asked when I came back into the dining room.

"Charly's cab driver."

"Her what?"

"Apparently, she didn't go to Bay St. Louis. The cabbie said he dropped her off at McSwain's late yesterday afternoon."

"The marina?" Cookie asked. "Why on earth would she want to go there?"

"I don't know," I said. "But when she opened her wallet to pay the driver, her emergency contact card with Punk's number must've fallen onto the floorboard. The next fare spotted it. And the driver said he'd had an uneasy feeling about Charly from the moment he picked her up. When he saw the card, he decided to follow his instincts and call."

Punk jumped up from the table and hurried to the telephone. She had just enough time to flip through the phone book before I heard her dialing and talking to someone at the marina. She thanked them for their help and came back to the table. I couldn't remember the last time I saw Punk look so worried.

"They said she bought supplies and booked a charter to take her to Horn—to take her there and drop her off," Punk said. "She told them she was joining friends who were camping on the island. As far as I know, Charlotte's only friend down here, besides all of us, is the one in Bay St. Louis. And why charter a boat when Cap's is right out there at the dock?"

"Pardon me, is Edie home?"

We were surprised to hear Jason's voice through the open windows. Punk hurried onto the porch and opened the back door to welcome him. "Come on in, Jason. What brings you here?"

"Good morning, everyone. Please forgive the intrusion."

"Won't you sit down and let me get you something to eat—maybe some coffee or juice?" Punk offered.

"No, no—I'm a bit pressed for time. But thank you, Mrs. Cheramie."

"What's going on, Jason?" I asked.

"Just a few minutes ago, I received a call regarding a Camille survivor you've been trying to reach. I'm sorry, but I'm drawing a blank on her name just now, and I left in such a hurry that I didn't bring the notepad where I wrote it down."

"Has to be Sarah Parsons," I said. "She's the lady gathering scattered pictures from her yard in one of the Camille images. I've been trying to get ahold of her for two weeks."

"Yes, I believe that's the name," Jason said. "Her sister is looking after things while she's camping on Horn. While the sister was checking Sarah's answering machine, she found your message and called to say you can find her on the island until late morning today. She'll be camping on the eastern end. You should look for a purple tent with a bright gold flag. I believe it has something to do with football."

As worried as we all were about Charly, I couldn't help smiling at the thought of Jason at an LSU game.

"I would never tell you to give up your weekend," he said, "but in case this woman was important to you, I wanted you to know. Mrs. Cheramie's line was busy, so I decided to drop by since there was some urgency involved."

"Pierre wants to know who's minding the store," Coco said.

Jason smiled at the cat lounging in Coco's lap. "A couple of local college students I just hired to help on weekends till the holidays are over."

"Thank you for coming, Jason," I said. "I'll get right over there."

"Happy to help." He smiled at the needlepoint hanging behind the table, the companion to the piece he had admired over Punk's fireplace. "I still say that's beautiful work, Mrs. Cheramie. And now I must be going."

Punk showed him out and then rejoined us.

"Could you give a girl a lift?" I asked Cole.

"Done," he said.

"We can get to Horn in no time by plane, Punk, and I can check on Charly while I'm there. I'll make sure she's okay." I got up and hugged her. "And then we'll figure out how to tell her we found Connor. Try not to worry."

# thirty-two

**"YOU THINK CHARLOTTE WILL BE OFFENDED** that we're following her?" Cole asked me.

With all the plane noise, we were talking to each other through the mics in our headsets.

I shook my head. "We're pretty close, so I don't think she'll be offended—annoyed, maybe, but not offended."

As we approached Horn, Cole banked east and prepared to set the plane down near the tip. We were all the way down to five hundred feet when he pointed. "Somebody's in the water."

He circled back around and dropped another hundred feet to get a better look. I grabbed my camera out of the bag, snapped on the zoom lens, and had a look. "It's Charly. Nobody else has hair like that. It looks like she's really far out."

He frowned as he checked his instrument panel. "She could be even farther out than she looks from this altitude." Cole immediately radioed the Coast Guard, told them we had a swimmer in distress, and gave them the details they needed.

"They're on the way, but we need to move now," he said, quickly descending to land about twenty yards from Charly.

He was shutting the plane down when I shouted, "Cole! She stopped swimming!"

Within seconds, he had kicked off his shoes, tossed his aviators and T-shirt next to his seat, and grabbed a flotation tube from behind me. He was in the water, swimming toward Charly before I could even say, "What do we do?"

I took off my shoes, climbed over his seat, and stepped out onto the left landing float to get a better view of them. The second he reached Charly, who was floating facedown, Cole dipped the flotation tube underneath her and flipped her over onto her back. Then he swam all the way back, pulling her along and making sure her face stayed out of the water.

"Help me lift her up there with you, Edie, but don't get in the water." He was breathing hard. "You'll have better leverage from where you are."

I put my arms under Charly's and heaved as hard as I could, with Cole pushing from the water. Once we had her lying flat on the plane float, I started CPR while Cole caught his breath and hoisted himself up. "Here comes the rescue team." He pointed to a boat leaving a big wake as it sped toward us.

Soon we were swarmed by Coast Guard medics, who took over CPR until, after an eternity, Charly began to cough up water and gasp for air. Before she was even fully conscious, they had her on a stretcher and took her aboard their boat.

"We're heading for the ER in Ocean Springs, Captain," called one of the crewmen as they prepared to leave.

"We'll head right over," Cole called back. "Thanks, everybody." Then he turned back to me. "We'd better get going."

I didn't move.

"Edie?"

Still I couldn't move.

He took me by the shoulders. "Are you alright?"

I couldn't get a word out of my mouth. Everything had happened so fast that I couldn't wrap my brain around it. Cole had shifted into a gear I didn't have, and I was frozen. I just stood there shaking.

He put his arms around me and held me tight as we stood on the float. "Listen, I know you're scared for Charly. And I know it's hard to think right now. But we have to, okay?"

He triggered something Nora Gilliam told me during her Camille interview. *"If you mean to survive a tough situation, your brain better keep a-workin'."*

I looked up at him and took a deep breath. "Tell me what to do, and I'll do it. I'm not sure I can think for myself just yet."

Cole smiled and kissed me on the forehead. "I want you to climb over my seat and strap into yours."

I did exactly as he said while he got in behind me and strapped into the pilot's seat. Then he checked to make sure I was safely buckled. Once we were in the air, he radioed Punk, told her what had happened, and asked her to get to the ER. We'd follow in Rosetta as soon as we landed at her dock.

"Miss Punk," he said, "why don't you let one of the other ladies drive you? Just this once."

———

Cole and I hurried into the ER, where we found the Ten Spots waiting in the lobby.

Punk all but ran to us. First she put her arms around me and squeezed as tightly as she could. Then she did the same to Cole. "I don't know where we'd be right now if it weren't for you, honey," she said to him.

"Everything's gonna be alright, Miss Punk," he said. "I

think we got to her in time, and she's been in good hands ever since."

Punk stepped back and nodded. I knew she was attempting a stiff upper lip. "Come over and sit with us," she said. We took a loveseat right next to her. It looked a little worse for wear, but we were so drained it didn't matter.

"Oh, Edie, this must've been *horrifying* for you and Cole," Sugar said, "just *horrifying*." She had a tight grip on the short strand of pearls around her neck.

"Are the two of you alright?" Cookie asked.

"Yes, ma'am," Cole answered as he took my hand and held it. "Just a little shaken up."

"Edie, do you need a Coke or something?" Coco asked, a worried frown on her face. "You look a little pale."

I shook my head.

"What about you, Cole?" she asked.

"I'm fine, Miss Coco, but thanks," he said. "Did they tell you ladies how long it might be before we hear anything?"

"No," Cookie said. "I guess all we can do is wait."

I felt so strange, like I was in some sort of bubble that isolated me from everyone else. I was in the same room with them but not really. My mind kept flashing from long red hair floating in the ocean to Leni covered with tubes in a New York ICU, to Jason handing me a teacup, to Cole diving off his plane into the water, and back to Leni. I felt like I was the one drowning.

Cole took my chin in his hand and turned my face toward him. He was looking straight into my eyes as he pressed two fingers against my neck. I had no idea why. "Here, why don't you lie down for a bit," he said as he helped me turn around. "Lie on your back and rest your head in my lap. You can put your feet up on the arm of the seat."

I wordlessly obeyed and lay down, propping my feet up. He slowly stroked my hair until I couldn't hold my eyes open anymore. I didn't want to hold them open. I wanted to sink deep down into sleep, far removed from another terrifying trip to a cold, gray emergency room where the life of someone I loved hung in the balance.

---

When I woke up, Cole was looking down at me. I turned my head and saw empty chairs where the Ten Spots had been. Slowly sitting up, I smiled at Cole. "Hey," I said.

He smiled back. "Hey yourself."

I looked around the lobby, then spotted a clock on the wall. We had probably gotten to the hospital around eleven. Now it was one thirty.

"I slept for two hours?" I couldn't believe I had been out for that long.

"Just about." He brushed my hair away from my face. My head was clearing.

"Cole, you must be exhausted. First you swam for Charly's life and then you sat here like my human pillow."

"Don't worry about me."

"Can't help it." I kissed him on the cheek. "What happened while I was out? How's Charly?"

"She'll be fine physically. They admitted her for observation overnight. Just moved her to a room a few minutes ago. The ladies decided their whole group would be too much for her, so your grandmother stayed and the others went home."

"You said she'd be fine *physically*. What exactly does that mean?"

Cole ran his fingers through his hair a couple of times. "It means she's in the psychiatric ward, Edie."

"The *what*?" I sat straight up.

"The doctor who admitted her had reservations about her mental state, and he doesn't even know everything that led up to her swim. He saw enough cause for concern in her demeanor and her answers to routine questions."

"But was it really serious enough for something so drastic?"

"I've seen perfectly capable pilots get pushed beyond their limits and need help. It can happen to anybody. I mean, think about it for a minute. Think about how you'd read her actions if you weren't so close to her. She lied about where she was going. She didn't take your Pop's boat even though it was right there. She hired a charter, but only for a one-way trip. What does that tell you?"

I felt a little sick. "She didn't plan on coming back."

"She was swimming out to sea on purpose, Edie. But to be fair, we don't know if she stopped swimming intentionally or changed her mind after she was too exhausted to turn back. We don't know what she was thinking, only what she was doing."

"You're right. We don't." I tried to smooth my rumpled clothes, still damp from our ordeal with Charly. "Why have I been so foggy?"

"I think you were in shock. Your skin was cold and a little clammy. Your breathing was shallow and your heartbeat was fast. You had a hard time understanding things."

I rubbed my eyes, trying to wake myself up. "I sound like a real catch."

Cole laughed and put his arm around me. I rested my head on his shoulder. "Edie, you reacted just fine when it counted. You're the one who realized Charlotte had stopped swimming. You were quick to pull her up like I asked you to, and you started CPR on your own. You didn't let anybody down. But that first rescue—knowing that another person's life depends on what you do—well, it's mind-blowing. Everybody needs a little time to level off."

I looked up at him and smiled. "You really were something out there."

"Back at you."

"What are we going to do, Cole? About your uncle and Charly?"

"I think we need to make a trip to New Orleans."

# thirty-three

**"I CAN'T BELIEVE WE GET TO DO THIS."** Cole had never traveled my favorite route to New Orleans, and I think it was safe to say he was impressed. "It's so . . . *real*."

We had the top down on the T-bird, traveling through the waterscapes of US 90.

"I feel like I could reach out my window and touch one of those shrimp boats." He put his hand out the window just as we passed a trawler in the Rigolets, then looked at me and smiled. Windblown blond hair, aviator sunglasses, lethal right dimple.

"Well, did you touch it?" I asked.

"Just missed."

"How about an Otis search?" I turned on the radio and worked the dial till I heard Ben E. King singing "Stand by Me." "It's not Otis, but it's pretty righteous," I said.

Cole gave me a thumbs-up. Watching the wind blow his hair and the smile he couldn't fight off on this great old highway, surrounded by marshes and bayous just a stone's throw from the Mississippi *and* the gulf, well . . . I could've died happy right then.

The next thing we knew, the Temptations were coming at us with "My Girl."

"Now that's just too much," Cole said, pulling into a dusty gas station parking lot. Leaving the engine running and the radio on, he jumped out of the car, came around to open my door, and we danced to the Temps right there on a tiny Louisiana byway in front of a two-pump gas station with a big minnow tank by the door and a special on crab traps. We couldn't stop laughing. When the song finally ended, three guys in white shrimp boots—all standing by the entrance watching us—applauded. We took a bow and got back in the car.

Just outside of New Orleans, Cole pulled into a new-looking gas station where I felt confident the restrooms would be clean. I freshened up while he gassed up, trying to still my jitters about meeting not only his uncle, who was important to him, but the long-lost Connor. I had claw-clipped my hair to keep it from becoming a tangled rat's nest with the top down on the T-bird. Now we were close enough to the Garden District for me to take it down and brush it. I blotted my face with a damp paper towel.

Thank goodness Cole liked to travel in comfort, so we had kept the top up and the AC blasting until we reached a spot just over the Louisiana state line where the road got especially interesting. Then Cole put the top down but kept the cold air coming. Otherwise I'd be a sweaty mess. I had worn a sleeveless, lightweight cotton wrap dress and sandals, which I hoped would keep me as cool as it was possible to be in New Orleans this time of year.

Back at the car, Cole opened my door for me. "Ready for the last leg?"

"Ready," I said as I got into the car. "A little nervous but ready."

"You're entitled to be nervous." He leaned into the car and kissed me. "But you really don't have anything to worry about. You'll see."

Soon we left the real world behind and crossed the Mississippi River into the wonderland that is New Orleans. This time we'd bypass the French Quarter and head straight to the Garden District, a quieter neighborhood of gracious historic homes, iron fences, and oak-shaded streets.

"That's my uncle's house." Cole pointed to a pale yellow five-bay with white columns and trim. Tall windows with forest-green shutters flanked a centered main entrance that led off the deep front porch. I couldn't wait to see inside.

We pulled around back, where a security-coded gate opened to a brick parking pad. Cole opened my door for me, and I grabbed the straw tote that held three potentially life-changing photos. He took me by the hand as we followed a manicured path to the front door and rang the bell.

My heart began to pound. Cole's uncle. Charly's lost love. I flinched slightly when I heard the door opening. Cole squeezed my hand. And there he was, standing in the doorway—a tall man with gray-streaked blond hair and kind brown eyes. They had a few lines around them now, but I knew them from Charly's drawing just the same.

"You must be Edie."

"Edie, this is my Uncle Connor," Cole said. "Uncle Connor, this is *the* Edie."

His uncle smiled and took my hand. "I'm very happy to meet you, *the* Edie."

"So nice to meet you," I said. "Thank you for having us."

"Come on in," he said. "How are you, buddy?" He put his hand on Cole's shoulder as he welcomed us into the house, which had a long central hallway and heart pine floors.

251

"Doing great," Cole said. "We had the best drive over. Edie introduced me to the US 90 route from Mississippi."

"Now that's a good one," said his uncle. "I make a point to drive it now and then just to see how close a stretch of pavement can get to water."

"I think the answer's 'pretty darn close,'" Cole said as his uncle led us down the hallway to a comfortable sunroom overlooking a shady walled garden. A slight woman who looked to be in her late sixties brought in a tray holding a pitcher and three glasses already filled and iced. The drink looked like tea but had a hint of red that I didn't recognize.

"Porcine, what are you doing carrying that tray?" Cole's uncle got up and took it from her. "You can't lift anything heavy or you'll strain your knee."

The woman put her hands on her hips. "Dr. Conny, you gonna help me right out of a job."

"No, I'm not." He smiled at her as he set the tray on an iron stand and began serving us. "But if I don't see an ice pack on that knee next time I come in the kitchen, I'll operate on you again."

"Have to catch me first." Porcine handed us napkins and strode out of the room as well as she could with a slight limp.

"I think she might be the boss o' you, Dr. Donovan," I said.

"Please call me Connor. No formalities here. And yes. She is absolutely the boss o' me."

"How long has she worked for you?" I asked as he sat down with us.

"Forever. This house would cave in without her. She spends more time in it than I do. I did a knee replacement on her about two months ago, and she refuses to take care of herself. She says I'll fire her if she doesn't do her work. I'd sooner fire my charge nurse, and the whole orthopedic wing would go down without her." He took a sip of tea and nodded. "That's a good batch. I have no idea how she makes it, though. Say, how's the photography going, Edie? Cole tells me you're really good."

"Cole is kind," I said. "But I'm excited about the possibilities. And we've had a lot of fun flying over to Horn Island to take pictures. I might be gettin' a little uppity with all these private plane rides to my shoots."

"Something tells me you're not prone to that," he said.

Cole spoke up. "Not one bit. She won't brag on herself, but I've never seen better pictures of Horn."

"Thank you," I said. "And I'll reciprocate. You're a *fine* pilot . . . and you fly well too."

Cole and his uncle both laughed. "Edie, consider me in your camp, one hundred percent," Connor said.

I raised my glass to him. "Happy and honored to have you."

"How's the T-bird, Cole?" he asked.

"Running like a train. And the new radio we put in last time sounds terrific."

His uncle smiled and nodded. "Good to see you've got your priorities in order."

It's strange, but as we laughed and talked and he did everything he could to put me at ease, I temporarily forgot who I was with—not just Connor, Cole's uncle, but *the* Connor, the missing piece in Charly's life all these years. And something else. I was beginning to think he had a missing piece too. He gave us a tour of his home, which was elegant and refined, but it could've belonged to anybody. There were no signs of attachment, no sense of personal history, of a place treasured and lived in like Punk's house. It held not one hint of who he loved and what his life was about, a contradiction for one so warm and welcoming.

Eventually, the three of us moved to a veranda with ceiling fans stirring the air to keep us cool. It overlooked the garden we had seen from the sunroom. Porcine had arranged glasses of lemonade and a plate of tea cakes on a small table, where we all sat down in some of the most unusual antique wicker rockers I had ever seen—heavy on the Victorian, but in a good way.

"Doctor—sorry, Connor—you said that Porcine spends more time in your house than you do. You must work long hours at the hospital."

"I do, but that's not the only reason. I've just never been much of a city dweller. Whenever I'm not working late or on call, I head to my fishing cabin south of New Orleans. That's where I feel the most at home."

"The one Dad helped you build?" Cole asked.

"That's the one. Whenever I've got a choice between sitting here in a rocking chair or sitting there on my dock with a fishing rod in my hand, well, no contest."

"When did you buy this house?" Cole asked.

"Two of my nurses picked it out five or six years ago. Before, I had a little shotgun house that suited me fine. But once the hospital made me chief of orthopedics, the nurses said I should be better prepared to entertain prospective recruits and donors."

"That doesn't sound like you," Cole said.

"Believe me, it's not," his uncle agreed. "I know I'm a dinosaur, but I've always believed that doctors—everybody, really—ought to serve wherever they feel called, not wherever they can claim the biggest paycheck. And the donors I choose to work with believe rich people ought to help poor people because it's the right thing to do, not because they want to be wined and dined while they rub elbows with each other. I'll probably sell this place pretty soon and buy another shotgun that's easier on Porcine."

"That's just so sad." The words popped out of my mouth before I could stop them.

"What is?" Cole's uncle asked me.

"I just hate to think of you living in a house that doesn't feel like home."

"Don't worry," he said with a smile. "I promise I'm not some lost soul wandering these well-appointed but lonely hallways at night. I'm not here much, and when I do stay, it's because I'm entertaining for the hospital or I'm so exhausted I just want to sleep."

"If you don't mind my asking, what made you stay in New Orleans if you'd rather be someplace in the country?" I asked.

He took a drink of lemonade. "I've just always felt a pull to this coast, and New Orleans was the best place for me to practice because the hospital is big enough and bankrolled enough to offer outreach care to the small communities around the city, which is probably what I enjoy the most. I guess I've stayed here mainly for the hospital. And I've grown close to the staff. I'm lucky to have a lot of good friends in New Orleans."

We sipped our lemonade, and Cole had a tea cake. Finally, his uncle looked from one of us to the other and said, "I should probably tell you both that one of the skills I've acquired as a doctor is the ability to tell when one of my patients is holding something back. Not that I wouldn't be happy to see you for any reason, but I get the feeling you came here to talk about something in particular."

Cole and I looked at each other. "I guess I'll start," he said. "Uncle Connor, Dad always told me that I shouldn't ask you about Hurricane Camille. And I can understand why you wouldn't want to talk about it."

"It's not so much that I don't want to. It's that I can't. My first clear recollections begin after I had been in the hospital for two weeks. Everything before that is a weird mix of hazy images that don't make much sense." Connor turned to me. "Is this about the exhibition Cole mentioned to me, Edie? I'll help you however I can, but I doubt I have much to offer."

"No, sir, it's not about the exhibition, not directly anyway. You see, two of the survivors I've talked with had memories of a young man they met in the storm. We think he might be you."

"Me?"

"We're not sure," Cole said, "but it looks that way." He turned to me. "Want to show him the pictures?"

I went back to the sunroom and took them from my tote bag. The first image I handed to Cole's uncle was the man on the stretcher. "Could the injured man be you?"

We watched as he studied the picture. "That's me alright. See?" He pointed to something I had noticed in the picture before but didn't know how to pursue—a small bowie knife tattooed on the inside of the man's forearm. Connor held up the same arm. And there it was. "Not one of my better choices, but I guess I thought it would make me look tough in the Army." He looked at the picture again. "So this is how it all started, I guess. Strange to see myself as a patient. Man, would you look at that leg. It's a thousand wonders I didn't bleed to death before they found me on that island. And a thousand more I can walk at all."

He returned the picture to me. I took out another and passed it across the table. "She might be the reason why."

He frowned as he stared at the image of Nora. "Who's this?"

"That's Nora Gilliam," I explained. "She's one of the Camille survivors I wanted to tell you about. She described a young man who washed ashore on Deer Island with her and two other women. His leg injury was just like the one in the other picture. Nora tore off the bottom of his pants leg and led him down to the saltwater, hoping it would cauterize the wound and keep him from bleeding to death. She also built a fire to keep the mosquitoes away. That fire helped the Coast Guard spot you. The picture you're holding is Nora right after she saw a couple of airmen put the man on the stretcher—put you—onto a helicopter. She was photographed in a triage center."

He raised his eyebrows. "Well, would you look at that." He tapped the image with his finger. "I've had so many dreams about a fire with water behind it. I always thought it had something to do with the hurricane, but the storm came in at night, and the fire in my dreams always burned in daylight. Now I know who built it. Your Nora saved my life."

"What she remembered most about you was your kindness," I said. "Even though you were badly hurt and probably in shock, you still gave her your shirt to protect her from the mosquitoes. They airlifted you before she could return it. She told me she held on to it for years, hoping to see you again and thank you."

Connor slowly stood up from the table and walked to the edge of the veranda, where he stood with his hands in his pockets, his back to us. "Edie," he said, "did Nora mention anything about a beautiful girl with long red hair and blue eyes?"

Cole and I looked at each other. "No, sir," I said. "But we know who she is. She's the other survivor who remembers you. She's actually been looking for you. For a long time now."

"Charlotte," he said quietly, turning to face us. "That's her name, isn't it?"

"That's right."

"Then she's real? I didn't hallucinate her in some fever dream?"

"No, you didn't."

Connor came back to the table, sat down, and leaned back in his chair as if he were suddenly very tired. "I just can't believe this."

I handed him the last picture I had brought with me, one of the environmental portraits I had taken for the merchants' walk. It was Charly sitting on the beach, the water behind her, the morning sun on her face, an ocean breeze in her hair.

"She's my godmother, my mother's best friend from childhood. Her full name is Charlotte Moran. She grew up in Louisiana but moved to Biloxi right after high school, the summer of '68."

"Do you remember her, Uncle Connor?" Cole asked.

He took a deep breath and let out a long, weary sigh. "I've dreamed about her so many times over the years. I thought I had invented her when I was on heavy pain meds for so long. I always see her in the same two spots—a sunny street where she smiles up at me and says, 'Well, I guess I owe you dinner,' and in the water at night, swimming in huge waves and calling my name as I call hers."

"Both of those are real," I said. I explained why she'd

owed him dinner and how Camille had destroyed Louella's house, throwing them both into the water, where they swam for their lives, calling each other's names. "Charly landed in a tree," I told him. "Then she was flown to a hospital in Pensacola for a week. After that, she came back to Biloxi to look for you. But she didn't even know your last name, and everything had been destroyed by the storm. She had no way to find you."

"What about you, Uncle Connor?" Cole asked. "What happened to you after that chopper picked you up in Biloxi?"

"Nothing good, at least not for a while." He handed me the portrait and took a sip of lemonade. "They flew me to Houston with a concussion, a splintered tibia, and the beginning of an infection in the deep gash on my leg. That turned septic. I had multiple surgeries and a battery of intravenous antibiotics during a month-long hospital stay. Then I went into rehab for a month, where I got another infection. Went back to the hospital, back to rehab—I bounced between the two for six months after Camille."

"That sounds awful," I said. "Were you all by yourself?"

"I had my share of miracles along the way. The medevac pilot who flew me to Houston had served with my brother, Jeff—that's Cole's dad—in Vietnam. He got a message to Jeff, who got one to my parents. The pilot volunteered to fly up to Arkansas and bring our baby sister down to Houston. Ruthie stayed with me for almost a year. She's the one who worked everything out with Tulane so I could start medical school with the next cohort after I recovered."

"Did you ever come back to Biloxi?" I asked.

He shook his head. "In more recent years, but not back then. Once I saw pictures of the aftermath, well . . . there wasn't anything left. And I thought Charlotte was somebody

I dreamed up when I was out of my head with infection and pain killers."

"She's very real," I said.

"You said she's been looking for me?"

"That's right."

"But why?"

"That's probably something for the two of you to talk about," Cole said. "She'll be at Edie's exhibition. Why don't you come? You and Charlotte can talk it over."

He smiled at Cole. "Be sure and tell your dad I said you're a lot smarter than he is."

# thirty-four

**"DON'T TELL LIBBA."** That was the first thing Charly said to Punk when she was fully at herself in the hospital. She knew Mama would be on the first plane to Mississippi and didn't want to ruin her time overseas with my dad. I guess that's why I felt a special responsibility to be there for her. I was trying to fill in as best I could for my mother—for Charly's Leni.

I pulled Rosetta into the parking lot of a private psychiatric clinic that Sugar had arranged. When Charly's ER doctor suggested a state hospital, the Ten Spots put their collective foot down and told him that would not be happening. Or, as Coco reportedly put it, "Over our soon-to-be dead bodies."

Sugar used the influence her philanthropy wielded and got Charly admitted to a top-tier clinic in Mobile. "It's where movie stars go when they want to keep it hush-hush," she said.

The grounds were gorgeous. Rolling, manicured lawns as lush as velvet, centuries-old live oaks, and a facility that looked more like an estate than a clinic. I followed a sidewalk through an allée of crepe myrtles, climbed marble steps to the front porch, and went inside.

The receptionist was probably in her fifties and wore an expensive-looking yellow suit. Her hair, nails, and makeup were almost Sugar quality.

"Good morning," she said. "My name is Leslie. How may I be of assistance?"

"Hello. I'm Edie Gardner. I've come to drive one of your patients home—a family friend. Charlotte Moran?"

She nodded as if she had been expecting me. "Yes, of course. Ms. Moran's discharge is complete. She's been given a folder with all of her paperwork. Allow me to escort you."

I followed Leslie down a corridor and out French doors that led to a large flagstone terrace surrounded by orderly flower beds.

"Ms. Moran is right over there," Leslie said, gesturing toward a porch swing hanging from an iron frame with purple clematis trained over it. "I'll have her suitcase brought down so it'll be waiting for you. Should you need anything at all before your departure, just let me know. Take as long as you like."

I thanked her and turned my attention to Charly. "Chouchou?" I said as I approached her.

"Hey there, chouchou." She got up and hugged me, holding on longer than she ever had. "You're a sight for sore eyes, kiddo."

"Glad to be going home?" I asked her.

Charly gave me a weary shrug. "Part of me is. Part of me would like to stay hidden away here from now on. But I'm told that's 'not in my best interest.' Would you mind if we sit for a minute before we go?"

We sat down in the swing. Charly reached over and took

my hand. "I really made a mess of things this time, Edie. You and Cole could've gotten badly hurt trying to help me."

"We didn't, though." I squeezed her hand. "If Jason hadn't sent us there—"

"Jason?" She frowned, trying to make the connection. "I thought Punk sent you to Horn."

"She was worried about you. Then Jason stopped by to say he had gotten word that a woman I needed to interview was on Horn but only till noon. Cole and I promised to find you and check on you when we flew over there for the interview."

"Did you find her—the survivor?"

I shook my head. "We never even looked for her. That reminds me—I need to call her. Cole spotted you in the water before we landed. After that, we forgot all about the woman Jason sent us to see."

"Jason saved my life."

"In a way, yes. If he hadn't sent us over there and made it urgent . . . I can't even think about that, Charly. I can't think about losing you."

She put her arms around me, stroking my hair the way Mama does when I'm sad or worried about something. "I did a mighty selfish thing, Edie. And I'm sorry—for scaring you most of all."

We sat there, rocking in the swing, before I had to ask the question lurking between us. "Charly, you don't have to answer me if you don't want to, but I think I have to ask. Did you want to die?"

"No," she said. "Not consciously anyway."

I sat up and looked at her.

"I've had some pretty major bouts of depression in my time, Edie, but nothing like the pit I started sliding into right before Miss Punk called and asked me to come down. I was

263

already halfway to the bottom when we started *Confessions*, and all the memories of Connor got churned up again. I started dwelling on all the things I'd missed—from parents who loved me to a husband and family. And I completely lost sight of all the ways I've been blessed—you, Libba, Punk, meaningful work that I love, the freedom and means to see the world. Everything just snowballed, I guess."

"What made you go to Horn?"

"I was hoping to see the light again."

"And did you?"

"Yes. I said a prayer on the island. I asked God to please let me see the light one more time. If only I could do that, I thought, I could find my way out of the pit. But when it appeared, so pure and clean and perfect, all I could think was, 'I don't deserve this. I'm not worthy of it.'"

"Charly, nobody's worthy. Punk says we live in a state called Grace, and God built us all houses there."

That made her smile. "Sounds like Miss Punk." Charly gathered her hair and pulled it all over one shoulder. She slowly braided it as we talked. "What I need you to understand, Edie—you maybe more than anyone else—is that I didn't go out to Horn to take my own life. I lied to Miss Punk about where I was going because I needed time alone but didn't want her to worry. And before you even say it, I know—nothing could keep her from worrying about the people she loves."

"True."

"Anyway, I needed some solitude. I needed to think. I needed to find some silence because there was so much noise in my brain."

"But how were you planning to get back?"

"The kids are still out of school. I guess I figured there

would be plenty of boat traffic the next day to hitch a ride back to Punk's, and I had enough supplies to last a couple of days. That way I could take all the time I needed instead of getting locked into a charter schedule."

"So you *did* plan on coming back?"

"Yes. At least I think I did. To tell you the truth, I'm not sure what my intentions were anymore. That's something I have to work on. I just remember seeing the light and then going into a not-good-enough spiral. That's when the idea came to me. I'd take all my regret and disappointment into the gulf and let the water wash it away. I just waded in and started swimming. No direction, no plan, no nothing. I guess I wanted to take my old lonely, confused self down into the gulf and let it be raised up new." She laid her hand against my face. "You know the rest."

"Charly," I said, "you're the bravest person I know."

# thirty-five

**I WAS ABOUT TO MEET** with an events specialist at the library and deliver the last of the plaques bearing photo captions I had written for all the images:

*Built in 1849, Trinity Episcopal Church survived eighteen hurricanes before Camille.*

*Airman Timothy Ellsworth carries eighty-year-old "Miss Helen" Jamison to a medevac helicopter bound for Pensacola, Florida.*

*Paul Williams stands behind the headstone marking thirteen family members lost to Camille.*

It was hard to read those captions and feel anything close to professional pride. What I felt was sorrow for the overwhelming loss, but also encouragement from the faith and strength of the survivors. I might have cataloged the storm, but they lived it. I could only hope that Jason and I had done them justice.

The night before the opening, Cole came to dinner at Punk's. When I answered the doorbell, he was standing there with a large gift box wrapped in satiny white paper with an enormous yellow department-store bow. "A little break-a-leg present," he said before he kissed me hello.

We sat down together in Punk's living room. "Did you make this swanky bow yourself?" I asked.

"I did not."

"It's impressive." Tugging it off, I tore the paper away and gasped when I looked inside the box.

"Thought you might like to wear a yellow dress to the opening," Cole said.

I stood and held it up to myself—a marigold-yellow crepe sheath dress. Simple, elegant, and respectful. But also hopeful.

"Cole, I absolutely love it! It's perfect. Thank you." I laid the dress across a chair as he stood up, put his arms around me, and kissed me.

"It's a beautiful thing you're doing, Edie. I thought you should have something beautiful for yourself."

I looked up at him. "Are you as anxious about tomorrow as I am?"

"I've got combat-level jitters. But Miss Punk and the ladies were right. After all they've been through, Charly and Uncle Connor deserve to find each other for themselves." He kissed me softly. "Just like we did."

# *thirty-six*

**A BIG SURPRISE GREETED ME** at the library—two mammoth banners hanging on either side of the main entrance:

## MISSISSIPPI & CAMILLE
A Photographic Retrospective
Presented by The Trove
Edie Gardner, Curator
August 17–September 1

"What do you think?"

I turned to see Jason standing behind me. "I think your name should be on that banner," I said.

He shook his head. "No. I merely approved your good choices. This is your exhibit, Edie. You did all the hard work—the painful work—of gathering and interpreting survivor stories. Your grandmother and her friends will be very proud. Where are they, by the way?"

"Cole's bringing them. He said he thought I might want a few minutes with the exhibit before I share it with everybody."

"I couldn't agree more," Jason said. "I'll keep myself busy and give you time alone."

"No, Jason. We've come this far. We should finish together, don't you think?"

He smiled and led me inside to the exhibit hall. Even though I had studied these images a million times and watched the exhibition come together, nothing compared to seeing it complete like this, the pictures enlarged so that every detail came to life. The exhibition hall was rectangular, the walls and ceiling clean and white, the floor reclaimed cypress. Track lighting was arranged to leave dim spaces between the images, putting the focus on the subject matter—Camille and the lives it changed forever.

Jason had agreed with me on the bookends for the exhibit: two large, mounted Scripture passages. Verses from Psalm 89 marked the entrance to the exhibition hall:

> You, Lord, are mighty,
> and your faithfulness surrounds you.
> You rule over the surging sea;
> when its waves mount up, you still them.

Just outside the exit doors, we had filled a large wall with words from Psalm 107:

> Then they cried out to the Lord in their trouble,
> and he brought them out of their distress.
> He stilled the storm to a whisper;
> the waves of the sea were hushed.

As Jason and I silently toured the exhibit, we passed images I knew like the back of my hand. The church ladies in their yellow dresses, young parents dedicating their baby,

Sarah Parsons grasping at a picture in her yard. That was the one I had been trying to learn more about when Cole and I flew to Horn and found Charly in the water.

I pointed to Sarah. "Jason, do you realize that if you hadn't sent me to Horn to talk with this woman, Charly wouldn't be alive today? Even if you had waited just thirty minutes more to tell me, Charly wouldn't have survived because Cole and I wouldn't have gotten there in time."

He gave me The Stare, which I was expecting. "You're seeing mercy, Edie?"

I nodded. "You saved her life, Jason. You might've been sending me to do an interview, but you got me there in time for Cole to pull Charly out of the water."

"All things together for the good?"

"Yes. And I'm very grateful."

He smiled. "So am I, Edie. If you'll excuse me, I'm going to leave you to see the rest of the exhibit on your own."

As he started to walk away, I said, "Jason? That's two out of three."

He stopped and turned back to me. "What do you mean?"

"The writing in the sand you translated for me: 'Help one, save one, lead one home.' You helped me. You saved Charly. Who are you going to lead home?"

For a moment, we stood there looking at each other in the empty exhibit hall. Finally, Jason slowly shook his head. "I don't know, Edie. I never know until it's time."

He backed away from me a few steps before leaving me alone, surrounded by images that were equal parts heartbreak and hope.

I made my way through them until I came to the picture that had been circling in my mind since I first saw it. The lone image hanging on the rear wall of the exhibit bridged pictures of destruction on the left wall and those of recovery on the right. The solitary man on a stretcher—Connor Donovan—looked lonelier and sadder than ever.

"Edie? Are you here?"

"Be right there, Charly." I hurried back to the entrance and found her standing before side-by-side pictures of the Biloxi lighthouse and Beach Boulevard before and after the storm.

She put her arms around me and held me tight. "You've done an amazing thing, chouchou. So many people still have wounds from Camille. You're going to help them heal. I just know it." She let go and stepped back.

"Sure you're alright, Charly?"

She smiled and nodded. "I'm fine, sweetie. And I want to be here. Mind if I drift on my own?"

I hugged her again before she began working her way to the picture I knew was calling to her most of all. And then I heard the Ten Spots.

"Sweet girl, I'm so proud of you!" Punk came to me with open arms and held me in one of her wonderful vise hugs.

When she finally let go, I kissed her on the cheek. "A hug from you is better than the keys to the city."

She laughed and gave me another clench embrace, whispering in my ear, "Forget that newspaper and work for yourself! Just look at what you can do!"

"This is impressive, kiddo," Coco said.

"I think it's just *mahvelous*!" Sugar squeezed my hand. "And you look *gaw-uh-geous*!"

"Thank you, Miss Sugar."

"In case you're wondering, we didn't do away with Cole," Cookie said. "He's parking the car."

Just as she said it, he came in and kissed me. "I like the banners out front," he said, "and you're a stunner in yellow."

271

"This old rag?" I said, which made him laugh. "Jason was mighty generous with the banner."

"Jason was truthful," Cole countered.

"I see Charlotte came even earlier than we did," Punk said.

"Yes, ma'am," I said. "She wanted a little time to herself."

Thank goodness Sugar had worn a strand of pearls because she was clutching it like nobody's business. "Oh, I just don't know if I can stand this. I *so* hope it goes well, I truly do."

"We all do, Shug," Cookie said.

"But are we absolutely *suhtain* we were right not to tell her?" Sugar was working herself into a full-blown tizzy.

"Oh, for heaven's sake, Shug," Coco said. "What if we'd told her and then he got called into surgery or something? What if he changed his mind and didn't want to meet her? We couldn't risk it. Besides, the two of them deserve their moment."

We could hear noise beyond the closed doors to the exhibit hall as visitors gathered, waiting for the doors to open. A docent cracked one just enough to let Connor inside. Cole shook his hand and was about to introduce him to the Ten Spots when his uncle spotted Charlotte, her back to us, standing before the picture of him lying on that stretcher, injured and alone after a great storm. She slowly raised her hand as if she were about to touch his face but then must've remembered where she was and pulled it back.

He started walking toward her, slowly at first, but then faster as he crossed the length of the long exhibition hall, stopped a few yards away from her, and called her name. "Charlotte?"

She slowly turned. For a moment, she stared at him in silence, her lips slightly parted. At last, she said, "Connor?"

Her soft voice echoed in the exhibit hall, empty now except for us.

They both froze, arms at their sides, like two birds who might at any moment frighten each other into taking flight, never to land in the same place again.

She took a step forward.

He quickly crossed the space between them and held her face in his hands. "I thought I dreamed you."

"Where were you, Connor? You've been lost to me for so long."

He looked up at the picture. "I was there, on that stretcher. And then I was sick, for almost a year. I didn't know you were real, Charlotte. I've been seeing you in my dreams for years. I thought I made you up to help me get through all those awful months after the storm."

"You didn't make me up." She began to cry. "I just couldn't find you."

# *thirty-seven*

**"THERE YOU ARE, EDIE."**

"Jason, can you believe this? I never dreamed so many people would come on the first day. It's almost closing time and the crowd is just now thinning out."

"You have much to be proud of," he said.

"You mean *we*."

He smiled. "Alright then. What I came to tell you is that I ran into your newspaper editor earlier, and he said he might be able to hire you as early as October. Something about bean counters. I just want you to know that I'll not hold you back if that's what you'd like to do."

"I appreciate it, Jason. I really do. But the truth is, I'm having second thoughts. Punk says I should consider working for myself—shooting for myself. What do you think?"

"I think your grandmother is wise beyond her years. By the way, I understand some space will soon be available on Howard Avenue."

"Where?"

"We can talk about it on Tuesday. I believe you have a visitor."

I turned to see Cole coming into the exhibit hall. He had driven the Ten Spots home but came back to stay with me. Almost everyone had left when I spotted her—Sarah Parsons—standing in front of the picture I wanted to ask her about.

"Cole, look. That's her. The woman we were supposed to meet on Horn. Can we talk to her for just a minute before we leave?"

"Sure."

We walked over to Sarah together. "Excuse me, Mrs. Parsons?"

"Yes?" She dabbed at her eyes with a handkerchief as she turned around.

"My name's Edie Gardner. This is my friend Cole. I worked on the exhibit for The Trove."

"You're the one who left the messages for me?"

"Yes, ma'am. I hope I wasn't a pest."

She reached out and squeezed my hand. "Oh, no, dear. Not at all. Please call me Sarah."

"I wanted you to know that Cole and I flew to Horn when we heard that you were over there camping and were willing to talk with us. But we had a family emergency and had to leave. I'm sorry we couldn't make it to your campsite."

Sarah was frowning and shaking her head. "There must be some mistake. I've never camped on Horn in my life."

Cole and I glanced at each other. "Well . . . Jason—he's my boss at The Trove—he said he got a message that a Camille survivor I had been trying to reach was camping on Horn. You were the only one I had been calling, so I assumed it was you."

"Wasn't me on that island," Sarah said with a shudder. "I'll never let myself get surrounded by water again. One awful night of that was enough to last me a lifetime."

275

"I understand. Jason and I must've miscommunicated somehow. I'd still love to talk with you sometime but only if you're comfortable with it."

She was smiling again. "Of course."

"I want to give you the opportunity to speak to the picture so that we can have a plaque made with a photo caption. Those are important, I think, in helping visitors understand what they see."

Sarah turned and gazed at her own image. "You know, I listened to the people around me when they looked at me up there. One woman said she couldn't understand why anybody would be desperate to save pictures when they didn't even have a roof over their head. But that's a picture of my husband I'm reaching for. He drowned in the storm. I knew that all I had left of him was lying there scattered on the ground. Everything else got blown away."

Without thinking, I put my arms around her. She held on and cried on my shoulder.

When she finally stepped back, she said, "You let them know, Edie. Let them know things aren't always what they look like. Those people standing around me in this libr'y looked at my picture and thought they saw foolishness. But what they were looking at was the deepest kind of grief a woman can feel. You tell them that, Edie. Okay?"

I reached out and held her hand. "I promise."

# thirty-eight

"HAVE YOU LANDED YET?" Punk kissed me on the cheek and handed me a cup of coffee.

"I'm not sure, Punk. That was one amazing weekend we had."

"Yes, it was, sweet girl. Yes, it was. I thought you could use a little extra fortification." She handed me a bowl of shrimp and grits.

"Bless you, Punk." We sat down at her table.

"I have news," my grandmother said. "There's going to be a wedding."

My fork stopped in midair. "Whose?"

"Charlotte and Connor's."

"I thought they were getting married at the courthouse today."

"They are, but Coco has talked them into what she calls a real wedding in her garden."

"Miss Coco? Not Miss Sugar?"

"I know. It surprised me too. But I think Coco has always had a soft spot for Charlotte. She said a marriage this long awaited deserves to be properly celebrated. No word yet on whether Pierre will be officiating."

"When is it?" I asked.

"This coming Saturday morning at ten. Coco says there's no reason to dillydally. As it turns out, Connor hasn't taken a vacation in two years, so the hospital is happy to give him a little time off."

"Where do you think they'll go on their honeymoon?"

"Biloxi, Mississippi."

*"Ma'am?"*

Punk clapped her hands together and laughed. "They're going to spend their honeymoon house hunting. Charlotte has always loved Biloxi. And Connor says he's never felt at home in New Orleans, even with all the friends he's made and the work he loves. He'll adjust his schedule so he can commute—part of the week here and part there—till they figure out the long term."

"And all this happened in the past two days?"

Punk took a bite of her grits and blotted her mouth. "I guess once you've waited thirty years, you don't want to wait any more. I'm taking the crew dress shopping. Want to come?"

"No, ma'am, I'm heading over to the gallery."

"I thought you didn't work on Mondays."

"Not usually. But the exhibition occupied so much of my time that I don't know much about everything else. I thought I'd spend the morning over there and get everything situated in my mind before I have to tell the garden club ladies whether I can give them a ten percent discount on the Victorian birdbaths."

I took one last swig of my coffee and put my dishes in the sink before kissing Punk on the cheek and grabbing my purse and camera bag—a habit I had developed getting ready for the merchants' walk.

"Edie," Punk said, "I know this will sound like I'm meddling, because I am. But I hope you'll give some serious thought to that bug I put in your ear." She got up from the table and laid her hands on my shoulders. "You've got real talent, sweet girl. Sometimes we have to take a chance on ourselves."

Mississippi in August is an oven, plain and simple, and it'll bake you in a heartbeat. The only place to be is in the water or as close as you can get to an air conditioner on full blast. Five seconds away from Rosetta's AC and I started sweating. I couldn't wait to get inside The Trove.

Hurrying down the side street from a city parking lot, I was about a half block from the gallery when I could see something in the display window, and it wasn't merchandise. In fact, the whole window looked empty. I crossed the street and stood on the sidewalk in front of a sign propped in the window: CLOSED FOR REMODELING.

I tried the door. It was locked. I looked for the thin streak of light usually visible to the right of the black curtain behind the window display. It was dark.

My heart pounded and I struggled to breathe. Jason had no reason to remodel the gallery if he intended to stay. That meant he intended to leave.

# thirty-nine

**BY THE TIME I DROPPED ANCHOR,** the sky was mercifully overcast, though the air was still heavy with humidity. For once, I hadn't brought my camera. Or much of anything else.

Cole was flying. The Ten Spots were shopping. I needed a shoulder to cry on, so I had taken Pop's boat to Horn, which never failed to offer consolation.

Jumping off the side, I felt the cool, refreshing saltwater swirl around my legs as my feet sank into the sand. The tide stubbornly tugged at me with each step.

I spread a beach towel in the sand and set down my cooler, then started walking the beach, letting the surf wash over my feet. The initial panic I had felt at The Trove began to subside, and I could breathe again. I heard the loud flap of large wings overhead and looked up to see a solitary white pelican. It was amazing. Snow-white against an overcast sky. I watched it sail through the blue, over the waves, and disappear in the distance.

That's when I saw a brilliant flash of light so silvery white and clear that I gasped and dropped to my knees. The whole tip of the island was bathed in it for maybe thirty seconds, and then it was gone. It was the most spectacular, inspiring thing I'd ever seen. I couldn't move—or maybe didn't want to. Now I knew why Charly had been desperate to see it a second time. Once you've caught a glimpse of something so glorious, you want more than anything to see it again so you can believe it's real, that you didn't invent it.

Now a cooler wind was blowing. I sat in the sand looking out at the gulf, one minute sparkling under a bright summer sun, the next cooled by a cloud drift blocking the light. A familiar and distinctive sadness washed over me, just like the waves coming ashore. I felt my eyes sting just before hot tears streamed down my face. Then I heard his voice, calm and quiet.

"This is not what I intended."

I hadn't heard him approaching, hadn't seen him in my peripheral vision, but there he stood—Jason. He was barefoot, dressed in white joggers and a white T-shirt.

Struggling to "straighten my face up," as Punk would say, I shaded my eyes with my hand and looked up at him. "What are you doing here, Jason?"

He sat down in the sand next to me. "You'd probably call it a feeling. I was given a sense that you were troubled. And I thought I knew where you would go under those circumstances."

We both looked out at the gulf, not at each other.

"You've been to the gallery?" he asked.

"Yes. Did you see the light?"

"I did."

I turned to face him, staring into ice-blue eyes that had looked straight through me so many times. "Are you the light, Jason?"

"No."

"Would you tell me if you were?"

"I would."

"I'm not sure I believe you. I don't think you told me the truth about Sarah Parsons."

He picked up a seashell and turned it over in his hand. "I persuaded you to go where you needed to be."

I reached over and touched his hand so that he dropped the seashell and looked at me. "But you're not the light?"

"No, Edie, I'm not the light. But I am often near it. And when it speaks to me here—"

"You mean here on Horn?"

"I mean *here*." He waved his arm in a wide, slow circle, taking in everything—the sea, the sky, the sand. "When it speaks to me here, I suppose it shows itself to you in a new way."

"Does that mean you're an . . ."

There it was. The Stare. "That I'm a what?"

I shook my head and sighed. "I don't even know how to ask."

He smiled at me. "That's understandable. We don't know what we don't know, remember?"

"I remember."

The two of us grew quiet as we watched a crane wade into the surf and catch a fish. "It's so strange how everything is connected," I said as much to myself as to Jason.

"How so?"

"If I hadn't stopped by The Trove on the day that I decided to look for a job, I might not have told you I needed one, and you might not have given me the Camille project, and I never would've seen the picture that brought Connor home to Charly."

"That's true."

"Now you're three for three. You helped me. You saved Charly. And you led Connor home to her."

"I suppose you could say that."

"And you're leaving."

"Yes."

"Were you going to leave without saying goodbye?"

Jason turned to look at me. "No. I wouldn't do that to you, Edie. It's just that I didn't expect you today. I was planning to tell you tomorrow. I was also planning to give you the keys to my building and my garden. I still am."

"You can't give me a whole building, Jason."

"Actually, I'm not. It's a gift from . . . that is . . ."

"From your director?"

"You could say that." He was smiling again. "You performed a selfless act of service with other people's images, Edie. Now it's time to take some of your own. I know you'll use them for the good."

I shook my head. "I don't know who pulls the puppet strings more, you or Punk."

Jason laughed with me, something he rarely did. "From what you've told me about her, I would never presume to outmaneuver your grandmother."

We were both sitting cross-legged in the sand like a couple of old college friends catching up. But we weren't that. We weren't that at all.

"You really have to go?" I said.

"Yes. My work here is finished. I'm needed elsewhere."

"Will I ever see you again?"

"Probably not for a while."

"I'll miss you, Jason."

"I'll miss you too." He frowned and added, "I don't think I've ever said that before."

It made me laugh, which felt so good right now. "I'm honored, Jason. Truly, honored."

He stood and helped me up, then looked down at me and smiled again. "I seem to have missed my ride. Give me a lift?"

# epilogue

**"WHAT DO YOU THINK OF THESE TWO?"** I had asked Cole to come down to the studio and help me make some tough decisions.

"I think I can't believe we flew through that storm and lived to look at pictures of it."

We were studying images taken inside the eye of Hurricane Katrina. Back in 2005, Cole had flown his crew through it as I photographed it for NOAA and the Hurricane Center in Miami.

Some pilots call the eye of a hurricane "the stadium" because they say the circular wall of clouds looks like a giant football arena floating in the air. Cole always said "stadium" was far too celebratory a name for something so deadly.

"I don't know, Edie. It's hard to choose, but I think the color is maybe a little better in the one on the right."

I nodded in agreement. Cole was rarely wrong about color and contrast, and I had come to trust his judgment over the years.

"Look at this one," I said. "It's not for the show, but I stumbled onto it when I was pulling images together. You took it, remember?"

He held the picture and smiled. "Look at you with your newlywed glow."

"I'm pretty sure that's sweat since all the power was off. We had been married, what—not quite two years when Katrina hit?"

"Sounds about right."

Cole had captured all the women—the Ten Spots, Charly, and me—on the grand staircase at Sugar's. She had invited us all to camp there after Katrina. Of all our group, Sugar had the only house that survived, and she somehow managed to make us feel safe and welcome until we could get ourselves situated during the long recovery.

After the storm, Punk had her house rebuilt exactly as it was before. Cookie bought a houseboat and found a spot on the back bay. Coco said she was done digging in the dirt and went condo. Charly and Connor moved to Pascagoula and built a house in a protected cove on the river.

As for Cole and me, both of us wanted to stay on the gulf. Our first house was in Ocean Springs, not far from Punk's. When she passed, she left her Creole cottage to us. We've made years of happy memories at "Punk II."

Sometimes I can almost imagine I see my grandmother and her crew gathered around the dining room table, Sugar driving Coco to distraction, Cookie doing her best to referee, and Punk making sure no one goes hungry, not for a second. I imagine I smell a pot of gumbo simmering on the stove and hear the sound of raucous laughter.

In those moments, I often think of Jason. And I'm grateful to Punk, who was never forgetful to entertain strangers.

*For more from*
## VALERIE FRASER LUESSE,

---

READ ON FOR AN EXCERPT FROM

# ALMOST HOME

---

*Available now wherever books are sold.*

*April 3, 1944*

*Dear Violet,*

    *How's everything over in Georgia? I bet you thought you'd never hear from your big sister again! What with getting the lake ready to open and looking after all my boarders, I'm about half crazy. I told Si that if I don't soon get a minute to prop my feet up and catch my breath, he might as well run on down to Trimble's and pick me out a casket.*

    *Did I tell you they've gone to selling caskets upstairs at the mercantile? They've got big yellow name tags you can tie on the handle once you make your selection. Then you just pay at the register, and that sweet little Gilbert boy that stocks the shelves will haul your purchase to the funeral parlor on a flatbed truck. It's so much more convenient than driving all the way to Childersburg when a loved one passes, but it's a little spooky to shop for your dry goods, knowing what's overhead. And anytime you cross the river bridge, you're likely to meet a casket bound for the funeral home. How about that? Before we can cross Jordan, we've got to cross the Coosa.*

    *I have to tell you, sister, I've been sorely missing somebody to talk to since you and Wiley moved away to Georgia. I've got people all around me from morning till night, but now and again you just want to have a conversation with somebody that doesn't need you to fry something, iron something, or mop something up. You got anybody to talk to over in Georgia?*

*Back to my boarders. Granddaddy Talmadge must be rolling over in his grave. I can hear him now: "Yankee carpetbaggers!" I'm a little ashamed of myself for renting to them, what with his Confederate uniform still hanging in the attic, but we sorely need the money. They say this Depression's near about over, but I reckon somebody forgot to tell Alabama.*

*My boarders seem to come and go in cycles. The ones that rented from me at the beginning of the war have all left, and I just filled up with new people. We rented the last of the upstairs rooms a couple of weeks ago, one to a perfectly horrible couple—the Clanahans from Reno, Nevada—and one to a young husband and wife from Illinois, name of Williams. I did NOT show those Reno people our old room—just put them in that drafty back bedroom and saved ours for Mr. and Mrs. Williams when they get here, which ought to be any day now. Something tells me they need it. (Little Mama's house is talking to me again!)*

*I'm babbling on and on about nothing, but I sat down here with a purpose, Violet. What with all the comings and goings at home, I've decided a thing or two. I think God gives us soul mates—not many but enough to get us through. And I'm not just talking about husbands and wives. I'm talking about those one or two people we meet on life's journey who see straight through all our nonsense and love us one hundred percent, no matter what. You're my soul mate, sweet sister. And I never fully appreciated that till now.*

*Well, I'd best go before I have to reach for that pretty handkerchief you embroidered for me. Some days I hold to it like a lifeline. Hope y'all are still coming for the Fourth. It wouldn't be a fish fry without my Violet.*

*Kiss the young'uns for me and give Wiley a hug.*

*Your loving sister,*
*Dolly*

# ONE

Anna Williams leaned out the truck window and let the wind blow her damp auburn hair away from her face. She remembered her grandmother's parting words: *I fear Alabama will suffocate you.* With each warm gust of wind, Anna felt a fresh wave of loneliness. The family she had left behind in Illinois seemed a million miles away right now. She had yet to see her new home but already missed the old one so much she could hardly bear it.

"Need to stop?" her husband asked without taking his eyes off the road.

"I'm alright." She took a sip of the soda he had bought her at a Texaco station just outside of Birmingham. It wasn't ice-cold anymore, but it was better than nothing. A quick glance in Jesse's direction told her nothing had changed—not yet, anyway—but she was hoping and praying.

Jesse had what radio newsmen at the front called "the thirty-yard stare"—a vacant, somber gaze. It had settled onto his face like a heavy fog and hovered there for the past year. Even though her husband wasn't a soldier—flatfeet and hardship had kept him out of the service—he was fighting a battle just the same.

Some men collapse under the weight of a failing farm, but Jesse had stood firm—sadly, for both of them, by turning to stone. Now he had decided that the only way to revive their farm was to leave it behind, at least for a while. He was driving them away from everything and everybody they loved, but Anna was determined not to cry in front of her husband. She had to believe that somewhere deep down, he still had a heart, and she didn't want to break it by letting him know just how desolate she felt.

She looked out her window and took in the countryside. Alabama was so *green*—a thousand shades of it. Everywhere you looked were towering pines, their branches thick with needles that faded from deep olive to sage to pale chartreuse at the very tips. With the truck windows down, Anna could occasionally catch the heady fragrance of honeysuckle, which draped the fence lines and mounded so heavily in spots that it threatened to take down the barbed wire and liberate the cows. The lush pastures made a thick carpet of grass that looked like emerald velvet. You couldn't look at grass like that and smell its perfume without wondering what it would be like to stop the truck, strip off your sweaty clothes, and lie down in a bed of cool, green sweetness. That had to be a sin. And it would likely stampede the livestock.

Anna thought to herself that this Southern landscape didn't so much roll as billow, like a bedsheet fluttering on a clothesline, as the mountains and foothills of Tennessee sank into flatlands around Huntsville, only to soar up again just above Birmingham. The pickup was headed down a two-lane highway that had carried the couple straight through the Magic City—that's what the radio announcers called Birmingham, though Anna had no idea why—and now she and Jesse were getting their first glimpse of rural Shelby County, where they would be living for the next couple of years.

"Help me watch for a dirt road off to the right." Jesse was turning off the Birmingham highway and onto a county blacktop. "It's supposed to have a sign by it that says 'Talmadge Loop' or something like that."

They drove past several white clapboard churches and what Anna guessed were cotton fields. She spotted a soybean field or two—at least that much was familiar.

"There it is," she said, pointing to a crooked wooden sign nailed to a fence post.

Jesse followed what did indeed appear to be a big loop— more a half-moon of a road, really, connected to the county highway at each end. It was sprinkled with houses, some noticeably nicer than others. Anna saw a yard full of children —colored and white—playing around a tire swing in front of a rickety little house. The walls looked as if they would collapse like a line of dominoes if you so much as leaned against them.

"I thought they didn't believe in mixing down here," she said absently, though she knew Jesse wouldn't answer. Sometimes she felt as if her husband had an overwhelming need to pretend she wasn't there.

Jesse pulled into a narrow driveway that led to a stately white two-story house surrounded by oaks and pecan trees so imposing that they had to be a hundred years old. As she stepped out of the truck and felt a breeze, Anna did her best to fluff out her skirt and loosen her sweaty blouse, which was sticking to her like wet tissue paper.

She took in her surroundings. Weathered and in need of fresh paint, the old house still had an air of grandeur about it. Both stories had deep, L-shaped porches with scrolled bannisters wrapping around the front and southern side of the house. The windows were at least six feet tall and flanked by dark green shutters.

Across the road was a long, narrow building that looked a lot like a barn, except for a gigantic side porch big enough to hold a row of Adirondack chairs. Steps led from the porch into a hole almost as big as a football field. Nailed to one of the few pines left standing was a plywood sign that read, "Future Home, Lake Chandler."

"What do you make of that?" Anna asked, pointing to the sign. "How do you build a lake?"

Jesse just shrugged and motioned for her to follow him to the house. He pulled the cord on a small iron bell mounted beside the front door and waited.

Standing on the porch, Anna realized that the only thing separating inside from outside was screen wire. The front door and all the windows of the house were wide open, but there were screens nailed over all the windows and a screen door at the main entrance. Anna had heard horror stories about the mosquitoes down South and prayed she could get back home without catching yellow fever.

She could hear a distant female voice singing "Praise the Lord and Pass the Ammunition." Jesse looked agitated, shifting his weight and running his fingers through his hair again and again. He gave the cord another yank. The singing abruptly stopped, and a woman who looked to be about fifty came hurrying through the house in a fusillade of footsteps.

"Can I help you?" she said with a smile as she reached the screen door.

"Name's Williams," Jesse said. "Here for our room."

Anna knew he had never rented a room from anybody in his whole life. When they married, they were so excited about the farmhouse he had inherited from his grandparents that they spent their honeymoon there. Last night she had slept in the cab while he slept on a quilt in the truck bed. They just pulled off the road and parked till they were rested enough to keep moving.

"My land!" the woman exclaimed, opening the door and ushering them inside. "I bet y'all are burnin' up. Come on in here and cool off." She led them to a worn but elegant Victorian settee in front of tall windows in an octagonal parlor, where two rotary fans aimed manufactured breezes all over the room. "Now you two just sit there and collect yourself while I go get you some tea."

"There's no need—" Jesse tried to stop her, but she was long gone.

Soon their host returned, carrying a tarnished silver tray with two goblets made of fine etched glass. They were filled with iced tea, each with a big wedge of lemon on top. "Here you go," she said. "Are y'all hungry? Supper's not till six, but I can get you a slice o' pound cake or make you some sandwiches with the roast beef I had left over from supper last night. Would you like just a little bite o' somethin' to tide you over?"

"No," Jesse said.

"Are you sure? Because it wouldn't be a bit of trouble. I could just—"

"Ma'am, we really just want—"

"We appreciate it, we really do." Anna interrupted her husband for fear he might be outright rude. "But we had lunch on the way down."

"Well, alright then. You just let me know if you change your mind."

"We will—and thank you, really. I'm Anna. This is my husband, Jesse. Could you tell us how we might meet the owner of the house and get settled?" Anna thought it best to relieve Jesse of any need for conversation. He sat slumped on the settee, cupping the tea goblet as if he needed an anchor to cling to.

The woman, who had taken a seat opposite the two of them, looked startled. "You want to meet the—oh, honey, you just did! I mean, I'm her. You'll have to forgive my bad manners. I've been runnin' around here like a chicken with its head cut off, tryin' to get my latest boarders situated, and when y'all went to ringin' that bell, I got so flustered I plain forgot myself. I'm Mrs. Josiah Chandler, but you can call me Dolly, and you can call my husband Si—if you ever see him, that is. He's so busy workin' on the lake, I've about forgot what he looks like."

"It's nice to meet you," Anna said. She smiled at her host and took a sip of tea.

Dolly was petite, with what Anna's grandmother would call a "feminine frame." Her chestnut bob was slightly curly, with just a few streaks of gray, and that dark hair made her periwinkle eyes look all the bluer. She wore a cotton shirt-waist dress in a yellow floral print.

"I like your tea," Anna said. "I've never had any quite this sweet."

"All my boarders comment on my tea," Dolly said with a smile. "The secret is lettin' the sugar melt while it's hot and then quick-chillin' it with ice. I just hope we can keep it sweet with all this rationin'. Oh, well, that's why Si keeps bees. If we run outta sugar, we'll just switch to honey. How long have y'all been on the road?"

"Two days," Anna said.

"Mercy!" Dolly shook her head. "My back hurts just thinkin' about it."

"Is it always this hot in April?"

"Oh, no," Dolly said. "In fact, it can get downright chilly. I thought we were just havin' a little heat wave, but *Farmer's Almanac* is predictin' an early summer—it mighta done started. Believe you me, it's gonna get a lot worse before it gets any better. July and August are always scorchers. That's how come we're hurryin' to get the lake done. Si didn't come up with the idea till February, so that put us in a bind to get it done by summer. We always have a big fish fry on the Fourth o' July, and since ever'body on the loop and quite a few folks from church will come, Si figured that was as good a time as any to promote our new business. He says we're entrepreneurs. I say we're poor as Job's turkey and sellin' everything but the family silver to stay afloat!"

Anna and Dolly laughed together while Jesse stared into his tea.

"What will you charge to swim?" Anna asked.

"Fifty cents, but you only have to pay once a day, and we're plannin' to stay open till five o'clock in the evenin', so you can swim till you prune up if you want to. We'll be closed on Sunday, o' course. As long as I've got my right mind, there will be no money changin' on the Sabbath Day."

"What's that building next to the hole—next to the lake, I mean?"

"Why, that's the skatin' rink," Dolly said. "It's been open for a whole year now. Got a dance floor in there too, and Ping-Pong tables down on the far end o' the porch. The concession stand's right by the front door. It costs a quarter to skate if you bring your own, fifty cents if you need to rent a pair o' ours. Ping-Pong's a dime a game, but we don't charge folks anything to dance or sit on the front porch and visit. We figure they'll end up feedin' nickels into the jukebox or

299

buyin' a Co-Cola if they stay long enough, and we can't see any point in bein' greedy. Ever'body needs a little enjoyment right now, don't you think?"

"Yes," Anna said. "I think you're absolutely right."

"Now listen," Dolly went on, "I know you're a long way from home and prob'ly missin' your mama already. But don't you worry. You'll make it back to Illinois. Alabama's just a little stop on your journey. And there's nice people here and good churches to go to. And if you need anybody to talk to, why, I've been told I'm a pretty good listener, so you just feel free."

"Thank you, Dolly." Anna was trying hard not to blink as her eyes began to sting. It's strange, she thought. Sometimes, when you're so sad that you're barely holding yourself together, it's the kindness of another person—a simple gesture from someone trying to bring comfort—that unleashes the tears. And she knew that Jesse, as usual, was far too preoccupied with his own frustration to notice that she too had reached a breaking point.

"If we could—if we could just get our room," he said, standing up and holding out the tea goblet.

"Why, of course," Dolly said politely as she took it from him. "I'll do whatever I can to make you comfortable. You're a guest in my home."

"About time," Jesse mumbled as she left the room. "Can't she see that we just want to get this over with?"

Anna knew he was prepared to go on and on about Dolly wasting their time and meddling in their business—and she knew she couldn't stand to listen to another word of it. But just then he turned to look at her, perched on that elegant settee, wearing the clothes she had slept in, and for once he was struck silent.

She could guess why. All these months, all this time, she had worked hard to make sure she never showed any sign of disappointment in him—not a hint of frustration, let alone anger. But what she felt now—and what she was sure he could see on her face—was an unsettling mix of fury and disgust.

For the first time since their downward spiral began, Jesse actually tried to explain himself. "Anna, all I meant was—"

"I don't care what you meant," she said without raising her voice. "What *she* meant, in case you missed it, is that she doesn't have to put up with any nonsense. You saw all those caravans coming down here. Dolly's probably got a waiting list a mile long. My father said all I have to do is make one collect phone call and he'll send me a bus ticket home."

Dolly came back into the parlor and could no doubt see that she had interrupted something. "Well then, let's get y'all settled," she said. "Come on upstairs, and I'll show you where everything is."

She led them up a sweeping staircase that opened into a spacious sitting area on the second floor. Bookcases big enough for a library lined the walls. The floors were covered with tapestry rugs that looked a little threadbare. There was a settee like the one in the parlor, along with a couple of armchairs and a rocker. Between two tall windows overlooking the lake-to-be was a door that opened onto the upstairs porch. Unlike the one below, it was screened. Anna thought how lovely it would be to sit here and read a good book or embroider on a rainy afternoon. Narrow hallways led from the sitting area to what she imagined were bedrooms.

"The porch there is a nice place to pull up a rockin' chair and have your mornin' coffee or a glass o' tea on a hot summer day," Dolly said. "And it's here for ever'body, so just make yourself at home."

As Dolly walked them through the upstairs, Anna watched her straighten lampshades and make quick swipes with her hand to clear any dust that she spotted. "Now, the two bedrooms on the opposite side there—one belongs to a Mr. and Mrs. Hastings. Actually, Dr. and Dr. Hastings. They were both college professors up in Chicago, but I guess times are hard there too. Both of 'em lost their jobs, which is a cryin' shame, if you ask me. They're the nicest people—and all that knowledge just goin' to waste. He works at the plant, and she substitute teaches over at the high school from time to time. 'Course, it won't be long till school lets out for the summer, so I imagine we'll be seein' a lot more o' her."

Dolly let out a tired sigh as she pointed to the room in the back corner of the house. "That room there belongs to the Clanahans from Reno, Nevada. They're out for the afternoon. Both of 'em work the early shift at the plant, so you'll only see 'em at suppertime, and that'll be plenty. I'll confess it right now—those two try my patience and test my religion."

"Why?" Anna asked.

"They're rude in that kinda way that makes *you* feel like the one who made the misstep—like *you're* the one with no raisin'. They're gone before Si gets up, and I've been carryin' his supper to him over at the lake so he can work late. The Clanahans have been livin' in this house for two weeks, and Si's never laid eyes on 'em. He will tonight, though. We'll see what he has to say then. In the meantime, just try not to get your feelin's hurt by whatever meanness they might decide to spew."

Dolly led Anna and Jesse to two rooms at the front of the

house. "Mr. Joe Dolphus has that small room right there. He lost his wife a year ago and moved here as much to get away from that empty house as to find work, I expect. He's just as kind and pleasant as he can be."

She gave them a big smile as she pointed to the other door, adorned with a wreath made of corsages. Their flowers were long gone, but the ribbon and crinoline that Anna imagined had once adorned ball gowns for dances and cotillions offered a cheery welcome from the heavy old door.

"Now, this room right here—this room is yours." Dolly opened the door to an immense bedroom. The ceiling must have been fourteen feet high. Anna loved the smell of old polished wood and the way her footsteps echoed when she walked across the floor. There was a walnut four-poster bed, a dressing table with a round mirror, a washstand, and an armoire with full-length mirrors on each of its wide double doors. A small rocking chair had been placed in front of the fireplace opposite the bed, and tall windows overlooked the lake. Best of all, the room had its own private door onto the porch. Anna wasn't sure why, but something about this grand old bedroom both excited and comforted her. For the first time in forever, she felt hopeful.

"It's beautiful, Dolly," she said. "It's just beautiful."

Her host smiled. "When me and Si first decided to take in boarders, I had a feelin' somebody was comin' who would need this room—this one in particular—so I've been savin' it. This room belonged to me and my sister when we were growin' up. If these walls go to talkin', you let me know because they've overheard a lotta our secrets. Wouldn't want 'em to start tellin' on me in front o' my comp'ny."

"I'll let you know if I hear anything you'd want to put a stop to," Anna assured her.

303

"You do that. Oh! I almost forgot. There's a bathroom up here, but with seven people, it can get a little crowded. We've still got our old bathhouse and outhouse in back. And you're welcome to use me and Si's downstairs bathroom, as long as the Clanahans aren't around. Far as they know, our bathroom's off-limits. I shudder to think what that man could do to a sink."

Jesse finally spoke. "Is there a key to our room? We'll want to keep it locked when we aren't here."

"There's no keys to the rooms, but there's a latch on the inside for privacy," Dolly said. "Also, you can flip down that doorstop on the bottom—won't nobody come in on you with that heavy ol' thing holdin' 'em back. And if you're worried about your valuables, that wardrobe locks, and the only key to it's right there in the keyhole."

"But how can we make sure—"

"I'm sure it will be fine," Anna said. "Thank you."

"Well, that about covers everything," Dolly said. "Breakfast is on the table at six every mornin', and whoever's here at lunchtime can fix a sandwich or somethin' outta the kitchen. Supper's at six every night. So just remember 'six' and you'll never go hungry in my house."

"We'll remember," Anna said.

"Well, I'll leave you to it then," Dolly said. "If you need any help bringin' in your things, just come and get me. I'll be in the kitchen." She suddenly clapped her hands together and laughed. "I'll bet you that's what they put on my tombstone: 'Here lies Dolly Chandler. She was in the kitchen.'"

Anna laughed with Dolly, following her down the stairs of a grand old home and out to a dusty pickup that held everything she owned.

# acknowledgments

Much love and gratitude to my husband, Dave, for so many reasons but especially for his endless patience with my right-brained eccentricities. That has to be tough for a logically minded fellow who appreciates a good rule book and can do math.

My thanks and a giant, never-letting-go hug to my parents for a lifetime of love, encouragement, and support. To all of my extended family and dear friends, you're the safety net that gives me courage to keep trying. (Nellah McGough and Carole Cain, you get a special thank-you for saving me this time around!) Thanks also to my *Southern Living* family for their continued support.

I have a hard time remembering life before Leslie—that would be my agent, Leslie Stoker, of Stoker Literary. Maybe that's because I don't want to. I appreciate her wisdom and friendship more than I could ever say.

To Kelsey Bowen, my editor at Revell: Kelsey, if you're excited, I'm excited!

Sometimes Kelsey knows what I'm trying to accomplish

even before I do, and I'm blessed to have her shepherding my stories.

I have benefited tremendously from the expertise of another fine editor, Jessica English, whose attention to detail refines every manuscript she touches.

Thanks also to three talented and vigilant proofreaders, Marti Shaver, Shelli Littleton, and Christy Distler.

For a beautiful cover that makes me so proud to see my book on the shelf, I thank senior art director Laura Klynstra and her team at Baker Publishing Group.

I'm blessed with an outstanding marketing and publicity team at Baker and would like to thank publicity manager Karen Steele, fiction marketing director Raela Schoenherr, and assistant marketing manager Lindsay Schubert.

My unending gratitude to four incredible authors—T. I. Lowe, Robin W. Pearson, Amanda Cox, and Sarah Loudin Thomas—for taking time away from their own work to read mine and offer their endorsements. I appreciate their support more than I could ever say.

Special thanks to Chris Jager, fiction book buyer at Baker Book House, just for being Chris, which is to say a great friend to all writers.

I am deeply indebted to the Center for Oral History and Cultural Heritage at the University of Southern Mississippi in Hattiesburg for guiding me to their phenomenal collection of interviews with Hurricane Camille survivors. Their harrowing stories shaped the survivor accounts in my book. The courage and resilience of those who lived through Camille—and powerful storms before and since—will forever amaze and inspire me.

Another invaluable resource was the 1971 documentary *A Lady Called Camille*, featuring actual footage of the Mississippi coast preparing for the storm and dealing with its devastating aftermath. I'm thankful for the storytellers who captured and preserved this painful chapter in the history of the gulf.

Finally, I thank all the readers who are kind enough to journey through a story with me. You make the trip worth taking.

**VALERIE FRASER LUESSE** is the bestselling author of *Missing Isaac*, *Almost Home*, *The Key to Everything*, *Under the Bayou Moon*, and *Letters from My Sister*. She is an award-winning magazine writer best known for her feature stories and essays in *Southern Living*, where she retired as senior travel editor. A graduate of Auburn University and Baylor University, she lives in Harpersville, Alabama, with her husband, Dave.

"Rich with historical details, Luesse's fascinating glimpse into the Old South combines an engaging mystery with sweet romance and social justice."

—*BOOKLIST* STARRED REVIEW

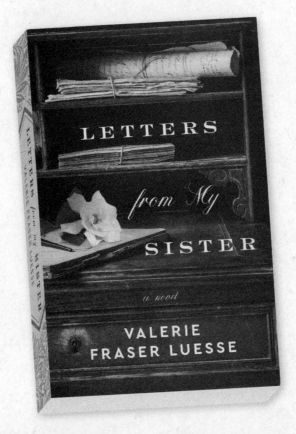

Sisters Emmy and Callie have no secrets between them until a mysterious accident robs one of a crucial memory and sparks troubling visions. Only through letters they exchange while painfully separated do the sisters reveal hidden truths leading back to a fateful springtime day—and a chilling September night—that changed them both forever.

R Revell
a division of Baker Publishing Group
RevellBooks.com

Available wherever books and ebooks are sold.

"Luesse's multifaceted, lyrical tale dazzles with larger-than-life villains searching for a big payday, a mythical albino alligator, a mysterious 'esprit Blanc' that allegedly roams the swamps, and a lovable cast. . . . Readers who enjoy Southern romances will love this."

## —*PUBLISHERS WEEKLY* STARRED REVIEW

A young, restless Alabama teacher searching for a sense of purpose accepts a position at a tiny Louisiana bayou school, where a lonely Cajun fisherman, a tight-knit community, and a legendary white alligator will change her life forever.

"Valerie Fraser Luesse once again directs a symphony of characters, charming readers with her storytelling expertise and captivating dialogue."

—BookPage

Through poignant prose and characters so real you'll be sure you know them, Valerie Fraser Luesse transports you to the storied Atlantic coast for a unique coming-of-age story you won't soon forget.

Ⓡ Revell
a division of Baker Publishing Group
RevellBooks.com

Available wherever books and ebooks are sold.

# Meet Valerie

FOLLOW ALONG AT

# ValerieFraserLuesse.com

and sign up for Valerie's newsletter to stay up to date
on news, upcoming releases, and more!

 Valerie Fraser Luesse

 ValerieLuesse